PEDAL TO
THE METAL

Visit us at www.boldstrokesbooks.com

By the Author

The Chase

Seneca Falls

Pedal to the Metal

PEDAL TO
THE METAL

by

Jesse J. Thoma

2015

PEDAL TO THE METAL

ISBN 13: 978-1-62639-239-7

This Trade Paperback Original Is Published By
Bold Strokes Books, Inc.
P.O. Box 249
Valley Falls, NY 12185

First Edition: February 2015

Credits
Editors: Victoria Villasenor and Cindy Cresap
Production Design: Susan Ramundo
Cover Design By Sheri (graphicartist2020@hotmail.com)

Acknowledgments

Writing a sequel was a unique and wonderful writing experience. Thank you to everyone who finished *The Chase* and e-mailed me, sent a note through social media, or elbowed me on the couch and said, "When's the sequel coming out?"

To my editor, Vic, once again, I count on your skill, encouragement, and kick in the pants to produce a product that is better than anything I imagine when I first plot out the beginnings of a story. For that, I am very grateful. Thank you to the entire Bold Strokes team, from cover design to final comma placement, a tremendous amount of work goes in to each book arriving on eReaders and bookshelves, and this author is in your debt.

As always, family and friends have been wonderfully supportive of my writing and have allowed me to run story ideas by them at very odd times.

Finally, to my wife, what a year this has been. Publishing a new novel feels like icing on a very large, very spectacular cake. I could not love you more.

Dedication

For Alexis
Love rocks when we're together
Love rocks, gonna love you forever
Love's got me rockin and I only wanna rock with you

CHAPTER ONE

Isabelle Rochat stretched before setting her book on the bedside table. She glanced at the clock next to her. It was late, again.

"Sweetheart, are you coming to bed?"

Holt Lasher emerged from the bathroom in her boxer shorts, toweling her ear-length brown hair. Isabelle wasn't disappointed to see Holt hadn't bothered to put on a shirt. She sighed happily, thinking she still had trouble recognizing her life sometimes. Six months ago, if someone had told her she would be sharing a bed with Holt, every muscled, tattooed, superhero-sexy inch of her, she would have checked the person for symptoms of a stroke. Now, however, she was enjoying being Mrs. Captain America.

"Are you picturing me in a Lycra suit with a cape again?" Holt asked.

"You are wearing your Green Lantern boxers."

"And no shirt," Holt said. "I thought that might keep you focused."

"I noticed," Isabelle said. "Are you going to tell me what's on your mind, or are you going to stand over there in your underwear fretting by yourself?"

Holt seemed amused by Isabelle's gentle prodding to let go of whatever was troubling her. She tossed her towel back into the bathroom and pulled back the covers on her side of the bed. Although it took some time, Isabelle was finally getting used to

Holt's newest tattoo. Angel wings spread from the spot she'd been shot in the chest. At first, Holt said she got it for Isabelle, which had freaked her out. It felt too soon, and too permanent, so Holt had changed her story. Now she said it was because a guardian angel had been keeping her safe. Who she named as her guardian angel was her own business.

"Why do you smell like a baby's butt?" Isabelle asked.

"Excuse me?"

Isabelle gave Holt a sniff, trying to find the source of the unusual smell. "It's your new tattoo. Your angel smells like a baby's butt."

"It's A&D ointment. My wings are itchy."

"Well, it is also used for diaper rash. Didn't you ever change Superman's diaper?" Isabelle couldn't believe Holt had never performed that particular task for her godson.

"Of course I did. Now I'm thankful his diaper rash cream was something completely different. That's not an association I want with my boobs."

"There's still time to make that a memory if we have kids, my love," Isabelle teased her.

"Speaking of kids, have you talked to Lola about her AWOL pregnant girlfriend?"

"We're having coffee tomorrow."

"Thank you for being there for her. Lola and I have known each other for years, and I'd happily take a bullet for her," Holt said. "But—"

"No more bullets for you." Isabelle could still see clearly the moment Holt was shot.

Holt smiled gently and smoothed away the frown line on Isabelle's forehead. "I've walked into more sketchy situations with Lola by my side than I can count. But when she started crying, I was completely helpless."

"You deal with your newest team member tomorrow, and I'll handle Lola."

"How did I let myself get talked into that terrible idea?"

"There was a damsel in distress who needed your help. You can't ever resist that. And someone stole your truck and pissed you off."

"I won't tell the state police commissioner you called him a damsel in distress," Holt said.

"How would you describe him?" Isabelle asked. "He was practically batting his eyelashes at you. Anyway, didn't you say you were putting Max in the lead on this? You trust her don't you? She's an adorable mini version of you with a serious case of mentor worship."

"She's one of my best. She's barely older than a toddler, but if I need anything hacked, coded, or computerized, then yeah, she's my go-to. But she's not worked the streets like the others. She's like a big fluffy golden retriever. Sometimes the streets require Dobermans. Moose, Tuna, Lola, they're Dobermans. I just don't know how Max will do."

"Well, I'm letting you take care of my dry cleaning bill this week, because one of your 'Dobermans' cried so hard on my shoulder she slobbered and snotted an allergy season's worth of mucus on my shirt."

"Ah, come on, that was about a woman. Women can make even the toughest pup whimper," Holt said. "Would you like me to show you what I mean?"

Isabelle saw Holt's blue eyes darken. Her gaze was intensely focused on Isabelle's face, her body. She never felt more beautiful than when Holt looked at her like this. It lit her soul on fire and fed her in ways only true love could.

"I've been waiting all night for you to get around to that idea," Isabelle said. "But go wash off that A&D lotion. I cannot take you seriously smelling like that."

She couldn't remember seeing Holt move so fast.

CHAPTER TWO

Max sat next to Holt, trying to exude a small percentage of the calm Holt seemed to be feeling. They had been sitting on the bench in the park, in the sun, for the past forty-five minutes and Holt had barely moved. Max knew that Holt probably knew what every person in the park was doing right now, could pinpoint their exact location, and describe their clothing and demographic particulars with uncanny detail, despite the fact that it looked like she was asleep.

Max, on the other hand, was having trouble sitting still for more than ninety seconds at a time. She tried to adopt Holt's posture and fully relax her body. Her butt felt like it was going to sleep. She shifted again.

"Do I need to take you for a walk?" Holt asked, still appearing to be sleeping.

"We can't leave," Max said. "They're meeting us here." She didn't know if Holt was serious about making her walk off the nervous energy, and she was embarrassed at not being able to control herself, especially in front of Holt.

"I know that," Holt said. "But with you twitching like that, so does everyone else in this park. Sit still."

"Sorry, H. I'm not used to being out of the office. Computers don't care if I'm a little twitchy."

"I'm asking a lot of you on this one. And they're late. Just try not to reposition every forty-five seconds. Someone is going to think I'm holding you hostage. And since the police commissioner is about to dump a state prisoner in my lap, I don't want people talking."

"This is Rhode Island. Everyone talks. I'm sure half the people in this park already know as much about what's happening here today as we do."

"I wish I knew a little more about it," Holt said. "Maybe you should go ask that nice looking man two benches down to give us his information. I don't like this deal. It could blow up on us. That's why I need you. You're the pin in the hand grenade. No pressure, kid."

Max wondered what it was she should keep from blowing up. She knew a little about the deal Holt had made with the state police commissioner and the prisoner they were about to take charge of, but she felt unprepared to keep the situation from "blowing up." *What the hell does that mean?* She was the computer geek. She didn't do much for Holt that didn't involve electronics of some sort. Until now. She also had no interest in talking to the man two benches down. He didn't look terribly talkative.

"I think we have company heading our way. You ready to meet your charge?" Holt asked. Max didn't know how Holt saw anyone coming.

"Boss, you got slits in your eyelids to see things with your eyes closed?"

"Appearances are important in our job. And even more important is having those appearances be deceiving. You should work on your surveillance skills. It might help you sit still, too."

"Maybe I'll start with my eyes open first."

"So tell me what you see."

Max slowly looked around the park. She took in each individual and how they were interacting with the groups they belonged to. Then she focused on the approaching car. It was a standard issue unmarked government vehicle, American made, nondescript gray. The guy driving looked like a casting director's dream applicant for the role of "stereotypical white male." Next to him, she recognized the police commissioner from the news. There was a third person in the car, in the backseat, but she wasn't easily visible from their vantage point.

"Standard issue cop, driving obvious unmarked government vehicle approaching from D north. Police commissioner is riding shotgun. They have a passenger in the backseat. Based on the size of the head and height, either a short woman or a child. You said state prison though, so I'm guessing a woman. The driver is moving slower than my grandmother on her way to church with her walker, probably trying not to call attention to their arrival, which means everyone in this place is now staring at them. What do they teach them at the police academy?"

"Look at him again, Max. He looks younger than you, if that's possible. He's driving the commissioner and a high value prisoner. He probably wet himself before they exited the highway."

"Not to mention he's now got to deal with you. You're right. This poor fool is having a really rough day on the job."

"I think I should be offended."

Max knew she should be paying more attention to what Holt was saying, or to what was happening around her in the park. She had a vague recollection that that was her job. Her attention, however, was focused entirely on the woman casually strutting along behind the two police officers making their way to Holt and Max. The woman was handcuffed and walking two paces behind the two larger men, but by her body language and calm demeanor, it looked as though she were an important figure out for a walk with her muscle. That the men left her to walk behind them suggested she wasn't exactly a flight risk.

She was short, with long, straight, dark brown hair, and fine, delicate features. Her lightly tanned face was incredibly beautiful. Max was having trouble looking away.

"Oh no, kid. I've seen that look. You might want to rein it in a little. She could very well eat you alive. Possibly literally. And you have a job to do, a very important one. If you are all googly-eyed, it's going to be an unpleasant one. Besides, we're the good guys; we catch the bad guys, and I don't know where she stands yet. You deserve someone who knows what side they play for."

Max was shaken from her trance by Holt's frank assessment. "How do you know she doesn't know?"

Holt shrugged. "Time, experience, gut. Be careful. And for God's sake, don't let her see you drooling over her."

Max watched the newcomer as the police officers and Holt chatted. The woman didn't take her eyes off Max, although there didn't seem to be a direct challenge. It was more of an assessment. The look felt like the one Max got when she was assessing the hackability of a database, a firewall, or a computer system. She didn't like it.

"This is Whitney Williams," the police commissioner said. "She's all yours."

"Oh please, not even my father calls me that," Whitney said. "Everyone calls me Dubs." She smiled at Max. "You know, like Wonder Woman, dubbya, dubbya, Dubs."

"Wonder Woman was an Amazon. You're the size of a tadpole," Holt said. "Want to give me a number between one and ten, just your best estimate, on my chances that you'll keep yourself out of trouble while under my care?"

Max was confused by Holt's brusque demeanor. She usually treated the folks who declined their court dates with more courtesy. Something was happening, but Max hadn't seen it yet. She kept one eye on Dubs and scanned the area as best she could.

"You're the boss, boss," Dubs said. "But you can ask these nice gentlemen here. I didn't serve my full sentence, so I wasn't fully rehabilitated. You should keep that in mind."

"I thought you might say something stupid like that," Holt said. "May I please have your handcuff keys, officer, and your extra set of cuffs?"

The young state trooper handed both items over with slightly shaking hands. Max felt for him. It wasn't long ago that she felt that way around Holt too. When one half of the trooper's handcuff closed around her left wrist however, disbelief was a better description of her feelings. They turned to anger when Holt unlocked the left wrist of Dubs's handcuffs, pulled them next to each other, and connected their handcuffs together.

"H, what are you doing? You can't tie me to her."

"For the record, boss, I'm not complaining. I like your leadership style," said Dubs.

"Max, I need you to keep your eye on her. This whole plan is based on her, and I don't trust her. I trust you."

Max lifted their connected wrists and shook them slightly. "And this is necessary?"

"Yes."

Max was going to argue, but then she saw what she assumed had Holt acting out of character.

"Uh, H. You do see the two dudes D west, right?"

"Max, you're going to need to work on your surveillance skills. They've been enjoying a picnic since before we arrived, noticed us when our guests got here, and have been frantically packing up since. Our window is closing."

"Mind filling me in?" the police commissioner asked.

"A couple of high value targets we've been searching long and hard for were enjoying a day at the park until you showed up," Holt said. "Now they're looking for a way out of here. I'm going to go and apprehend them."

"Who are they?"

Holt relayed their names and both officers drew their guns. Holt's body stiffened, a sure sign she was fighting her temper. Max took a step back, keeping her eyes on their targets. She jerked the handcuffs connecting her to Dubs, indicating she should step back out of the way as well. Dubs complied.

"Boss lady looks a little pissed. Is she going to get into fisticuffs with the cops? I haven't seen a good cop brawl in years. She looks like she could hold her own."

"Shut up," Max said.

"Put your guns away," Holt said. It wasn't a request.

The troopers were a little too slow to comply. Holt removed the young trooper's gun from his hands with speed only hours in front of a boxing speed bag could produce, and stripped it in seconds. She dropped the pieces at his feet. She looked at the commissioner.

"Yours is next, sir. Do you know how many children are in this park right now? Put your gun away."

"Holy shit," Dubs said, close to Max's ear. "This might be the greatest show I've ever seen. Who are you people?"

The commissioner's eyes were no longer casually friendly. Holt may not have made a new friend today, but Max didn't think she cared. Holt was adamant about not carrying a gun herself, and Max knew she disliked them with good reason.

"So how are you going to arrest them? Walk over and ask nicely?" the police commissioner asked.

"You're going to stay here with her, and I'm going to do what I do. Dubs, are you done getting out of those handcuffs yet? If not, you're a worse criminal than advertised and I'm starting to have second thoughts about you," Holt said.

Max spun around and looked at Dubs, who had moved slightly behind her. Her focus had been so laser-like on the men across the field, she had lost track of what her charge had been up to. Apparently, Dubs had been "up" to removing her handcuffs. She wiggled her fingers in response.

"Sorry, Hot Stuff. If there's going to be shooting, I'm not interested in being tied to you. You had that look, like you were going to be in the middle of it."

"Cuff her to that bicycle rack, Max. Let's move."

"You can't just leave me attached to a bicycle rack," Dubs said. "How do you know I won't take off? I'm not sitting here waiting around, watching this shit blow up in your face, or mine."

Holt got right in Dubs's face. She was a good six inches taller and a much more commanding presence. Max, totally inappropriately, thought the contrast between power and beauty was stunning.

"If you are not right here when I get back, your life will be much less pleasant than you can imagine. I don't have time to explain further. Do I need to?"

Dubs shook her head and Max wanted to laugh. She had seen that look many times before. She was sure she had produced it herself.

"Let's go, Max."

Max's heart was racing. She had never worked on a capture. While she technically worked under Holt as a bond enforcement agent, just like all the other members of Holt's crew, she usually did computer work only. She'd been asking for the opportunity to learn more fieldwork, and Moose, Holt's right-hand man, had been helping her learn a thing or two, but this was trial by fire. Holt was moving fast enough that Max had to jog to keep up.

"They see us coming, H. What's the plan?"

"Don't let them get away. They saw us moving ten minutes ago. You hold back and prevent an escape if they get past me. I'm getting the short one first. Sorry to throw you in the deep end."

"I'll be okay. What do you want me to do with the short guy? After you get him?"

"Keep him," Holt said, smiling.

Max was pretty sure it wasn't really as simple as that.

As they got closer to the two men, Holt started moving at "Holt speed." It didn't seem human, but Max had raced against her before. She knew Holt could run this fast for miles. She almost felt sorry for the short guy when Holt zeroed in on him. His eyes widened and he tried to run, but he didn't have warp speed, so he turned to fight. That was even stupider.

Holt easily caught the first punch and swatted it away. She didn't look like she wanted to engage in a true fistfight, and Max guessed that she was trying to break his spirit by showing him just how fruitless his efforts really were. Max tried to keep an eye on Holt while also keeping an eye on the second guy. When Holt engaged with Stumpy, the second one circled back around, apparently unconcerned with Max's presence. Max didn't think Holt would appreciate if she let the other guy sucker-punch her.

As he closed in, Max stepped up and kicked him in the shin. He howled and hopped on the un-accosted leg. Max tried to channel Holt and punched him in the gut. He had looked a little soft, but it still hurt like hell and she wanted to shake her hand out, but now he was mad and didn't seem as interested in Holt. He swung at her, and she barely avoided taking a square shot to the jaw. She spun away, turned around, and was horrified to see a knife in his right hand. Panic set in. A shin kick probably wasn't going to work now.

"Care to switch?" Holt asked. "That guy needs some handcuffs, and I didn't bring any." She motioned to the guy kneeling, clearly dazed, on the ground.

The knife-wielding attacker must have gotten bored waiting. He lunged at Max, who was still standing closer to his knife than Holt was. Max was paralyzed at the sight of the metal heading for her abdomen. Luckily, Holt was not. She lifted Max by the back of her shirt as if she were a small child and swung her behind Holt's body, out of harm's way. Holt must have also used the momentum of Max's swinging body for offensive purposes as well, because when Max turned back to the action, Holt was crouched low, with one leg extended where the man's knees had been when he was standing. He, however, was now flat on his back, the knife a few harmless feet away.

Max turned to the other man, the one she was now in charge of subduing. She was surprised he hadn't taken advantage of the situation and run, but Holt had a magnetic draw on many people, so perhaps he couldn't get out of her orbit. He moved to stand and she got into a defensive position.

"I'm a wicked shin-kicker, and not above a crotch shot. You missed your chance to run. And if you do now, she's got nothing to do, so I'll send her after you. What's your decision?" Max asked.

The man put his hands above his head and slowly lowered himself back to his knees.

"I think it was the threat of the shin kick," Holt said softly as she retrieved a pair of cuffs from Max's back pocket to restrain the knife wielder, while Max used another pair on Stumpy.

When they returned to the two state troopers, Holt turned their two captures over to them. They were high value, wanted in multiple states, and the troopers were happy to have them.

"Can I get out of these now?" Dubs asked, shaking the wrist attached to the bike rack and looking a little put out as she sat cross-legged in the dirt.

"Of course," Holt said. "But now that I know you can get out of them on your own, I'll be more careful with you. I was also curious how much you were willing to trust me. Now I know not at all.

Something you should know about me, Dubs. I never put my people in harm's way unnecessarily. I take care of my own. Neither one of us has to like it, but you are my people for the moment. You were in no danger."

Holt unlocked the cuffs from the bike rack, hoisted Dubs by the armpits, and walked her to Max's side. She pulled another set of cuffs from her pocket.

"Just how many of those things do you people carry around?" Dubs asked.

Max complied when Holt snapped the cold metal around her left wrist and coupled the other end to Dubs's right wrist, even though she didn't like it. At least the look of terror on the young trooper's face when Holt approached and demanded his chewing gum, was worth something. She split the gum in two and shoved half in each key hole.

Dubs looked like she was ready to explode, but she wisely didn't say anything. Max felt her shoulders slump. What was she going to do, tied to this woman? How was she going to work? How was she going to assist the mission in any way? She was a glorified babysitter.

"That should slow you down, what twenty, thirty seconds?" Holt asked Dubs.

"I make a living getting in and out of places people don't want me near," Dubs said. "Your gum is hardly an insurmountable obstruction. If I wanted to get away of course, which I'm not saying I do. I'm here for the greater good, remember?"

"Of course," Holt said. "But if you change your mind, that's why you're tethered to Max. She's very good at delivering a painful kick to the shins. Hard to drive a car that way. Keep that in mind."

CHAPTER THREE

Hey, Pulchritudinous Girl," Dubs said. They sat in the office, wasting time until Holt gave them instructions. "What did you call me?" Max asked, looking offended.

"It means physically beautiful. I played a lot of Scrabble when I was locked up. I always won because I was smart and studied the dictionary in my downtime. But like I was saying, I was worried your boss just stuck me with a pretty face to keep me happy. I mean, don't get me wrong, your face, it would totally make up for it if you didn't have anything else going for you, but now I know you've got some serious skills. Maybe not like your boss—what is she by the way? Some kind of human, ninja, assassin, alien, superhuman, Amazon, superhero, robot, cyborg, terminator hybrid? Anyway, like I was saying, now that I know you've got some wicked skills, I think we should be friends. Maybe an extra special kind of friend, if you know what I mean. Eh, what do you think?"

"I'm not sleeping with you," Max said. "And don't call me a polka-rude-girl. You sound like an idiot." Dubs thought she detected the slightest hint of a smile.

"Who said anything about sleeping together? Although we are back in these." Dubs held up their handcuffed wrists and waggled them back and forth. "So I think that's going to happen no matter what. Something to look forward to. But I was talking about getting your beautiful self into the passenger seat of a hot little car and going for a spin around town. I promise it feels so damn good if someone else is making the car payments." Dubs had been "clean" for a long time. The idea of stealing cars again, with permission, was almost as enticing as sex, booze, or any other vice she could think of.

"Not to burst the bubble on this perfect fantasy I can see playing out in your mind," Max said, pulling Dubs out of her daydream, "but I think the point of the handcuffs is that I'm always by your side, passenger seat or not. And I get the feeling you're a little intimidated by Holt, which is a healthy state of mind."

Dubs didn't like being so easily read. "Please. You saw how easily I can get out of these bracelets. And I only steal fast cars."

"You've never seen Holt run," Max said, her face straight.

Dubs had seen Holt in action at the park. She stuck by her earlier assessment of Holt's superhuman makeup. She didn't know whether to take Max seriously.

"What's Holt's deal anyway? She got a lady? I would like to see the woman who could take someone like Holt." As Dubs was saying that, she felt the air in the room change. It was as if everyone, Max included, simultaneously experienced the competing emotions of excitement and reverence, and all eyes were focused on the door. Dubs felt like a celebrity was entering the room. "Oh shit, never mind. That must be the boss's lady. You're all looking at her like she's the queen. And it's a title she wears well. She looks like a benevolent ruler, though. Not my type."

"Good Lord, you're insufferable," Max said. "But I wouldn't say a word about Isabelle in front of Holt. They're insanely into each other, and Holt is protective of what is hers. That's true of Isabelle, and all of us. Probably not you. You're just a dull instrument of destruction, bait in her trap, but the rest of us, she protects."

"Hey, she said I was one of her people." Dubs was offended until she caught Max's eye and realized she was teasing her. "Oh, so now we're going to play each other a little? Now you're going to like me, Pretty Girl? We'll see about this. So, what is the queen doing here? She doesn't look like the rest of the crew."

"Please, for your benefit, and mine, call her Isabelle. And she's here to meet Lola, I think."

"Lola's the starter-house sized one, right? Tuna's the four-bedroom house in the nice neighborhood, and Moose is the McMansion in the gated community?"

"I dare you to say that to one of their faces."

"I steal cars. I don't make a living being stupid."

"And yet, you ended up in the can," Max said, definitely teasing this time.

Dubs was sensitive about that fact, even though Max was only teasing. Truth be told, it was stupidity that got her arrested. Or arrogance. Maybe they were the same thing. And being locked up had cost her a lot. She was out to right some wrongs.

"So, do we just sit around here all day? What did you bust me out for?" Dubs asked.

"We've got a strategy meeting in four hours," Max said. "With the whole team. I've collected as much information as I can about thefts in the past three months, and the strange influx of money throughout the city. That's where you come in. We want your thoughts on the way it's being run. Is there anything else that would be helpful to you?"

"Do you have make and model of the cars?"

"And the neighborhoods where they were taken, and the time of day. As much as I could gather. If it was on the police report, I have the info. And some of them made news reports and other media, so I pulled data from those sources too. Although their accuracy is iffy."

Dubs felt like she was in the Twilight Zone. Stealing cars wasn't this technical. "I've got to see a few people. It will look weird if I'm out and don't stop by. I would prefer to do it alone, but I know our fearless leader would put the kibosh on that. I also need clothes."

"Sure. Let me check in with Moose." Max rose quickly and headed for the largest man in the room. She set off at a quick pace, but stopped short, jerking both of their arms painfully when she quickly reached the end of the handcuff's length. "Care to join me?" Max asked.

❖

Dubs was nervous as she approached the front steps of the home she knew so well. She had climbed these stairs more than the steps to her own home, but they felt so different now. Sadness hung from the worn rafters, shoddy shingles, and pieces of peeling paint now. The guilt and anguish she felt threatened to consume her.

"How do you think this is going to go?" Max asked. "Your father didn't make it sound like she was going to be happy to see you."

Max was right. They had just come from seeing Dubs's father, and he hadn't provided any assurances about the type of welcome they would receive from Mrs. Otis, but Dubs needed to be here. She just wished she wasn't handcuffed to Max. It was hard enough talking to her father, and she'd felt like she was speaking in code the whole conversation.

"We're about to find out, Pretty Girl."

Dubs knocked. The door opened and Mrs. Otis stood blocking the entrance. Dubs wanted to hug her, seek the comfort this woman had always provided, but she didn't. She waited.

"No one else thought you would come, Whitney. But I knew you would. How long have you been out?" No one else could get away with calling her Whitney.

"About six hours, ma'am," Dubs said.

"Have you seen your father?" Mrs. Otis asked.

"Yes, ma'am."

"Do I want to know why you have a young woman handcuffed to your arm?"

"It was a condition of my release. She's sort of like my parole officer." Dubs winked at Max, who glared at her.

"I'm Max Winters, ma'am. Nice to meet you."

"Come on in, you two," Mrs. Otis said.

Dubs settled on the familiar couch and was bombarded by memories of Levi. She had stayed as far away from his room as she could, but the house was small. She felt the pull of the space from across the living room. Max seemed uncomfortable next to her, and Dubs suspected it was because of how uncomfortable she was.

"His dying wasn't your fault, Whitney," Mrs. Otis said.

"Yes, ma'am, it was."

"Oh, sweetie, he was young and full of beans. He was going to do what he did. You know that."

"But if I wasn't locked up, he wouldn't have died. I could've stopped it." Dubs felt a strong urge to punch Max in the head, knock her unconscious, do anything to keep her from hearing this conversation.

"That still doesn't make it your fault. He would have found a different way to try to prove himself to you. Maybe killed himself that way, instead."

Dubs wasn't ready to let herself off the hook for her best friend's death. She appreciated his mother's forgiveness, though.

"Are you back in the game?"

"You can't ask me that kind of question in front of my parole officer," Dubs said.

"Max, if you're a parole officer, then I'm Spiderman, no offense of course," Mrs. Otis said. "You've always been a terrible liar, Whitney."

"That's not true. I'm a terrific liar. I just don't lie to you."

"Because you and Levi knew what was good for you. So I ask you again. Are you back in the game?"

"Do you want me to be?" Dubs asked. The answer was surprisingly important.

Mrs. Otis stood right in front of Dubs. She grabbed her by the jaw, the meaty hand resting on her chin. "If you get back in, you had better promise me to be more careful than you were last time. When you're focused, there is no one better. But I hear it's a different world out there now, so no more stupidity like what got you caught. You understand me?"

Dubs nodded, although most of the nodding was courtesy of Mrs. Otis's helping hand.

"If you're back in, Shorty's car is two houses down."

"You said it was a different world. What good would stealing Shorty's car do? That guy's just a pontificating minor leaguer."

"You and your big fancy words," Mrs. Otis said, holding Dubs in a long stare. She clearly wasn't going to elaborate on her earlier suggestion. She obviously didn't trust Max's presence, and probably wasn't sure she should trust her either. Dubs knew the feeling.

"And you." Mrs. Otis turned on Max. "I don't know who you are, but you take care of her. Watch her back. You hear me?"

"Yes, ma'am."

Dubs was amused to see how intimidated Max was. This woman worked for Holt Lasher, the most feared woman in Rhode Island, a bounty hunter whose reputation alone scared most criminals into keeping their court date. But here Max was, terrified of a grieving mother. At least Dubs knew Max was intelligent. Everyone should be scared of Mrs. Otis.

"I can't bear to lose another child."

CHAPTER FOUR

Did I miss a wedding announcement? You two are so adorable. I think you're taking the 'til death do us part' thing a little seriously, though," Moose said when Max and Dubs walked into the full staff briefing back at the office. The handcuffs were hard to miss.

"You're hilarious, big man. Jealous? No one to handcuff yourself to on the long, lonely nights?" Max felt much more comfortable here, among her friends, than she had out in the world, alone with Dubs on turf she wasn't familiar with.

Poor Moose looked confused when everyone in the room burst into laughter. Everyone except Jose, that is. Lola had snuck up behind Jose and forcibly raised his hand when Max was teasing Moose about not having a special friend to share his handcuffs. Everyone in the room, with the exception of Moose, knew Jose was desperately into Moose. Apparently, it had been that way since Moose, Jose, Lola, and Holt were kids.

Max made her way, with Dubs following, to her usual seat at the table. Her laptop, and a sense of normalcy, were waiting. However, only one chair was in place. They were a crew of routine. Everyone sat in the same order around the table, and all the chairs were accounted for. Today they had to squeeze extras in for Jose, who was visiting from the mechanic shop he ran next door, and Isabelle. And now they needed one for the convict attached to Max.

The one chair dilemma didn't seem to have escaped Dubs's notice, either. Max wasn't sure anything escaped her notice. "I'm happy to sit on your lap, Pretty Girl. I'd be real content."

"You never stop trying, do you?" Max said. She wasn't sure whether to be flattered, offended, on guard, or annoyed. Dubs was hard to get a read on.

"I'm not trying for anything. Just making a truthful statement. There's only one chair, and I'm sure I could get real comfortable in your arms."

"Can I get another chair, please?" Max said.

Isabelle gave up her chair. "It's nice to meet you, Dubs. Holt said you'll be joining her team for a while. I see you and Max will be getting to know each other."

For all her earlier digs about Isabelle being the queen they all bowed down to, Dubs seemed to be at a loss for words. Which, from the limited time Max had spent with Dubs, seemed unusual.

Max gave Dubs a little handcuff wrist jiggle to get her talking. "Oh, yes, ma'am. A little time. Seems my skills are useful for something good. And anything is better than jail."

"I don't doubt that," Isabelle said. "There's no one better around here to look after you than Max. And Holt will keep you safe. Welcome."

Isabelle retreated and took her seat on Holt's lap, since there weren't any more chairs. One could have been brought from the other room, but no one was going to suggest that. Dubs was right about everyone in the crew adoring Isabelle. They loved her for who she was, but also for how happy she made Holt.

"Oh, so she can choose any lap she wants?" Dubs asked, plopping down grumpily in her chair. "Did I even make any sense when I was talking to her? I'm not sure I put together a coherent sentence. What's wrong with me?"

"Not any lap," Max said, sort of enjoying Dubs's discomfort. She hadn't been sure Dubs was flappable until now. "I dare you to suggest Isabelle test out yours."

"Is that when Hulk gets angry?" Dubs asked, smiling genuinely, or so it seemed, for the first time since they met. It was a beautiful thing.

Max squeezed Dubs's hand in her own and returned the smile, feeling like maybe they were laying down the first tiny building block of connection. "Now you're catching on."

"All right, let's get started," Holt said. "We've got a lot of work to do, and limited intel. Max has a new houseguest I'm hoping can help us. This is a special assignment, so business keeps running as normal, but I'm going to pull a few of you in to work this too. Isabelle is on this one as well, but only behind the scenes. We all know what happened the last time she went in the field."

"Yeah, boss, you got yourself shot and Isabelle had to save your ass."

"That's funny, that's not quite how I remember it," Holt said, smiling.

"We do," the group said, almost in unison.

"Fine. I can see I'm outnumbered. I'll be honest. I'm concerned about employing a group of individuals with such horrible memory." Holt didn't seem to mind the teasing. "This time, no one gets shot, okay? I really, really hate getting shot."

"And I really, really prefer her in one piece," Isabelle said. "That goes for all of you."

"Enough," Holt said. "Isabelle swears she's staying, and I don't need to give her a reason to lock all of us in a dark dungeonous room until our business goes under, just to keep us all safe."

"This might not be the time," Moose said, "but how did you end up crossing off two of our most wanted during a meet and greet with Max's new houseguest? This is just a rumor, but I hear you were stripping down weapons again."

"Who, me? Nah. I mean, I had to disarm the state troopers who were waving their guns all around the park. Maybe that's where that rumor started. The bad boys were only armed with knives. And Max took care of them. I mostly just watched and waited with handcuffs. Right, Dubs?"

Max wanted to argue. That wasn't at all how the encounter in the park had occurred. But she knew better than to challenge Holt in this setting. She was curious to see if Dubs did.

"Yep. Holt moved like the Flash, stripped the young cop's weapon to pieces, and Max was awesome fighting both dudes. I was tied to a bicycle rack, so I had a perfect view."

While it felt good to accept the congratulations from the rest of the crew for the captures, it was false praise. Holt had to swoop in and save her when the guy pulled the knife, and Holt was the one who subdued the first guy. If she ever had a free moment again, she was going to ask her about it.

"Why do you keep tying this poor woman up?" Isabelle asked Holt.

"She left out the part where she let herself out of the handcuffs when the fighting started. The bicycle rack was more of a rallying point. She just happened to be cuffed to it, but she could have left at any time. I'm glad she didn't though, because then she wouldn't be here now. But I'm still not entirely sure she's not going to make a run the moment she gets bored with us."

Max wanted to laugh. It wasn't a good idea to challenge Holt so openly, especially not in front of her entire crew. Dubs had tried to play the sympathy card, insinuating she was being mistreated, but it backfired. Now everyone knew Dubs was a mini Houdini, if they didn't already. They also knew she wasn't yet a team player. Max wondered if Holt had been baiting Dubs a little, as she now understood she had been in the park. It was going to be hard being so close to someone, living with her, and not knowing if you could trust her.

"Back to business," Holt said. "Let's talk about what we know. A few months ago, there was a dramatic increase in the number of cars stolen in the Providence area. The pattern of thefts, and methods used, don't match any that police recognize from known car thieves in the area. The most notorious and well respected of those known thieves was cooling her heels in prison anyway." Holt pointed at Dubs, who mimicked taking a dramatic bow.

"And then they went and pissed in your morning Wheaties. Right, boss?" Lola said. "No offense, Isabelle."

"Why does everyone around here think I have these delicate little lady ears that need to be protected all the time?"

"They don't know you like I do." Holt planted a kiss on one of Isabelle's "lady ears." Sometimes, Max was totally infatuated by how much they loved each other, caught up in their current, hoping she too could find that one day. And sometimes, she wished they would keep it to themselves and not rub it in to all the rest of the poor fools in the office who weren't so damned happy, and adorable, and in love.

"Don't play all nice with me, trying to distract your crew. I think a few of them are wondering where their fearless leader went, by the way. We all know what happens when someone pisses in your Wheaties. Or in the general vicinity of your Wheaties, Cheerios, Grape-Nuts, oatmeal, Fruity Pebbles, or Cap'n Crunch." Isabelle tugged gently on Holt's hair.

"I end up handcuffed to Dubs," Max said. The room cracked up. Holt shot her a look, but Max was getting better at reading Holt's expressions. This wasn't the look of death.

"Would you and your new BFF like to run us through the data you've been collecting? The state police, Providence police, and some of our informants on the street, all seem to think the uptick in thefts is due to a new power player entering the arena. The police don't know who the new player is, and if our contacts know, they aren't saying."

"They probably won't tell you," Dubs said. "Some of the crews out there are mixed up in drugs, guns, sex. Some pretty nasty stuff. I'd keep my mouth shut, too. It's a smarter way to stay alive."

"So what can we provide you, from here, to help narrow down our list of suspects?" Moose asked.

"You said you have a list of all the stolen cars?" Dubs asked, looking at Max.

Their handcuff-necessitated proximity made everything they did feel intimate, but there was something about the way Dubs asked her about the list that felt like it was tickling her spine. Max knew Dubs was playing with her. She just didn't know how she was doing it. She put on her best Holt style game face and focused on her computer.

"I'll put it on the screen, then I guess we'll tag team it since we're a three-armed monster," Max said. She clicked a few buttons and sent all the data she had been scooping up recently to the big screen hanging on the wall. The screen made her geek out every time she got to use it. Holt bought it for her after she beat her during the fundraising challenge last year. No one had ever beaten Holt, so it was a big deal.

"We're up," Max said, pulling Dubs to her feet.

"What are we going to do up there? Don't you need your computer and your fancy fingers on those keys, Pretty Girl?"

"Do you do anything without talking about it first?" Max asked, hoping she didn't have to drag Dubs to the front of the room.

"Nope. I even talk to myself when I'm relieving someone of their vehicle."

"Fantastic." Max didn't think she would ever sleep again.

She tapped the large screen on the wall, and it came to life. The map of the greater Providence area she had sent from her computer was now displayed on the screen. The cluster of stolen cars was in the lower right-hand corner. She put her right index finger in the center of the grouping and flung the whole cluster toward the center of the map. They aligned with dots on the map.

Next she put her finger over a second group of data, this time vehicle makes and models. As she flipped them onto the map, the data points lined up, one each with the vehicles.

"What kind of voodoo magic are you doing?" Dubs asked, trying to back away from Max, but only getting so far.

"Just look at the screen. Tell us what you see. Please don't tell me now, of all times, you're at a loss for words." Max liked Dubs being off balance for a change. Since they'd met, it felt like she was always the one on her heels.

Dubs studied the map. Max wasn't sure the rest of the room could see the look on her face, but it looked as if Dubs was reading a really good book, or a letter from a friend. The map clearly meant more to her than it did to any of them.

"Okay," Dubs said. "These two aren't your new crew." She pointed at two of the map dots. "Neither are these, or these." Dubs identified a few more thefts.

"Any that aren't related, put your finger on, and flick off the map," Max said. "It will be faster if you do it."

"Flick them off the map? Are you insane? It's a television screen." Dubs didn't seem as convinced of the awesomeness of Max's toy as she was.

Max demonstrated.

Dubs looked much more impressed after she saw it in action. "All right, I've got the idea. Move over."

When Dubs was done sorting, about fifty-five percent of the thefts had been eliminated.

"Do those belong to the new guy?" Moose asked.

"I don't know for sure," Dubs said. "But they don't belong to anyone I know. And from what you said, this new player has upped the total volume by a lot. This is a lot. Most of these cars are high-end, too. You're chasing an enterprising little fireball. I mean, we're chasing, of course. It's just, I have some professional admiration for his balls."

"Speaking of which, isn't that your truck on the map, H?"

"Oh, you happened to notice that, did you?" Holt said, looking amused.

"So what's the plan, H? Do we start causing a ruckus in the areas still lit up on the map? Lay down our own gauntlet?" Lola asked.

"Any luck on the money, sweetheart?" Holt asked Isabelle.

"Not yet. I need more time. Forensic accounting is new to me. I'd be much faster if these guys needed their taxes done."

"Maybe you should stand on the corner in one of these neighborhoods in one of those Statue of Liberty costumes, you know, the ones for the cheap tax services. Maybe you can actually do their taxes." Tuna laughed at his own joke.

"We're not laying down any gauntlets just yet. And no costumes," Holt said. "But we do have the best thief in the state." Holt paused and stared at Dubs, who stood glaring at her. "What? You need your ego stroked? I can do that for you. I understand it's been lonely in prison." Holt was clearly enjoying herself. "Okay, I'll start over. We do have the best thief in the country."

Max heard Dubs let out a breath. When she looked over, Dubs was shaking her head, looking both entertained and exasperated.

"Too much?" Holt said. "Fine, you tell me how good you are."

"New England, at least," Dubs said. "Probably Eastern Seaboard."

"Best east of Denver?" Max asked.

"That's just bragging," Dubs said.

"It's okay," Holt said. "You're among friends here."

"I don't know that yet, ma'am," Dubs said seriously.

"Well, friends at my table get to help plan the attack. What would you suggest our next move is?"

Max wondered if Dubs knew she was being tested. Max wasn't sure if that was Holt's intention, but it felt like it might be. Holt had said she didn't feel confident about this new job, and none of them knew Dubs. Max had already gotten the impression she was moving to her own beat, which may or may not line up with what Holt wanted from her. Max wasn't sure what was giving her that sense, since they'd only spent a short time together, but there was something that wasn't sitting quite right.

"You want to find out who this new crew is," Dubs said. Her voice sounded strong, but Max could see her hands were shaking slightly. Maybe Holt could even scare the pants off a cocky car thief.

"So I need to start stealing some cars. In my old territory. I saw my father and an old friend today, so everyone knows I'm out. They also probably know I'm here. If you cut me loose and let me get back to work, I'll have the new crew's attention by the end of the week."

"Not going to happen," Holt said. "You don't get cut loose. The rest we can talk about. What do you think, Max?"

Max didn't expect Holt to seek her opinion on fieldwork. She thought the park demonstrated pretty definitively that she had a truckload of things to learn.

"Well, we need to find this crew. It's been surprisingly hard. Dubs test-driving a few cars seems like the best, and fastest, way to do that. Besides, I'll be with her. What could go wrong?" Her last statement got the laugh it was intended to elicit.

"I can't steal cars like this," Dubs said. Max thought she might actually be pouting a little.

"Start with something easy," Holt said. "Make sure you still got your mojo. And Max stays by your side. Bring me back something pretty, and then we'll talk handcuffs. And then you drop it off where the police will have no trouble finding it. No one gets hurt long-term in this, understood?"

"Damn, boss, talkin' dirty to me and in front of your lady, too."

Max noticed Dubs had her swagger back. She wasn't sure if she should be happy about that or worried.

"Let's go, Pretty Girl. We've got work to do."

CHAPTER FIVE

Holt pinched the bridge of her nose, hoping it would either help clarify the day, or make her head stop hurting. It did neither. Instead, she ran her hands through her hair and let out a sigh. She relaxed when she felt Isabelle's hands on her shoulders.

She was perched on the side of the bed, but now that Isabelle provided an alternative, she slumped back against her, resting her head against Isabelle's chest.

"This seems a little dramatic," Isabelle said, waving her hand at Holt. "Need a little help feeling sorry for yourself?"

"Hey," Holt said, "I thought you were supposed to be supportive and understanding. You know, help me lick my wounds when I've had a rough day."

"I am being supportive. I'm giving you a solid kick in the ass. What is going on with you? You've been stomping around for the past hour, and now you've moved on to dramatic sighing. The loft isn't that big. Headphones are my next move."

"I've got them handcuffed together. What am I thinking? And of all people to put on this fresh-out-of-prison, probably unreformed thief, I chose Max. That was the stomping."

"And the sighing is because you don't see any other way?" Isabelle asked.

"Are you some kind of accountant mind reader?" Holt felt like she shouldn't be surprised by Isabelle's uncanny ability to know what she was thinking, but she still was. "I don't trust Dubs. I don't think she trusts herself, and she has no reason to trust me. I need someone close to her at all times, and Lola has other things on her mind right now. And Dubs is young, so Max is more likely to connect with her. But Jesus, Max is so damned green."

"You said she did well in the park," Isabelle said.

"She kicked a guy in the shin and almost broke her wrist punching his teddy bear gut. But she didn't completely panic until he pulled a knife, so I'll call it a win."

"Sweetie, I love you. I really do. But two things. First, I could do without hearing about people swinging knives at you. It's still too close to your getting shot for me. And second, not everyone is you. If you want Max to fight like you, teach her. But if she does, and she gets hurt, I'm holding you responsible."

"Does it defeat the weight of your message if I find it sexy when you so clearly show me who is in charge around here?" Holt asked. She arched back as far as she could in Isabelle's arms and lifted her head toward Isabelle's. Their upside-down kiss calmed some of her roiling emotions. "You're my safe harbor," Holt said.

Isabelle kissed Holt's nose and put her palm against her cheek. "I'm glad you feel that way. Every superhero needs a safe place to call home. I want it to always be right here."

"I don't know how I got so lucky," Holt said. "Did I see you meeting with Lola today?"

"That poor woman is turned inside out right now. Tiffany left her the positive pregnancy test and offered her the baby, but now Lola can't find her. She's been looking since we found her on our doorstep. She doesn't even know how far along Tiffany is."

"Is she going to keep the kid?"

"I think so. I don't think she can imagine what will happen if she doesn't. Tiffany's note indicated she didn't want the baby, so Lola feels like she doesn't have a choice. While we were talking, it seemed like the reality of it was starting to set in. That's a lot of responsibility."

"She's going to need a lawyer," Holt said. "If she's going to go through with keeping the baby. And she should get it in place as soon as she can, so everything is ready once we find Tiff. I'll call in a favor and get her hooked up. Sometimes it's convenient being connected."

"Do you want kids?" Isabelle asked.

"I love kids," Holt said.

"Not an answer to my question. Spending five minutes with you and Superman sort of gave away your love of that little guy. What about your own, our own?"

Holt felt a little short of breath. She hadn't thought about it, ever. She figured no one would want to partner with her, given the life she led, so being a parent seemed like the last thing on her mind. Sure, her friend Amy was a single mom, but she was an amazing woman. Holt didn't think she could do what Amy did. But now she had Isabelle.

"What about my job?" Holt asked.

"I still hate how dangerous it is, despite you saying it's boring and mostly paper pushing. But I don't think it's more dangerous than if you were a police officer or firefighter. Certainly not more dangerous than if you were a soldier. They all have children."

"Did my mother put you up to this?"

"Your mother calls me 'Adele.' Although she might learn my name if we produce a grandchild."

"Ugh. That woman gives me migraines. Do you want children?"

"I think so. I wasn't sure for a while. Daddy issues and all. But lately, I've changed my mind. And now, the image of you holding our baby in your beautiful, tattooed arms...Well. I like that idea a lot."

"You do have a soft spot for my ink," Holt said.

"Just something to think about," Isabelle said. "But if there is a baby in our future, this loft, as beautiful as it is, won't work. So think long and hard, Hot Stuff."

"I do think I might like to give mothering a shot one day," Holt said. "But what's wrong with my loft? You don't seem in a hurry to leave. You even made me put my boxers and boxer briefs all in the same drawer so you could move in here."

"Someone was murdered in my house. Considering that is my alternative, your underwear drawer problems seem minor."

Holt felt guilty about the fact that Isabelle didn't feel comfortable in her own home anymore. If she had gotten to Isabelle sooner that night, or if she had been by her side, as she should have been, it might not have happened. Not that Holt was complaining about Isabelle moving in. Coming home to her every day, and waking up next to her each morning, had enhanced her life in ways she didn't think possible.

"I'm sorry about your house," Holt said. "I'll buy you any house in the state that will make you feel safe."

Isabelle shook her head and smiled, as she always did when Holt offered. "If you're here, then I feel safe. I like the loft. For now, it works just fine. Someday we'll consider something else. And when we do, we won't let any of your work acquaintances know where we are."

"Sounds like heaven," Holt said. It really did.

CHAPTER SIX

Dubs knew Max was annoyed, but they were about to head out onto her turf to play her game, and she needed to feel comfortable. Since they were handcuffed together, that meant Max had to sit on the toilet awkwardly while Dubs put on her makeup. She never stole cars without it. It was part of her routine. At least she didn't have to do her hair too. A ponytail was good enough for work.

"I'm almost done, Pretty Girl," Dubs said. "We've got to look the part."

"I don't think too many car thieves look like you, Dubs," Max said. "Makeup or not."

"Is that a compliment? Are you flirting with me, even though I know you really don't want to?" Dubs couldn't get a read on Max. Maybe they just hadn't spent enough time together. It hadn't even been twenty-four hours yet. Usually, though, Dubs knew all she needed to about cars and women in less than half that amount of time. Either she had lost some of her edge in prison, or Max was unlike anyone she had ever encountered. She really hoped it was the latter, since she was about to take them out for a joyride. She might be technically working for Holt Lasher, Superwoman extraordinaire, but she was sure there were still more than a few Providence cops who would be happy to forget that and toss her back in jail for the night. Holt had done half the job of cuffing her already.

"I don't flirt. Certainly not with you," Max said, clearly grumpy. "Are you almost done? How long does it take to put on all this stuff?"

"A lot less time if I didn't have to do it one-handed. And it would help if you could sit still," Dubs said. She didn't believe for one second that Max didn't flirt. She'd caught her staring more than once today. "So, did our genius boss give you any ideas on how exactly we are supposed to blend into a crowd while handcuffed together? Stealing cars is all about not being noticed. These are pretty noticeable." Dubs held up their joined wrists.

Max moved like a blur. Dubs's mascara tube clattered to the floor as her cuffed wrist was wrenched behind her and her face was pressed against the bathroom wall. Max stood behind her, holding her there, forcing submission.

"There are a few things we need to get clear," Max said, from the sound of her voice, clearly very angry. "Don't lie to me and we'll get along just fine, but until I know you're not lying, I have no reason to trust you. Stealing cars is your thing. You figure out how we do it. If it was easy, probably everyone would do it, so a few extra hurdles doesn't require whining. And finally, when I'm around, which, given the cuffs, is going to be always, Holt gets the respect she deserves, from you and everyone else. Got it? Bow at her feet, kiss her pinky ring, whatever you think is appropriate, it's probably still not enough. At least not in my eyes. And not in the rest of her crew's eyes either. You're lucky to be in the position you're in. Take advantage. And don't blow it."

"Did you just burst out of all of your clothes and turn green?" Dubs asked.

"What?"

"You know, Hulk mad, Hulk smash. 'Cause I'm feeling a little like a mosquito here." Dubs's words were a bit slurred since half her face was pressed against a tile wall.

Max released her slightly. "You hear what I said?"

"Yes, yes. Don't lie or cheat. You and the rest of Holt's crew have a major hard-on for her. I got it. Well, I don't get it, but I got it. She's not been the most welcoming though. Just have to say that."

Dubs felt Max tense up on her right arm, which was still behind her back, once again.

"Hey, wait a minute. No need to get all tyrannical again. I won't say another word about Holt." In truth, she hadn't really formed an opinion about Holt yet. She was intimidated by her, and respected how much power she commanded. Until just now, she thought she must rule mostly by intimidation, but Max didn't seem scared of her. Holt had seemed to be trying to intimidate Dubs earlier in the day, though. She was another one who was hard to read.

"She's testing you," Max said. "She's not going to let you get close to any of us if she can't trust you. She puts our safety and well-being above her own on every job we do. It's just how she is."

"And yet here we are," Dubs said.

"If I needed her, she'd be here."

Max seemed so sure of that statement, Dubs wondered if the room was bugged. Maybe the handcuffs?

"So do you want to go and cool off as far away from me as possible while I finish getting ready?" Dubs asked. "Maybe you could sit on the edge of the tub, and I'll use this little mirror and sit on the toilet seat? If we stretch our arms out, it might work."

The attempt at humor seemed to work, as the air in the room didn't feel so charged, and Max actually smiled. Pretty Girl wasn't just something Dubs called her; it was an accurate description. Especially when she smiled.

"Well, I don't want you to think you're the only one working around here. I actually did think about us blending in out and about. I asked Jose to make some modifications to our jackets. We now have zippers on our sleeves, and there is a tear-away Velcro closure inside each sleeve too. We can hide these pretty well, hopefully."

"Jose the mechanic?"

"We're a multitalented group. Do you play an instrument? Write poetry? I don't think we currently have anyone who does face painting."

"Okay, now I know you're flirting with me," Dubs said.

"Are you done with your makeup?" Max asked. "It's almost dark. You promised me a joyride."

❖

"This isn't quite what I had in mind for the evening," Max said. "Don't get me wrong; watching you consume five lattes in the past two hours has been awesome. Not so much when you have to evacuate all those lattes and I have to go with you, but didn't we have something else in mind for tonight?"

"Pretty Girl, you sit still worse than I do. And we're doing exactly what we planned on doing tonight. I told you, we're waiting for the match. Until then, we're just two beautiful women, enjoying a nice evening on the patio of a lovely coffee shop, on a long, luxurious date. Now snuggle closer, our cuffs are starting to show again." Dubs had been holding Max's hand, or snuggling up close to her, or somehow keeping their hands in very close proximity, in order to keep the handcuffs joining them hidden beneath their jackets, for the past couple hours. It was incredibly distracting. Sure, they were both simply putting on a show, but Max was hot, and Dubs had been in prison for a long time. If the end goal wasn't getting behind the wheel of a sweet BMW tonight, all this hand-holding would have changed her plans for the evening.

"Why don't you trust me?" Dubs asked.

"I don't have any reason to," Max said. "And any time you've been given the chance to provide a straight answer, you don't. You have something snarky to say. You didn't join this team willingly, so I don't know what your motives are."

"Well, that was honest," Dubs said. Max wasn't really that far off the mark. Her life prospects had changed so much in the past few days even she wasn't sure what, or who, to trust. All she knew was once she found out about Levi dying, she had needed to get out of prison. Holt Lasher and this new group of thieves had provided that opportunity. She would figure the rest out later.

"Is it going to be a problem that some of your people saw you with me today?" Max said. "Do they know you date girls?"

"Please," Dubs said. "My father set me up on my first date. If anyone has a problem with you being with me, it's because they know who you work for. They'll think this means I've turned snitch. My father, Mrs. Otis, they're old school. In their world, you're either good or bad, no gray area. If I'm there with you, I've crossed over."

"Are they going to tell other people that?" Max looked worried.

"Hell no," Dubs said. "That would get me killed. People will have to come to their own conclusions. But Holt is putting us both in danger by chaining us together."

"I'm sure she has her reasons." Max seemed a little less convinced.

"Don't throw your coffee in my face or anything, but why do you follow her so unconditionally?"

"It's not unconditional," Max said. "And it's not without foundation. You just have to know her, I guess. If you've been through the shit with her, you tend to be a believer."

"That's some pretty strong Kool-Aid," Dubs said. "Does the really big dude mix it up special every morning? I bet with his biceps, he can practically froth it to a boil. Is that what makes it so powerful?" Dub hoped Max could tell she was teasing.

"No, they leave me in charge of that," Max said. "It requires a featherlight touch. It's like egg whites. You can't over beat."

"Tell me more about your featherlight touch," Dubs said. "Tell me about the unstoppable badass, Max Winters. From your absolute spaztastic freak-out over that screen thingy in the office, I'm going to guess you lean slightly techy. Am I right?"

"I'm the data acquisition specialist and technology advisor for the crew," Max said.

"You know I have no idea what that means, right?" Dubs said. "Wait. Are you like Tony Stark from the Iron Man movies? With all the fancy computer toys and tricks?"

"That's just a movie, Dubs."

"Oh." Dubs was disappointed.

"My skills are so much better than Iron Man's."

Dubs caught Max's eye as she grinned wryly. When it came to computers and whatever "data acquisition" was, Max was clearly the shit and she knew it. Dubs couldn't think of anything sexier.

"Maybe you can show me some of your wicked skills soon," Dubs said. "I am prepared to be very impressed. But right now, we should think about wrapping up. Our ride just arrived."

"What do you mean it just arrived? From where?" Max looked around. She must not have seen the car Dubs had been waiting for for the past two hours.

"Did you really not notice that we've been enjoying our evening coffees right across the street from an extremely busy valet drop-off for half the restaurants around here?"

"Of course I noticed that," Max said. "But I'm not a car thief, so I don't understand how that is relevant to our situation. This is part of the trust issue. You could have shared your plan for the evening when we sat down like I asked. Instead, you said you were planning on people-watching and having coffee."

"I was watching people," Dubs said. It wasn't really a lie. She'd only ever told her secrets to Levi, when she was teaching him. It was habit to not let anyone in on her thinking.

"And apparently more than that," Max said, looking a little more cooperative than earlier.

"Well, the car we're going to steal just got dropped off with the valet. The couple that got out looked like they were dressed for dinner. We have at least an hour, but the sooner we move the better. That gives us the longest head start before they notice the car is missing."

"It's a busy night. Won't the valet notice us?"

"I don't plan on being in there that long," Dubs said. "But if we get spotted, we'll have to improvise. You willing to play along with whatever we need to do?"

Max didn't look like she particularly liked the sound of that plan, but she nodded in agreement anyway. Max paid for their coffee and pastry and they crossed the street, hand in hand.

Dubs made sure they moved at a casual pace, keeping their focus more on each other than their destination.

"You seem familiar with this setup, the coffee shop, the valet stand, the lot. Done work here before?" Max asked.

"I'm touched you noticed," Dubs said, snuggling a little closer to Max's neck.

"What car are we looking for?"

"That beautiful black BMW they parked right over there." Dubs had watched the car all the way into the lot. That was another reason she had used this place to scout cars for so long. The valet lot was open-air. She could watch the attendants park the cars she was interested in. It made accessing them much easier.

"Convenient," Max said. "What do you need me to do once we're there? How long do you need?"

"I'm usually on my own, but it will be nice to have someone keeping watch. If all goes well, we'll be driving out of here thirty seconds from the time I first put my hands on that car." Dubs hadn't felt this particular brand of excitement in years. It was hard to force herself to calm down. She was already four steps ahead and behind the wheel driving away. She had to focus or they were both in trouble. Even though this was an easy steal, things could still go wrong.

"Thirty seconds?" Max seemed incredulous.

"Maybe forty-five, because you'll have to climb through the driver's side to your seat. That will slow us down. Good thing you're so little."

"You better not be all talk."

"I guess we're about to find out." Dubs tested the driver side door. It was locked. She pulled out her lock pick kit and moved to the trunk. Max followed close. "Watch for anyone coming. I'll have this open in a second."

"Why are you opening the trunk?"

"Because I would much rather have a key to drive us out of here than have to hot-wire this thing and set off the alarm. The owner didn't use a valet key when he dropped it off. I'm banking on the valet key still being in the BMW-issued toolkit in the trunk. Most people don't even know it's back here. Not all the models have them that way. Some have a spare key adapter in the glove box, but this one does."

"Car approaching, D south," Max said, sounding stressed.

"What?" Dubs didn't understand anything but the first part.

"Company. We've got company."

Dubs had the trunk unlocked, but she didn't want that to be obvious. She held it down, but not enough to relock, and spun Max around so that Max was leaning against the car and Dubs was pressed against her. "Go with it, okay?"

Max nodded and cupped the back of Dubs's head with the uncuffed hand. She pulled her in and kissed her. Dubs knew Max was playing a part, but she was still surprised at how exciting the kiss felt. Maybe it was because it was delivered during the commission of a theft, something that already excited her, or maybe because she knew so little about Max and that, in and of itself, was alluring. Or maybe it was all the coffee she had consumed. Regardless, she didn't think Max kissing her would be so enjoyable, especially when she knew it didn't mean anything.

After the car moved past and parked and the valet returned to his post, Max returned Dubs to her work.

"Damn, Pretty Girl. Where'd you learn to kiss like that?"

"That wasn't a kiss," Max said. "That was an undercover maneuver. If I had kissed you, you would know."

Dubs wasn't sure Max was as unaffected as she was pretending to be, but she got back to work. It wouldn't do either of them any good to stand here and argue about it. She located the valet key and unlocked the driver side door. They let out the full length of the cuffs for the first time all night and Max scrambled across the driver's seat and center console to the passenger seat. Dubs was hot on her tail.

She started the car and pulled out of the lot. Her pace was casual, and she used her turn signals and obeyed traffic laws and speed limits. This was not the time to burn up the pavement.

"The valet key only allows the car to run for ten minutes at a time," Dubs said. "We have to find an alley to restart in four minutes."

"There." Max pointed to the perfect location a few blocks ahead.

Dubs pulled in, stopped the engine, and restarted. She backed out and turned back into traffic. "Where are we ditching this thing?"

"Downtown. Somewhere easy for it to be found. How about by Kennedy Plaza?" Max said.

"You got it," Dubs said. "We might have to stop again. Find me another alley in about five minutes."

"This is a damn fine car," Max said, looking around for the first time.

"I told you there's nothing like it. Isn't it better knowing someone else is making the payments?"

"I didn't say that. I just said it's a nice car. I understand why you like them so much. Jose, too. He rambles on about cars so much and I never understood why. This car I can understand. Some of the crap cars he seems to love, those I don't understand."

"Oh, I'm going to make you love them all. You'll see. No friend of mine will be allowed to be a luxury car snob. I shouldn't have started you off so high-end. Now you've got a taste for it. Next time we're going to steal a nineteen eighty-four Lincoln Town Car."

"I can tell already I won't like that one," Max said. "Our next alley is ahead on the right. And just when did you decide we were friends?"

Dubs pulled the car into the alley and repeated the shutdown and restart procedure. "When you kissed me. That really brought our relationship to a new level. Didn't you feel it? Remember, we're building trust here. Be truthful."

"You're impossible," Max said. "Okay, I guess once you've stolen a car with someone, it would be rude not to consider them a friend."

"Pretty Girl, you and I did make a good team, but you're dancing around the kiss. Which of course tells me everything I need to know. I'm pretty good at data acquisition too. Just in my own Luddite way."

"Focus on the road, Dubs."

"Uh huh." Dubs liked working with Max. She didn't think she would have enjoyed it. In fact, she had been dreading it. But sitting here now, cruising along in a beautiful car, with Max sitting next to her, that was nice. It also made her feel horribly guilty. It used to be Levi sitting next to her. Was she going to take Max on as her protégé like she had Levi? Look how that had turned out. But Max wasn't here to learn from her, and she had never had any interest in kissing Levi. She shouldn't feel the similarities, but she did. Until she figured out how to do right by Levi, this was a burden she had to carry.

"What's wrong?" Max asked. "You look awfully brooding all of a sudden."

"Oh, nothing." She didn't realize she was so transparent. "This just reminded me of a moment from the past."

"Did it involve Levi, Mrs. Otis's son?"

"He's off limits, Max. We don't know each other that well," Dubs said. She didn't talk about Levi with anyone.

"Okay, then tell me about the best car you ever stole."

"That's a hard question. Do you want to know about my favorite car I ever stole? Or my favorite theft? Those aren't the same question, and they don't get the same answer."

"This sounds like fun," Max said. "Start with your favorite car."

"That's easy. Maserati GranTurismo. It was a matte black exterior with a red wine color leather interior. Even the steering wheel. You should have seen the pedals on this thing. I could have just stolen those and been happy until the day I died. I wanted to keep driving that car all night."

"Where did you find a car like that? I don't think I've ever seen something like that rolling through Providence," Max said.

"You should spend a little time in Narragansett in the summer. I'd love to see you killing it on the beach. If you did, you would also see a lot of really amazing cars."

"So how did you pull that off? Don't those cars have maximum security?"

"I would assume so, but I wouldn't know. The driver left the car running when he ran in to buy snacks at the gas station. Good thing I was there to relieve such a dumbass of that amazing car. He probably would have driven it into something. A beauty like that didn't deserve that idiot," Dubs said.

"You've got some funny ideas about deserving and ownership, but I guess I already knew that. What about your favorite theft?"

"It isn't the most complicated, but it is my favorite. There was this politician from a few years ago that had it out for a friend of mine. So I stole his car three times. I kept stealing it and leaving it a few blocks from where he had parked it. I always waited a few days though. Just long enough for the police to get involved and the news media to pick up the story. By the third time, he was considered a buffoon and his career was basically over."

"I remember reading about the politician who couldn't keep track of his car. The assumption was that he couldn't remember where he parked. That he was so rich and spoiled it wasn't important to him if he couldn't find his car for a few days. No one trusted him with a higher office if he couldn't even manage his own car keys. That was you?" Max was laughing.

"Yep. After the second time his car went missing, he knew it was me taking it. He had his security staff watching it constantly, but I still managed to get it one more time. That's all it took."

"Remind me not to make you mad. Although I don't have a car, so I'm probably safe, right?"

"You're safe with me, Pretty Girl," Dubs said. "You're safe with me."

CHAPTER SEVEN

Max waited until she was sure Dubs was asleep before she made any movements. She only had a twin bed in her small apartment and she hadn't felt like sharing a bed with Dubs, so for this evening, Dubs was in the bed, and Max was set up on the floor. It wasn't comfortable in the least. One of them had to have their hand extended up or down to accommodate the handcuffs.

Dubs didn't move when Max did, and her gentle snoring breaths stayed steady. Max pried the gum out of the handcuff hole, picked the lock quickly on the set attached to her wrist, and freed herself. She closed the open cuff around the metal bedpost, effectively cuffing Dubs to her bed, and slowly snuck out of the room and downstairs to the office.

Holt looked up when Max knocked. "Hey, H," Max said. "It's been one hell of a day."

"So I hear. Where's Dubs?"

"Handcuffed to my bed," Max said.

"I think I'm going to leave that one alone," Holt said. "How are you doing?"

"I can't really get a read on Dubs," Max said. "She's flirty and cocky, but I kinda like her. I don't know if I trust her though. You might have been right about that. Can I use your computer?"

"What's up?" Holt looked concerned.

"Dubs lost a friend named Levi Otis. It seems to be on her mind a lot. I want to know more about him."

"I remember when he died," Holt said. "It stirred up the debate of police engaging in high-speed chases with suspects again. I think another person may have been injured in the accident. A lot of ugly things were said on all sides. I don't know how you spend so much time online. I think that was the last time I read the comments section of a news article."

"Boss, don't ever read the comment section. That's where the trolls live. They go there specifically to rile up the rest of the world."

"Good to know," Holt said. "The car you and Dubs liberated from the valet lot this evening was reported stolen about two hours ago. Shouldn't be long before the Providence Police find it downtown. It's in one piece, correct?"

"Not a scratch. If I hadn't had to kiss her, Dubs would have had us out of there in under forty-five seconds."

"Excuse me?"

Max didn't think she was suddenly curious about Dubs's impressive skill. She played dumb anyway. "She's cocky as hell, but she delivered as advertised."

"Max."

"What? One of the valets was coming to park a new car, and we were going to be seen. We needed a reasonable excuse to be where we were. Strictly for allaying suspicion. You would have done the same thing in my shoes." Max didn't believe that for a second. For one thing, Holt had Isabelle now so she wasn't kissing anyone but her. For another, if it was only for cover, why did both of them come away breathing a little heavily? And why had Dubs tried to add some tongue to the equation? Either she took her cover scenarios very seriously, or she too had gotten a little carried away by the moment.

Holt didn't look like she was buying it.

"H, another thing. I don't think Dubs or I can work long-term with the handcuffs. I know you want me to keep an eye on her, but neither of us can do the job you want from us attached to each other. I can't see Dubs being able to sit still for hours next to me while I dig through leads here in the office. And frankly, she needs both hands to work if you're going to ask her to steal any more cars."

"Do you think I should?" Holt asked.

Max was surprised by the question. Holt often wanted input from her crew, but Max had spent so little time in the field, so she didn't expect Holt to seek her opinion.

"You've spent the most time with her. I want to know what you think," Holt said, clearly able to read Max's surprise.

"Dubs thinks getting her name out there again is important if we want the new crew to make contact. The valet lot we hit tonight was a place she worked a lot before she was locked up. She seemed to think those who mattered would know any car stolen from there was done by her."

"How can she be sure someone else hasn't moved into her territory while she's been away? It's been a long time," Holt said.

"I asked her that too," Max said. "But she said it wasn't possible, that no one would move on her turf. I don't know how she's so sure. She wouldn't tell me how she could be so sure. Do you think it's possible she's using us? That we're basically sponsoring her getting back to her old ways, making new connections, and then she'll ditch us?"

"Of course it's possible," Holt said. "I have no idea what her true motivations are. But right now, she's agreed to help us."

"But we keep her on a handcuff short leash?" Max said. "Until we can tell what her true motivations are?"

"You said yourself, neither of you can work that way. I would love to keep you locked to her constantly, but I imagine after being in prison and having someone else telling her what to do all the time, having me control her every move, through you, isn't a great way to make friends. But you're still with her constantly. If you can't be for some reason, and it better be a good one, get Jose to stick with her. They can talk cars until one of them goes hoarse or deaf. At night, either the cuffs go back on, or I put a man outside your door. Your choice."

Max didn't like the idea of any of her co-workers sitting outside her door all night. She didn't think she snored, and there wouldn't be anything else to hear, but it still seemed like an invasion of her privacy. Her apartment was tiny enough as it was. Having the lurking presence of another just outside would make it even more claustrophobic. Not that the cuffs were an exciting alternative.

"I think that will work," Max said. "But I'm really wishing I had taken you up on the offer of a bigger bed. Maybe if I had a king it wouldn't feel weird to share it with Dubs. There's a lot of spooning right now."

"Just make sure you're the big spoon," Holt said. "And face both of you toward the door."

"I think I'm learning a lot about you, H. Do you sleep with a knife under your pillow just in case, too?"

"Don't be ridiculous. Isabelle could get hurt accidently. I moved it to my boot by the bedside when she moved in."

Max had been kidding. She had a miniature baseball bat that she kept in the freezer. She couldn't remember the thought process that had led her to hide it there, but at the time it had made a lot of sense.

"Maybe when this case is over, I should brush up on my tactical skills. If I'm going to be spending more time out from behind my computer."

"We can arrange that. Your instincts are good. Trust those. You held your own in the park. You can learn fighting skills. When my back was exposed, you covered it. When you were in trouble, you backed up and sought reinforcements. Like I said, good instincts."

Holt's praise meant a lot. Everyone on the crew wanted to be like Holt, but few of them had an opportunity to prove themselves next to her. Most of their daily routine was rather boring, and Holt wasn't directly involved in many of the captures anymore. Max knew she used to be responsible for all of them, but now she was more a behind the scenes player, except on a big case, like this one.

"Thanks, H. I really feel like I've mastered the desperation attack, but a little more thought and planning to my fighting skills might serve me well."

"It certainly can't hurt. I'll let Moose know you're interested. And, Max, be careful with Dubs."

"Of course," Max answered confidently, but she didn't feel confident. She didn't know what Holt was cautioning her about exactly. Professional responsibility, personal entanglements, or something in between, maybe, but Max felt like she was in the dark in both areas. Normally, when she was having a problem at work she would talk to Lola or Moose. But Lola was having her own problems right now, and Moose would feel obligated to tell Holt about this particular problem.

"Good night, H."

CHAPTER EIGHT

G ood morning."
Max looked up from her bed on the floor and saw a smiling Dubs, who appeared quite awake and cheerful, peering down at her from her bed.

"What time is it? How long have you been awake? Why are you so awake?" Max asked.

"I waited as long as I could, but I really have to pee, and I can't sit still any more," Dubs said. "You sleep awfully late in the morning. We've wasted half the morning already. I thought we had a bad guy to catch. I've got some new ideas about that, by the way. I'm going to need a cell phone."

"Oh my God," Max said. "You're even worse with a full night's sleep. How is that possible? And what time is it?"

"What do you mean I'm worse, Pretty Girl? That sounds like a thinly veiled insult. But I really have to use the bathroom. Can you get up and insult me on the way to the can? And it's six thirty. How can you sleep so late? Half the morning is gone. How do you people catch any criminals?"

Max got up and stumbled after Dubs to the bathroom. "Six thirty. Really? Do you know how little crime is happening right now? We catch the criminals who keep normal criminal business hours. Can we try being silent for sixty seconds so I can wake up the rest of the way? It's my day off, and you've woken me at an ungodly hour. Not fair."

"Wait, Holt gives you days off? How is she, by the way? How was your chat last night? I have to say, in the movies, when someone is handcuffed to a bedpost, there's a little more of a happy ending than the wicked back spasms I've got from our two-tiered sleeping arrangement, but I know we're both new to this."

Max figured since Dubs hadn't yet stopped her morning updates that she wasn't going to get the requested sixty seconds of quiet. "Today's my usual day off, but I probably would have worked anyway. After I got some sleep."

"Man, your nose is really bent out of shape about that," Dubs said. "How was I supposed to know you needed twelve hours of beauty sleep? How many of your days off do you work? Never mind, don't answer. I bet you work all of them, right?"

Max tried to remember a day recently she hadn't spent in the office. She couldn't. Since Isabelle had found her camping mat and sleeping bag hidden in the broom closet downstairs and Holt had insisted she move into the apartment upstairs from the office, she had worked every day. She felt some obligation to repay the kindness Holt had shown her, but mostly, she didn't have anything else to do. Before she moved in, she had been briefly surviving on the street. That had required a lot of energy, time, and effort, almost more than she had to give at times. But now that she was stably housed, she had a lot more time on her hands. She didn't have many people she associated with outside of the people she worked with, though, so even her social life was tied to this building.

"No work today," Dubs said. "I'm taking you to do something fun. I haven't done any of the things I used to love to do around here in years. You know, that whole jail issue. So today, we're doing as many as we can squeeze into one day. Agreed?"

It sounded like fun, but Max felt guilty. She had a lot of work to do. Today was her day off, though.

"I can see you want to acquiesce. Just give in already."

"It's too early for the Scrabble words. I surrender. Fine, we'll go. But we take a map of the locations of the unaccounted for thefts you identified yesterday, and while we're out, we keep our eyes out for anything helpful. Deal?"

"How could I say no to something like that? Any chance we could lose the cuffs?"

"Depends on what the chances are you're going to try to ditch me on our super fun day," Max said, holding Dubs's gaze with a long stare.

"Pretty Girl, my day isn't any fun solo. I told you yesterday too, I don't make a living being stupid. I know if I ditch you, Holt will drag me back here before you get back to tell her I'm gone. My back spasms chained to you are better than prison."

"Maybe by the end of the day my company will outrank back spasms as a better deterrent for a return trip to prison," Max said. She wanted to trust Dubs, but she was wary. She would keep her close all day. Not an unpleasant thought. "So where are we going?"

"First, you're going to show me what you've got for bathing suits, then you're taking me shopping."

"I have no idea how those two things correlate. And why do I have to take you shopping?" Max asked.

"You think I made any money doing laundry in the can?" Dubs said. "I didn't exactly have a savings account. I don't know when payday is around here. If you own a bathing suit, you're taking me to get one, and if you don't, then you're buying us both one. And then we're going to the beach. I haven't been to the beach in years. We'll stop at your work locations on the way back."

Max wasn't sure she wanted to go to the beach with Dubs. She found her extremely attractive and was fighting that urge, and she didn't think a bathing suit was going to help. Maybe she was a glutton for punishment though, because a beach day actually sounded amazing. She hadn't been in a long time, either, despite living in the Ocean State.

After packing a beach bag, buying Dubs what had to be the most expensive per square inch piece of clothing Max had ever seen, and downloading a list of the locations of unaccounted car thefts, they headed off to the coast.

When they arrived at the beach, Dubs made them hustle across the sand. She seemed determined to make it to a specific location. Max would have protested, but the sand was so hot on her bare feet, she was happy to be moving at such a fast pace.

"Here," Dubs said, coming to an abrupt halt. "Best spot on the beach."

"Wow, you were determined to get here," Max said. "My feet may never be the same."

"I see who you are, Pretty Girl," Dubs said. "You have that sexy short hair, the muscly little body, the Holt imitation walk, but deep down, you are a delicate little flower with sensitive toes."

"Excuse me?" Max laughed, it sounded so ridiculous.

"You heard me all right. And if your delicate feet can stand it, I'll tell you what else I think, but you have to get across the sand to the water."

Dubs took off running for the ocean, weaving in and out of the many other blankets and umbrellas that littered the beach. After an instant of panic that Dubs was trying to escape, Max realized she was heading to the water, throwing down the gauntlet. Max wasn't going to let the challenge go. She took off in pursuit.

"Damn, the water's cold," Max said. She didn't usually barrel straight into the ocean. She was more of the dip a toe in, then retreat until she warmed up, kind of swimmer.

"See, that's what I was saying. Too hot, too cold. I've got your number now, Pretty Girl."

"Oh yeah, what about you?" Max said. "I notice you're only wet up to your waist. I think that should change." Max didn't know exactly what was driving her, but she reached under the water, grabbed Dubs behind the knees with one hand, and put the other behind her back. Then she flipped her into the wave about to break just behind them.

When Dubs resurfaced, Max regretted her impulsive maneuver. That tiny bikini was now soaking wet and clung to Dubs's perfect figure. Her small body was tight and toned, and her stomach was as close to perfection as Max had ever seen. She did her best not to look at her breasts.

"You are not getting away with that," Dubs said.

She was smiling, but in an evil, up to no good kind of way. Max started to retreat back toward the beach as fast as she could.

"Oh no, there's no salvation that way."

Dubs jumped out of the water and onto Max's back. She wrapped her legs around Max's waist, and her arms around Max's shoulders. The move caught Max off guard. It wasn't unpleasant, which was unnerving. She needed to be a little more careful around Dubs. While she was busy in her own head, Dubs leaned back and pulled Max off balance. When the next wave came crashing in on them, Max lost her balance and they both tumbled backward into the water.

Max came up sputtering a few feet from Dubs, who was casually treading water, clearly trying to look nonchalant. Max splashed water at her. "Very risky move, Dubs. I'd give you two and a half more waves before that bikini is nowhere to be seen." Dubs had teased her, saying her bathing suits looked like shorts and a sports bra, but now she was enjoying the security of board shorts and a racer back top. She chastised herself for hoping a rogue wave came and pulled Dubs's teeny top off and into the sea.

"Something you're hoping for, Pretty Girl?" Dubs asked, as if reading her mind.

"Just an observation." Max felt like the ocean was the size of a wading pool as Dubs moved into her personal space again.

"Well, no need to worry. I spent most of my teenage years at the beach, in less of a bathing suit than this. Never lost a top yet."

Max wasn't sure if she was relieved or disappointed. "A beach bum car thief? You should have grown up in LA. And how old are you anyway? Your teenage years must have been right before you got arrested."

"Hey, I'm not getting all nosy about why you live in Holt's attic," Dubs said.

"Whoa, okay. I'm going back to the beach. You coming?"

"If I promise not to swim to Block Island or Nantucket in a really dumb attempt at an escape from your charm, do you mind if I stay here for a while?" Dubs asked. "Like I said, it's been a while."

Max wished she had a better way of detecting bullshit from Dubs, but the request seemed sincere. Besides, she was in the ocean, where was she going to go? "Yeah, sure. Just don't be too long or I'll have to come and drag you back in."

"If you're going to threaten someone, Pretty Girl, you need to work on making it sound aversive."

Max made her way back to their beach towels and small cooler. She dried off slowly, enjoying the sun on her ocean-wet skin. She kept her eye on Dubs, but also scanned the beach for anything out of the ordinary. Dubs seemed to be lazily floating with the waves, occasionally repositioning or taking a few backstrokes to a new location if the waves got too intense. The rest of the beach seemed full of families, teenagers, and typical summertime occupants. She kept her focus though. Holt would expect no less.

When Dubs was finally done with her extended swim and exiting the water, Max noticed a young man, not much older than they were, leave his perch and head straight for her. She had noticed him before, mostly because he wasn't dressed for a day in the sun. He was wearing long pants, a dark T-shirt, and sneakers. Max got up and headed for Dubs too. She brought a towel with her. If this guy wasn't beelining it for her, she would seem a little overly eager to dry Dubs off, but there were worse things.

When she got closer, there was no doubt about the young man's destination, or that Dubs knew him. As soon as she caught his eye, Max could see the familiarity, and the warmth. Dubs hadn't looked that relaxed since they'd picked her up. She was a little jealous.

Dubs also saw Max approaching. She caught her eye and gave her a strange look…almost pleading. Dubs threw her arm around the man's neck, kissed him on the cheek, and behind his back shooed Max away. She hesitated, unsure. She had no idea who this man was, or what game Dubs was playing.

"Trust me," Dubs mouthed over the man's shoulder.

That was the problem. Max didn't trust her. She calculated the risks and tried to imagine what Holt would do. Holt would probably have some magical superhero action plan, but Max was a regular human. She was going to have to trust her gut. She backed away, wrapped the towel around her shoulders, and circled around Dubs and the stranger so she was behind them as they walked along the beach. She was glad she had had the sense to grab her cell phone when she left their things. At least she was able to take a few pictures of Dubs's companion.

She stayed at the point where the sand and water met, kicking at the softly lapping waves, stopping idly now and again to pick up a shell, never taking her eyes off the two in front of her. She wished she could hear what they were saying. It was making her crazy that she was stuck back here, following behind, too far to be useful. She imagined this was one of the situations Holt was trying to avoid when she handcuffed the two of them together. And once again, she'd been right.

Fortunately, she only had to stew about ten minutes. Whatever the stranger wanted to say, he clearly didn't need a long time to do it. He gave Dubs a quick hug and took off toward the parking lot. She tucked her phone in the pocket of her board shorts before Dubs turned back in her direction. She wasn't sure how Dubs would feel about the photo shoot.

"What are you doing here?" Dubs asked. She seemed genuinely surprised to see Max. "What if he had seen you?"

"You didn't even know I was here," Max said. "And you couldn't honestly think I was going to just let you wander off down the beach by yourself. You remember who my boss is, right? I'd like to live through the night. Who was that? What did he want?"

"That was an old friend. His name is Tony. He heard about our job last night, figured it must have been me. When he saw me here, he wanted to say hey. But even better than that, he's heard about the new group we're looking for."

"He just happened to see you on the beach?" Max wanted to believe her, but it seemed too good to be true. "Of all the thousands of people here, he got lucky and saw you? The dude was dressed for the roller derby, not the beach. What was he really doing here, Dubs?"

"Hey, I don't judge other people's beach attire. Tony doesn't wear anything but what you saw him in. At least not that I've ever seen."

"I want to believe you. I want to go back to Holt later and say we had a great day, you met a friend who gave you valuable information, and that you're going to be a great asset. But I can't do any of that if you don't stop bullshitting me. You said he told you about the crew we're looking for. Fantastic. I want to hear all about them. Not until we get past Mr. Beach Attire. I need to know that I can trust you. Or I need to know that you're going to hold back on me. Either way, what comes out of your mouth next determines a lot about whether we're going to get along well during our time together. Go."

Dubs looked stunned speechless. Max found that amusing and a little endearing. It was also one of the only times since she'd met Dubs that she hadn't had something to say.

"He probably came here looking for me. I told you I spent most of my teenage years here. And I told you where we set up was the best spot on the beach. That's my spot. I always set up there. You can see the ferries coming in and out, and the view along the coast is the best in the state."

That felt like an honest answer. "Why did he want to talk to you?"

"He wanted to know if our little joyride last night was my handiwork. He told me the game has changed since I've been gone. I think he came to warn me. That's when he told me a little about the new guys."

"And?" Max could tell Dubs was enjoying the buildup. She wasn't.

"And, I'm hungry. I'll tell you on the way to the snack bar."

Max was learning that Dubs liked to run the show. She let her lead, for now. They had a lot of day left in front of them. "This time you're buying. And for every minute you hold out information on me, I'm ordering something else off the menu."

"Playing dirty?" Dubs asked. "I didn't think you had it in you. All right, we'll get a feast, then we'll talk. Only one problem. I don't have my wallet. I came right out of the water, and there's no place to hide a credit card."

Max thought that was an understatement. She also realized she was now stuck paying for lunch. "Well played."

They walked silently to the beach bar, skirting kids building sandcastles and young couples rubbing lotion on one another. Max had a moment of wistfulness she quickly squashed.

"Aren't you glad you didn't spend your day off working?" Dubs asked between bites. "This is glorious. Look at this day."

"I am working. Or I'm trying to, but my interview subject is obstructing my every move," Max said, starting to get annoyed.

"Fine. Have it your way. The new guys in town aren't an offshoot of any of the other smaller groups that were already here. At least, not as far as anyone knows. Tony doesn't know, and no one Tony knows has any idea who the leaders are, but they're well connected."

"Does he have any idea where they're based?"

"Providence, but we already knew that."

"Did he give you anything else? Or is that tiny bit of info what you were building up to?" Max folded her arms.

"It doesn't seem like outsiders are welcome, but Tony thought a guy I used to know might do some work for them."

"It's a place to start," Max said. "Is that all he said?"

"He asked me about prison and my family. Told me about a couple kids we both know, what they're up to now. I can give you those details too, if you don't trust me." Dubs looked a little hurt.

"Would you trust you, if you were me?" Max asked.

"Of course, why would I lie?" Dubs said, giving what Max assumed was supposed to be her most earnest smile.

"For the record, that didn't help your cause. Just keep telling me what you know. All of it. That will build trust."

"So will the next stop on my list," Dubs said. "Do you know anything about the trampoline park? I've never been, but I think we have to go."

"Seriously? I thought we were spending the day at the beach."

"Yes, and here we are. We came, we saw, we conquered. Remember, long list, one day, lots to do?"

"I think I know why you like stealing fast cars," Max said. "You're looking for one that can keep up with you."

CHAPTER NINE

Holt had her feet up on her desk. She thought back to when this was the place she felt most at home in the world. It wasn't that long ago, but she didn't miss it. Now, Isabelle was home, wherever that was. When did she get so tame?

"I'm not sure I'll ever get used to that look on your face, H," Moose said. "It suits you, but I didn't think anyone could put it there."

"And what look would that be?"

"Bliss, happiness, joy. Take your pick. If she ever dumps your sorry ass, you're totally screwed, 'cause the crew around here is more in love with her than you are. You'll have to find a new job."

It meant a lot that her friends liked Isabelle so much. After the turmoil of the past few months, and Decker Pence's attempt on her life, Isabelle hadn't returned to her previous job. They might not have wanted her back anyway. She was an excellent accountant, but Decker had ransacked the office in an attempt to scare Isabelle, and in the process had really freaked out her bosses. It was a mutual parting of company. While she figured out what she wanted to do next, she had been consulting on some cases for Holt.

"I've been getting the sense she could stage a coup and I wouldn't stand a chance."

"Every reign must come to an end," Moose said, patting Holt on the shoulder. "What do you think of our newest team member? Max seems smitten with her."

"She certainly does. It looks like it's mutual, but I can't tell if it's sincere. Dubs gave us the name of someone who might be doing some work with our target car theft crew. These guys can't be ghosts, but no one knows who they are. It doesn't feel right to me."

"Spidey sense?" Moose asked.

"You don't think it's strange the state police commissioner asked us to get involved? A big case like this? Wouldn't they be eager for the bust and the credit?"

"I would think so," Moose said. "Maybe they really have no idea who they're looking for. At the risk of your head not fitting out the door, you are the best at tracking down people who don't want to be found."

"Our team is the best," Holt said. "I don't do anything alone."

"Has Dubs made contact with the guy her friend told her about?" Moose asked.

"Yeah. She's waiting for a call back. I still can't believe you talked me into giving her a cell phone."

"Come on, H. It would be weird for her not to have one. And Max bugged the shit out of it. At some point, we're going to have to trust her. It's not like you to be this paranoid."

"I don't want Max to get hurt. I threw her in at the deep end, not only without water wings, but with weights around her ankles. And Dubs is too damned cocky. She walks around here like she owns the place. Look at her right now. I could walk out there and ask her to steal the governor's car and she would bounce out the door, talking the whole time, happy to do it."

"She reminds me of a very good friend of mine at her age," Moose said, giving Holt a good long stare. "You were always on the path to good, though. She might need a push. You going to give it to her, or be a pain in her ass?"

"I can tell you who is a pain in my ass," Holt said. She hated when Moose was right about something she was completely blind to. Was Dubs reminding her of herself and thus annoying the hell out of her?

"I'm here to help," Moose said with a smile. "Lola asked me if you would be willing to sit in on her meeting with the lawyer. I guess she finally got in contact with Tiffany."

"I'll go talk to her," Holt said.

When Holt made it to the main area of the office, she found Dubs and Lola sitting next to each other, one facing the other, each with her feet up on a desk. Whatever they were talking about, they were enjoying. Lola was wiping tears from her eyes.

"H, I haven't laughed this hard in months. Probably not since that thing with Decker and you getting shot and all. You should keep her around."

"I'll take it under advisement," Holt said. "Moose said you were looking for me."

"Yeah. Tiffany finally came out of the weeds. She's six months pregnant. Can you believe that? She won't tell me who the father is. I guess it doesn't matter."

"Your pride is hurt, of course it matters," Holt said. She couldn't imagine what Lola must be feeling. She'd never liked Tiffany, or thought she treated Lola well, but she knew Lola cared about her.

"Is she still sure she doesn't want the baby?" Holt asked.

"Oh yeah," Lola said. "If she could give it to me now, she would. She said she's been taking vitamins and going to the doctor though. For some reason that surprised me. I didn't think she'd be so careful."

"Is she having a boy or a girl?" Dubs asked.

"I don't know," Lola said. "I never thought to ask, and she never said."

"Are you going to be able to get back in touch with her to get her to sign the adoption paperwork? Will she even let you know when she goes into labor?" Holt asked.

"Like I said, if she could, she'd give me the kid right now," Lola said. "I don't think pregnancy is agreeing with her. And I didn't get the sense the father was all that interested in being a dad. I think she'll be motivated to get in touch. After that, I probably won't ever hear from her again."

"Lola, I'm really sorry." Holt didn't know what else to say. Of their group of friends, Lola had always had the worst luck in relationships. Maybe because she put herself out there the most. But she seemed to have one bad girlfriend after another.

"So are you going to have a baby shower?" Dubs asked. "Is your place the same size as Max's? If it is, where are you going to put a crib?"

"I never thought of that," Lola said. "What else do I need for a baby, H? You've seen all the stuff Superman has. Diapers? Toys? Bottles? I don't know anything about kids."

"Slow down," Holt said. "We'll figure it out together. You set up the first meeting with the lawyer and I'll be there. Isabelle too, if you want."

Lola looked relieved.

"You two mind if we switch to work for a few minutes?" Holt asked.

Lola looked relieved at that prospect, too.

"Have you heard anything from the guy you contacted, Dubs?" Holt asked.

"Nothing yet. But if history holds, he's cautious. He'll get in touch, but it might be a day or two. He's probably asking around about me right now. Honestly, I doubt it's helping my cause that I'm sitting in your office talking to you. I'm sure everyone in Rhode Island knows I spend my nights handcuffed to Max."

"Well, that should only improve your status in the world." Lola winked.

"Very true," Dubs said. "But her association with you," she nodded in Holt's direction, "not so much."

"Hey, you've joined the Avengers now. Don't hide it, kid, flaunt it," Lola said.

Holt almost laughed out loud at the look of horror on Dubs's face. The Avengers was clearly not part of the self-image Dubs had for herself.

"You more the Legion of Doom?" Holt asked. She was curious how Dubs saw herself.

"Lone Ranger," Dubs said.

"That's not what I've heard," Holt said. "You used to work with others. What about your friend, Levi? He was your protégé right?"

"Don't talk about Levi." Dubs leaned forward, her teeth clenched.

Holt put her hand on Dubs's shoulder. She hadn't meant to upset her. It wasn't a test. "When I was younger than you, I lost my best friend, George. He was Lola's brother. He was shot and killed right in front of me. I felt like I should have been able to stop the man who killed him. I carried that guilt for a long time. I still have some of it."

"Why are you telling me any of this? Are you trying to get me to spill my guts? Trying to get me to like you?"

"No," Holt said. "I'm telling you because I might understand some of how you feel. And I thought you might want to know that. It's a hard burden to carry alone."

"We're not the same," Dubs said. She got up and walked away.

Holt thought she saw tears forming in Dubs's eyes, but she couldn't be sure. She wasn't sure if she should follow. Dubs didn't seem like her biggest fan.

Max walked into the office, just back from an errand. "Where's Dubs going in such a hurry?"

"I may have mentioned Levi," Holt said. "I was trying to tell her about George, and that I understand."

"H, I told you not to bring that up," Max said. Max put down the papers she had been carrying and hurried after Dubs.

❖

Dubs felt like a firecracker with a lit fuse, waiting for the explosion. The emotions were close to the surface, and she had no outlet for them. She didn't understand why Holt had to ask her about Levi. It wasn't any of her business.

She jumped and spun around, ready to fight, when she felt a hand on her back. It was Max. She wanted to tell her to go away, scream at her, because Max was there and she was hurting, but she couldn't. Max held out a bottle of Coke and looked so sweet. Even when she was swearing up and down she didn't trust her, she always had the kindest eyes.

"You okay? You look a little tense," Max said. "I notice you drink way too many of these a day, so I thought your blood supply might be running a little low."

Dubs wondered if Max was paying extra attention to her soda consumption for business or pleasure purposes.

"They calm me down," Dubs said. It seemed weird, but it was true. "I'm fine. Just not used to being caged up. I've never been on someone else's schedule. Well, in prison I was, but I thought I was out now."

"Come on," Max said. "The company has to be better than prison. At least give us that. And I got you a phone."

"I guess Lola is pretty cool," Dubs said. "And Jose does know a lot about cars." Dubs saw Max waiting for her to continue. She let her wait a few beats, then caught her eye and winked. "My jailor's a lot cuter here too. And I didn't get to sleep with the dude at the state prison, thankfully."

"I don't think that's a rumor you should be starting," Max said.

"And how would you describe it?" Dubs asked, feeling calmer. She enjoyed spending time with Max, verbally sparring with her. "At night, the cuffs come back, and we hop in bed together. I don't know what other name to give it."

"My back couldn't take another night on the floor," Max said defensively.

"I'm also irresistible."

"And modest."

"Oh, don't tell me you aren't into it," Dubs said. "You took the chivalrous route by sleeping on the floor. When I complain about something, you fix it. You're enjoying being my knight in shining armor. In return, I get to tease you. Which, I might add, I can also tell you enjoy. I saw your eyes glued to me at the beach."

"Dubs, half the people there had their eyes glued to you at the beach." Max was turning a little red. "You were wearing an eye patch and calling it a bathing suit."

Dubs was going to continue, but the prepaid cell phone Max had given her rang. She'd only given the number to three people, and it wasn't her father or Mrs. Otis calling. "It's our boy," she said. She turned away and took the call, speaking softly. Max frowned.

Dubs talked to Shorty for a few minutes. She had known him before she was arrested. They had crossed paths in their mutual professional engagements, but she didn't know him well.

"He wants to meet in person. He didn't want to give me details over the phone. It sounded like he'd done some work with our group though."

"Do you believe him?" Max asked.

"I don't know," Dubs said. "He's always been that kid who didn't quite fit in, and he always wanted to have information other people didn't. Sometimes that meant his info kinda sucked. He's a good thief though. I could imagine a new crew using him."

"Only one way to find out I guess. Let's go talk to Holt."

Dubs wished she could do the meet alone. She wanted the information he had, but she wanted to be able to screen what she gave to Holt and Max. She was willing to help them, but she needed to be thinking about herself long-term too. Either they weren't going to be able to take down this mystery crew and there might be a place for her among them, or they would bust them, and their absence would leave plenty of room for her to set up shop.

"You hear from your guy?" Holt asked when they approached.

"He wants to meet tomorrow afternoon," Dubs said. "He suggested the new frozen yogurt place downtown."

"It will be crowded," Holt said. "And right on the street. Not the easiest location to provide cover, but I like that it's public. I haven't had frozen yogurt in a long time. Maybe I'll pull rank and take inside cover."

"How many people are you going to have watching this meeting?" Dubs asked. So much for going alone. "I was thinking I could meet with him a little more privately. He's a little paranoid."

"You won't even know we're there," Holt said. "Remember what I said about protecting my people? This is one of those situations. If this goes bad, I need to be close to you, and to Max, to get you out. It's just how we work around here."

"So if someone tried to shoot me, you're telling me you would take a bullet for me? I don't believe it. I'm a criminal, and you're Captain America."

"Believe it," Moose said. He was leaning over a cubicle wall, half participating in their planning. With him draped over the wall, the divider looked like doll furniture. "It wouldn't do her any good though, 'cause if the first shot didn't kill her, Isabelle would be so furious, she'd finish the job. She'd have to get in line though. I'm not interested in you getting shot again either."

"I don't remember this being about me," Holt said a little testily.

Dubs couldn't remember ever being around people quite like these. They all seemed too good to be true. That said, she hoped she never had to find out if Holt really was willing to make good on her promise.

"Fine, bring all the Merry Men. I have no idea how you're going to hide him in a crowd though," she said, pointing to Moose.

Max laughed.

"I'll think of something," Holt said.

CHAPTER TEN

Dubs didn't know how Max and the others spent so much of their time sitting around. They had been waiting at the frozen yogurt shop for fifteen minutes, but still no sign of Shorty. She was getting antsy.

"I told you to eat slower," Max said. She wasn't even a quarter of the way through her dessert.

"How do you wait around like this all the time? It's making me crawl out of my skin."

"You get used to it," Max said. "Truth be told, I don't do that much out of the office. I'm behind my computer most of the time. This is a treat for me."

"Do you see how many beautiful cars have driven by, just in the time we've been sitting here? And how many people have butchered perfectly awesome machines with really bad custom additions? I mean, don't get me wrong, sometimes it's great to add on a little touch here, an improvement there, but some of the stuff that's out there? No way. What am I supposed to do with your janky ass custom job? I can't break that shit down and sell it. It's amazing how many 'car people' don't know the first thing about cars."

"I think I've heard this same rant from Jose a time or two."

"He's a smart man," Dubs said.

"Is this your boy?" Max asked.

Dubs looked around carefully. She had memorized everyone sitting near them. They were on the sidewalk outside the shop, in uncomfortable metal patio chairs, surrounded by couples and families enjoying the warm day. They had already had to scare off more than one person trying to take their third chair.

"Yeah, that's him," Dubs said. Finally.

He slid into the chair opposite Dubs, ignoring Max completely.

"I thought you still had a couple years left, Dubs," he said.

"Hello to you too, Shorty."

"Hey, I didn't mean nothing by that, just surprised to see you out is all. Not that I'm worried or anything. I've got my own game now. It's good to see you out. Yeah, good for you. Welcome back."

"Dude, I told you, I want to hear about your game. You willing to tell me?" Dubs had always found Shorty really annoying, and the last thing she felt like was small talk.

"Hey, after you left, things changed around here. It's not the same with all the little crews, or people working on their own. If you want to run your own show, you've got to either go somewhere else, or you've got to pay a percentage to the new bosses running the game now. That's who I do work for. I think I'm the only one they've allowed into their circle."

Shorty was clearly very proud of that fact. Dubs didn't think he should be quite as proud as he was, but she didn't say anything. This meeting was trying her patience, and she was sickened to hear how much things had changed.

"Who is 'they,' Shorty?"

"I don't know," he said. "And even if I did, I wouldn't tell you. Honor among thieves."

"I'm a thief too, you fuckwad."

"She's not," he said, acknowledging Max for the first time.

"She's with me," Dubs said, raising her eyebrows at him knowingly. "You know what I mean? And I say she's good."

"Oh man," Shorty said. "Still. I don't know anything. They get in touch when they need me to do something. I only have contact with some guy I'm pretty sure isn't that close to the main group. Holy shit."

Shorty's eyes got wide as the mood of the other diners changed rapidly and people started moving. Max stood so quickly the table flipped. She pulled Dubs and Shorty with her, away from the yogurt shop, toward the street corner. Dubs didn't know where they were going, or what Max had seen, but she followed.

Squealing tires heightened Dubs's anxiety. She glanced back and saw a black Escalade bearing down on them. The windows were tinted so dark the entire car looked like a black hole. She looked in front of them, trying to see where Max was leading. Instead, she saw another vehicle, this time a white passenger van, closing on them fast. There was an alley ahead, but she wasn't sure they would make it.

Max had her by the hand, but her grip kept slipping because Dubs's hand was sweating. Her heart was racing so fast, and so loud, it sounded like she was standing in a wind tunnel. She didn't know why those two cars scared her so much, but it was damn clear they shouldn't be there. Max was certainly taking them seriously.

When she peeked back over her shoulder again, she didn't need to wonder why she was so scared. One of the back windows of the Escalade was down and a semi-automatic assault rifle was clearly visible.

She wanted to say something to Max, to pull her to safety, to run in the other direction, something. But she couldn't. She didn't seem capable of doing anything as panic squeezed her throat shut. Max and Shorty were still moving, but Dubs wasn't sure if she was. She might steal cars for a living, but she wasn't used to people waving guns in her face.

Max turned to her and said something. She couldn't hear her, her heart was still too loud in her ears. It looked like "move your ass." She would have, but before she could, everything exploded in chaos around her.

She heard the gunshots because those were even louder than her pounding heartbeat, and at the same time she was hit hard in the back and lifted completely off the ground. At first, she thought she had been shot, but when Max, and then something even heavier, landed on top of her and she didn't feel any horrendous pain, she reevaluated. She was flat on her stomach, pinned to the ground behind a massive concrete flowerpot. If she weren't trapped under all the weight, she would have almost felt safe, given the situation.

Dubs had no idea how long the shooting lasted. It could have been ten seconds, or ten hours. It was too long. When it abruptly stopped, there were more squealing tires and she could hear the two vehicles leaving quickly.

"You two, don't move."

Dubs knew the voice sounded familiar. It was directly above her. Given how thoroughly pinned she was, it seemed comical that the woman speaking thought she could go anywhere. As soon as she thought it, the weight lifted and Holt came into her line of sight as she tore off down the sidewalk at a full sprint.

Max rolled off of Dubs so she was lying next to her.

"You okay?"

"Was she the sumo wrestler lying on top of us? I don't think I have any ribs left."

"Tell me about it," Max said. "I had your bony ass on one side and her on the other. That was a crappy Max sandwich. I'm serious, though. Are you okay?"

"I don't know," Dubs said. "That was pretty shitty. And I think I have road rash on my chin. Do you know what happened to Shorty?" Dubs hadn't wanted to ask. She didn't really want to know. He had been right next to them, and he wasn't with them now.

"I don't know," Max said. "I was trying to get us to that alley. All of a sudden, Holt literally had me by the back of my pants and she tossed me on top of you back here. Then she jumped over us both."

"Are you two okay?" Holt was back.

"What the hell just happened?" Dubs asked. She was mad, and scared, and wanted to yell at someone. "'Cause I've never been shot at until I came under your 'protection.' If this is how it's going to be, put me back in prison. It was a hell of a lot safer."

"You're right. I put you both in a risky situation. I don't think you were the target, but you were in danger. That shouldn't have happened. I'm sorry."

Dubs could hear sirens. The first police car was visible in the distance. She was already on edge enough without adding in the police.

"What happened to Shorty? Was he the target?"

"He's gone, Dubs. I'm sorry. I tried to get to all three of you, but I couldn't." Holt looked sad. "Can I get you back to the office? You don't need to be here for all the police questioning and cleanup. Do you need the hospital?"

Dubs shook her head. She felt okay, if a little disoriented, by what had just happened. *Gone.* How close had Shorty been to them when he'd been shot? How close had that bullet come to her? "Where did you take off to just now?"

"I wanted a license plate on the Escalade," Holt said.

"You took off, on foot, after a car full of guys with assault rifles?" Dubs couldn't believe Holt was serious.

"My binoculars are in my other pants."

"You're insane, woman."

"Calculated risk," Holt said. "They needed to get out of here fast, not continue shooting at me. And if they did start shooting, they were moving too fast to hit anything with accuracy."

"Does accuracy even matter with automatic assault rifles?"

"Like I said, calculated risk."

What Holt was saying didn't even sound like something a human being should say. What kind of person ran toward that kind of danger? What kind of person would jump on top of two other people to shield them from a shooting? She could understand Holt wanting to save Max, but why did she toss her to safety first? Because she was an asset? Then why not save Shorty? Dubs massaged her temples and sat up. It was all too much for an afternoon.

"Was it worth the chase?"

"Nah, no plates."

"That car was custom. Shouldn't be hard to track it. I'm putting money on it being stolen," Dubs said.

"Come on. You two head back to the office. I'll be back in a bit." Holt positioned herself behind Dubs and Max and waited for them to get up before moving them in the direction of the truck they arrived in. Dubs got the feeling Holt was trying to make herself as large as possible, a human shield against whatever was behind her. Dubs tried to look around her and caught a glimpse of a trickle of red and the sole of a sneaker on the other side of the flowerpot.

"Leave it, Dubs. You don't need to see what's over there. Go back to the office with Max. Today's been shitty enough. I'll take care of things here."

For the first time, Dubs and Holt agreed.

CHAPTER ELEVEN

Max could tell her pacing was adding to Dubs's agitation, but she couldn't sit still right now. She was going over and over the past few hours, dissecting every decision and move she had made, trying to figure out if she could have done something different to change the outcome. Holt trusted her with a lot of responsibility, and right now she didn't feel like she was living up to that trust.

"Hey, Pretty Girl, you need a cup of calming tea or something. You look wound even tighter than me. Not even sure how that's possible."

"I'm thinking," Max said.

"Well, be careful," Dubs said. "With as hard as you're thinking, it looks like you could pop a vein or something."

Dubs got up and caught Max as she passed on one of her laps. She put her hand on Max's back. "Look, I'm upset too. That was some scary ass shit."

"No Scrabble words to describe it? I'm a little disappointed." Max was getting used to Dubs's nonstop talking and vocabulary that was bigger than both of them. She even kind of liked it.

"My brains almost got Scrabbled. Kinda takes the fun out of a triple word score."

"You have a point," Max said. "You really haven't ever been in a situation like that before? I know it's a big assumption, but given your past life…"

"My father always told me to get in and out before anyone noticed you were there, otherwise the guns come out. He never let me carry a gun either, even though a lot of the other thieves did. He said it would slow me down and make me feel invincible. I made it a mission to avoid what we just experienced."

"Your dad sounds like he went to the same school as Holt. She has the same rule about guns," Max said. Given the chance, she suspected Holt and Dubs might actually get along.

"My pride is still a little bruised at having been flung like a rag doll over a flowerpot earlier. How did she do that?"

"Eventually, you stop asking 'how' with Holt," Max said. "You just accept that some things don't make any sense, but you're glad she can do them." Max wished she had some of Holt's confidence and instincts. She should have been the one keeping Dubs and Shorty safe today. She was embarrassed Holt had to swoop in and rescue them. And now Shorty was dead. He was their best lead, and she'd let that lead be compromised.

"Any chance we could do something? You know, some work, or go for a walk? Not outside or anything, but around the office. Maybe get a snack. Do you have any video games in here? Or coffee?"

"How about we see what we can find out about that Escalade? It must be related to the folks we've been looking for. You said you thought it was stolen. Why?"

"A car like that, it's really noticeable. And the tint on the windows is illegal. I mean, shooting people in the street is too, but why call attention to yourself like that? My thought is, they were using whatever they had and they'll dump the cars after."

"Couldn't they have just removed the plates off their own vehicle before coming out?"

"Sure. But there are probably only two or three of those Escalades around. It really narrows down the search if they used their own car. Maybe they're idiots, though. I would be all for that."

Dubs still looked a little wound up. Max moved closer to her and put her hand against Dubs's cheek, and her stomach jumped when Dubs leaned into the touch. It felt so intimate, Max's instinct was to pull away. She didn't know what she was doing, but she didn't move. Instead, she ran her fingers through Dubs's hair, which was down after being tied back for their meeting with Shorty.

"We're going to get these guys. We always get our guys."

"You've been spending too much time with me, Pretty Girl. You're starting to sound cocky," Dubs said quietly.

"Well, uh, should we get to work?" Max said. Dubs was looking at her too gently and they were standing too closely. She didn't know what the expectations were from here. It kind of felt like they should kiss, but she wasn't about to go there. Certainly not in the middle of the office. She also wasn't sure she wanted to kiss Dubs. It didn't seem like a good idea. She was already struggling enough with her new responsibilities.

"Whatever you say," Dubs said. "How are you planning on tracking this vehicle down? What if I'm wrong? Or if they didn't file a police report? A car like that, with illegal tint, probably doesn't belong to some upstanding citizen."

"If there's a DMV registration, a traffic violation, or a parking ticket, I'll find it," Max said. This was where she felt most comfortable. She knew she wasn't letting Holt down when she was behind her keyboard.

"Is that legal?" Dubs asked. She looked impressed.

"'Is that legal?' asks the car thief," Max said. "I got to watch you work, hot stuff, now it's your turn to be impressed."

"Lay it on me," Dubs said. "My socks are ready to fly right off."

They got to work. Mostly, Dubs sat and watched Max tap away on her keyboard, but she was a supportive presence. It felt good to do something after their stressful afternoon. As Dubs had suggested, no police report had been filed for a missing vehicle matching the car from earlier.

If Max had any doubts about Dubs's usefulness in this quest, they were quickly allayed when Dubs was able to give the trim level and year of the Escalade from memory. Max looked up a picture of that vehicle, and it perfectly matched her recollections as well.

"Never doubt the memory of a car thief for the details of a car," Dubs said. "Even with someone shooting at me, that was the first thing I noticed."

"I think you might need to work on your priorities," Max said, although in this case, it was coming in handy.

"So, how many are in the DMV database?" Dubs was worse at sitting still than Max.

"Dubs?" Max said.

"What?"

"I've been tense since we got back, but I'm finding the massage a little distracting."

"What? Oh, sorry." Dubs looked surprised, but not especially sorry. Max had been caught off guard when Dubs had first rested her hand on Max's knee, but she hadn't minded. Over the past fifteen minutes, though, Dubs had been absentmindedly stroking Max's leg until her hand was quite a bit farther from Max's knee than when she started.

Dubs moved her hand from Max's leg and rested it on Max's back, settling it against Max's ribs. This position actually brought them even closer, something that was significantly more distracting than her hand on Max's leg.

"Is this some kind of test?" Max asked. "Some examination of my iron will?"

"Is there a problem?" Dubs asked.

Max wasn't sure if she was playing dumb, or was actually clueless.

"I like being close to you," Dubs said. "Since we've started sleeping together."

"You've got to stop saying that."

"You get snuggly after you fall asleep. Turns out I kinda like it." Dubs ignored Max's protest. "It's better without the handcuffs, though."

"Oh dear Lord," Max said.

"So, how many Escalades?"

Dubs didn't move away, and Max was working on breathing. She wasn't sure if it was Dubs specifically, or the fact that anyone was giving her this kind of attention. She didn't want to get carried away by a beautiful woman playing with her.

"Five," Max said. "Two seem unlikely to be our vehicle, but we should still check them out."

"Well, do you have addresses? Let's get going."

"Hold on there, Tiger," Max said. "We've got a chain of command here. I've got to talk to Moose. We might not be the ones to go on this jaunt." Max wasn't sure if she wanted to be the one to be back in the field so quickly. Moose was across the room. "You wait here. I'll go talk to him."

Dubs put her feet up on the desk. Max made her way over to Moose. She could have brought Dubs, but she wanted the opportunity to talk to Moose alone. He had been in her corner since she started here, willing to lend an ear, or a gentle push in the right direction, when needed.

"You good, Max? Too much excitement out there today from what I hear. You know I don't like Holt getting shot at. How do you think I feel about you being on the other side of a gun barrel?"

Max didn't know why it would matter who was being shot at, but she was flattered Moose made a distinction. "Why would you care if it's me or Holt?"

"Holt's too damn stubborn to get shot for real. She'd just flex something and send it back where it came from. Maybe it's my own denial about her invincibility. But you, let's just say I can't imagine anything happening to you. Makes me want to put you in my pocket and keep you safe."

"I think I'd probably fit in your pocket," Max said.

"What's on your mind, Max? You look like something's gnawing at you."

"Couple things, I guess. First, we might have found a lead. The car from the shooting today was custom. Dubs thinks it was probably stolen. There are only five in Rhode Island that could be the one we're looking for. I thought we could pay them a visit."

"See if they're still where they're supposed to be? Do you think it's related to the people we're looking for?"

"Yeah. Otherwise, why come after Shorty? They seemed to target him when he was telling us about his working with them. Oh! I can't believe I forgot. Dubs," Max said.

"Yeah?" Dubs looked up from the cell phone Max had gotten for her. She must have been texting.

"Didn't Shorty say the new thieves get in touch with him when they needed his services?"

"Yeah. I think so, why?"

"We need that cell phone," Max said. "Do you think Holt is still there?" Max asked Moose.

"I'll call her. Tell me, why do you think knowing that one of the Escalades is stolen will help us? Think they're dumb enough to lead us to them?"

"Don't know," Max said. "But no police report was filed, so we don't have any other information to go on. Maybe there won't be anything worthwhile to learn, but we don't know anything at all right now."

"You're getting the hang of this fieldwork, huh?"

"Not at all. I almost got us all killed today," Max said. She hated admitting that to Moose, of all people.

"That's not what I heard. Holt said you were doing a great job of trying to get the three of you to safety in an alley. You reacted faster than anyone else, according to her. Fieldwork takes time to get the hang of. Give yourself the time."

"If I was so great at it," Max said, "no one would be dead, and I wouldn't have gotten tossed over a flowerpot and landed on by a two-ton tank."

"At least you weren't at the bottom of the pile," Moose said with a smile.

"Don't say that too loudly. She just stopped whining about it," Max said. Moose was good at making her feel better.

"Get out of here. You two have Escalades to hunt down. And find out what Dubs is up to over there."

Max looked over at Dubs. She was hunched over her phone. She felt like she couldn't quite keep on top of anything right now.

She walked over quietly and threw her arms around Dubs's neck from behind, leaning her head down so their cheeks were right next to each other. "Ready to get going?" Max felt Dubs jump. She quickly closed her text message. Max wasn't able to see who she was writing to.

"Who you texting?"

"My father. He heard about the shooting today and asked if I knew anything about it. I didn't want him to worry."

Max really wanted to believe her. She really did.

"I've got addresses for four of the five," Max said. "Let me run the VIN on the fifth and see if I can get any more information. The owner is listed as a company. They only have a PO Box."

It didn't take long for Max to find some useful information. The fifth Escalade had some service work done at a local garage recently. Maybe they would have more information about an owner.

"Do I need to send you with a bodyguard?" Moose shouted after them. "Maybe the bulletproof truck?"

"Shut it, Big Man," Max hollered back.

"Do you really have a bulletproof truck?" Dubs asked.

"I have no idea."

Max and Dubs set off on their Escalade hunt. They got through the first three quickly. For two of them, they didn't even need to talk to the owners. The cars were sitting in the driveway and didn't match. The third was tucked safely in the garage, which they could see when they looked in through the side window of the garage.

When they got to the fourth house, no one was home.

"Can't we just take a peek in the garage?" Dubs asked. "I think only five percent of houses in Providence have garages that actually fit cars. Why are we visiting all of them?"

"Just lucky, I guess," Max said.

"I'm starting to see why you like playing detective," Dubs said.

It was amusing watching Dubs try out a new role. Max noticed she had also been spending most of her time watching Max work. "Is that why you've been staring at me the whole time we've been out and about today?"

"I'm trying to learn from a master," Dubs said.

"Uh, huh," Max said. "Take a peek in there. But don't do anything illegal."

Dubs was back quickly. "Car's in the garage. Also, there is a really, really large spider hanging out over the doorway to the side entrance. I mean, massive. It's bigger than you. Let's get out of here before it decides it's hungry. I think the Escalade belongs to it."

"Really?" Max said. "You're afraid of spiders?"

"It's a reasonable fear," Dubs said. "If you had seen the size of this thing, you would be scared too. I think I can see it waving at us. It's giving us an eight-legged salute right now. Maybe that's how spiders flip people off. Seriously, let's get out of here. I feel like they're all over me."

"Okay, just for the record, that's not reasonable at all," Max said. "But as much fun as this is, we've got to get moving anyway. The garage is closing soon."

They got back in the car, which seemed to make Dubs happy, and took off. Max hoped Escalade number five would provide some useful information.

"We've passed four coffee shops," Dubs said. "How can you not want a latte or something? It's the middle of the afternoon. Perfect time for a stop."

"Are you Italian?" Max asked. She was amazed at the amount of coffee and other caffeinated drinks Dubs consumed. It didn't seem to impact her sleep though.

"No. I'm thirsty."

"Maybe less caffeine would help you sit still. I would be going out of my mind if I had what you have every day."

"I told you before, coffee calms me down. I don't know why. And I'm not complaining about our day. Well, that's not true. I'm complaining a lot about the first part. I'm blocking that out actually. But the last two hours? No complaints. I don't think I said it before, but this truck is really working for you. I mean, really working for you."

Dubs was looking at Max with that appreciative look that was both exciting and distracting. It didn't seem like a look that could be faked.

"The jeans, the sneakers, that A-shirt, and this truck. Damn."

"Are you flirting with me, hoping I'll be swayed enough to stop and get you coffee?" Max asked.

Max wasn't sure if Dubs would be offended by her joke, but she needn't have worried.

"You know what I might like the most about you, Pretty Girl?" Dubs said.

"I wouldn't even begin to know."

"You don't take yourself too seriously. And you have no idea just how hot you are. That's very sexy to a lady like me."

"If I was trying to attract a lady like you, of course," Max said, teasing her.

"Who wouldn't be?"

"Modest as always." Max grinned, enjoying their banter.

Dubs unclipped her seat belt and slid over to the center seat. She buckled back in and let her thigh rest along the full length of Max's. She pulled some form of makeup things from her bag and readjusted the rearview mirror for her own use.

"Hey," Max said. "I'm driving here."

"Use those," Dubs said, pointing to the side mirrors. "I need this one."

"Doesn't your little kit come with mirrors?" Max asked, thinking it was rather convenient Dubs suddenly needed to be half an inch away from her, using the mirror.

"Mine's broken. You complaining?"

"No elbowing me for mascara application, okay? You look beautiful without all that stuff," Max said. "No use getting us both killed for something you don't even need."

Dubs stopped what she was doing and glanced at Max. "Did you just call me beautiful?"

"I, uh." Max thought back to what she had said. She thought about what she meant. "Oh man, is your head even going to fit out the door now? The last thing you need is someone stroking that healthy ego of yours."

Dubs finished what she was doing and put away her makeup. She put her left arm around Max's shoulders and left it draped there. They rode the rest of the way silently like that.

Max parked in front of the repair shop and turned off the engine. She unbuckled her seat belt and was ready to go in, but Dubs hadn't let her go.

"Are we going in?" Max asked.

"This hasn't been like I thought it would be," Dubs said seriously. "That's because of you. I just thought you should know."

"Thank you?" Max said. She was confused by Dubs's seriousness and rather cryptic statement.

"Let's get going." She kissed Max quickly on the cheek and hopped out of the truck.

Max followed. Sometimes she had trouble keeping up with Dubs's rapid shifts. This felt like an abrupt change, even for her, though. Max wondered what it was all about.

No one was behind the desk when they got inside so they rang the bell and waited. A middle-aged man eventually made his way to the counter. He smiled at Max and seemed friendly, but his demeanor changed drastically when he saw Dubs.

"You are not welcome here," he said. "You have to leave. And if you're with her, you get out too. I don't know what you're doing here, but I'll call the police."

"Whoa, wait," Max said. She was confused. "There's no need for the police. I have a question about a car you did some work on about a month ago. I was hoping you could help us out."

"Oh sure, I give you information on that car and the next thing I know, it goes missing and who's to blame? Me. That's who. I'm not helping you punks steal any cars."

"Punks?" Max said. Who was this guy?

"Hey, pal," Dubs said. "I deserve your mistrust. Clearly, you know who I am. But I'm not here for that. I'm working with this wonderful woman to try to catch car thieves now. Do you know who Holt Lasher is?"

"Of course. Everyone knows who she is."

"Well, this is Max Winters. She works for Holt. And I guess I kinda do right now, too. I'm not here to case your shop, or see what inventory you're working with. I don't care about your security, which sucks by the way, or any of that. We really and truly just want to find out about a car you worked on a month ago. We don't want to steal it. We think someone already did."

"You say you're working for Holt Lasher? I'll just check that out," the man said.

He tapped on his computer and found what he was looking for. Max hasn't seen someone hunt and peck on the keyboard like that since she had to watch her mother try to check her e-mail, and watching him type was almost physically painful. It must have been Moose who answered the phone when the garage owner finally found the number for the office and called, if the tone of voice they could barely hear was any indication. Moose agreed to text over a picture of Max and confirmed that Dubs was currently consulting for Holt.

The text message came through a few seconds later. He did a thorough inspection of the picture, comparing it in great detail to Max's face. Once satisfied, he seemed slightly more willing to help them. "You are who you say you are," he said. "I still don't understand why *she* is working for someone as reputable as your boss." He was directing his conversation to Max.

"She's my colleague," Max said. "And has been invaluable to our current case."

"Watch your back," he said. "What car do you need to know about?"

Max didn't care for the guy, but she wondered if there was more to his warning than his displeasure at having a car thief in his repair shop. He seemed to have a visceral disdain for Dubs that went beyond what she would have expected.

She gave him the VIN number of the Escalade. "We don't have an owner for this vehicle. It's listed as owned by a corporation and the address is a PO Box. We thought you might have more updated information. We really need to talk to the owner."

"I can give you an address," the man said. "I'm not doing more than that. If you are really who you say you are, you can figure out the rest."

"Hey—" Dubs started. Max held up her hand to stop her. There was no use arguing with him.

"That would be very helpful, thank you," Max said.

The man leaned down to write out the address. He was as methodical a penman as he was a typist.

"Is that Lola?" Dubs whispered.

Max glanced into the auto shop. Coming into view was indeed Lola. Max couldn't imagine why she was here. Lola glanced up in their direction, and Max tossed her a casual wave.

Lola headed purposefully toward her. She didn't look happy to see them.

"What are you doing here?" she asked. "You've got to get out of here before she sees you. She's flighty enough as it is."

"Wait a minute. What are you talking about?" Max said. "We're here following up on a lead on the shooting earlier today."

"Shooting? What shooting? Is everyone okay?" Now Lola looked less angry, more worried.

"We're fine, thanks to Holt. A possible informant was killed. What are you doing here?"

"I'm talking to Tiffany. Trying to get her to tell me who the father of her baby is, so he can sign the adoption paperwork. The lawyer met with us this morning."

"And she works here?" Max had only met Tiffany a couple of times, but she didn't seem like the kind of woman who would spend any time under the hood of a car.

"I don't know. This is where she asked to meet."

"You guys almost done with the family reunion?" Dubs interrupted. "I've got the address we came looking for, and I think it's time to go. Do you know that fella at the other end of the shop?"

Lola and Max looked in the direction Dubs indicated. He didn't look familiar.

"Nope," Lola said.

"Well, he's been back there working on his power poses for Mr. Malevolent Rhode Island. I, for one, have had enough inexplicably angry outbursts for one day."

"Maybe he's a new member of your fan club," Max said. "This seems to be their headquarters."

"Hilarious as always," Dubs said. "Except he's been staring at you two. Seriously. Time to go."

Max thanked the shop owner and they left. She wished she had been able to get a picture of the threatening man across the room, but she couldn't do it without his noticing. Maybe he was upset Dubs was there, or perhaps he knew Tiffany. Max would add it to her report of the day's events.

They parted ways with Lola and got back in the truck. Lola said she'd keep an eye on the guy while she waited for Tiffany, but she wasn't worried about it. She just wanted them to leave so Tiffany didn't freak out and run.

"Still have some more adventure in you?" Max asked.

"Just what are you suggesting?"

"Probably not what your tone implied you had in mind," Max said. This day had gone from really horrible to enjoyable. Dubs was fun to spend time with. Max wouldn't have guessed that when they first met.

"You're no fun, Max."

"I'm plenty of fun," Max said. "You haven't found out where I'm taking you yet."

"I don't want to know, do I?"

"Depends on if your idea of fun includes visiting the head of the largest gang in Rhode Island?"

"That's whose address we just got? And we get to tell him his car was involved in a shooting today? How do we know he wasn't doing the shooting? How do we know he won't just shoot us when we show up?"

"That's where the adventure comes in," Max said. "You in or not? I can take you back to the office."

"Oh sure, and spend the night handcuffed to your bed, waiting for you to get home."

Max didn't respond. There really wasn't a response she could make. The handcuffs being introduced into their relationship had skewed it in all kinds of strange ways.

"You in or out?"

"I wore my adventure pants this morning. Let's go. But for the record, my life as a car thief was much tamer and a whole lot safer than this."

Somehow Max didn't doubt it.

CHAPTER TWELVE

Isabelle didn't know when she had grown so fond of the morning drive in to work with Holt. They didn't always have much to say, and when they did talk, it usually wasn't groundbreaking discussion. What it was, though, was comfortable, and intimate, and theirs. That space in the truck in the morning felt like a comfortable pair of jeans she never wanted to get rid of. There was a part of her that wondered what happened to the fiercely independent woman she was just a few short months ago.

She knew she probably needed to get a job with someone other than Holt, eventually. Living with Holt was one thing, but working for her was quite another. For now though, it was working. They didn't actually see each other all that much during the day, except when Holt made up a very important question to ask, just so she could steal a kiss. And they had the drive to and from work, each morning and evening.

She had worried at first that Holt's colleagues might resent her presence, but that had turned out to be the furthest thing from the truth. Sometimes Isabelle thought Holt might be a little jealous at how well she got along with the band of do-gooders Holt had assembled.

She tried not to think about the events of the day before. Holt had assured her the guys doing the shooting hadn't been aiming at her, but what did that matter if the bullets had hit her? What if Max had gotten hurt? She knew Holt came with her job, but she didn't have to like it.

"You look lost in deep thoughts."

"Taking a moment to feel content and thankful that you're okay," Isabelle said. "My life is pretty good. I thought it was before, but then you landed in it and made it better."

"I hope I keep doing that, every day," Holt said.

"Honey, you know you make me happy, but there are limits to how good things can be, even for you."

"You'll never convince me of that. I clearly just have to try harder."

"Do you have someone new starting work today?" Isabelle asked. She knew most of the cars Holt's crew drove.

"No, why?" Holt looked up. She slammed on the brakes. "What the fuck?"

"Not much of a parker." A black SUV was parked perpendicular to four or five parking spots right outside the main entrance to Holt's office building. The windows were tinted, too dark to see anything inside.

Holt backed the truck up quickly, away from the SUV.

"What's going on?" Isabelle asked. Holt's body language had changed. She was in full work mode, which scared Isabelle.

"That's the damn Escalade Max and Dubs ran all over town looking for yesterday. I want to know why it's sitting outside my front door. Call Max. Tell her and Dubs to get down here in the next thirty seconds."

"Sweetie, you know Max is never awake at this hour," Isabelle said. They got to work early, and Max wasn't an early riser.

"Don't care. She's been getting up early now that she has a houseguest. Dubs probably even talks in her sleep."

"Where are you going?" Isabelle didn't like the fact that Holt was getting out of the truck. She had seen her get shot once. She couldn't watch it happen again.

"I'm going to go knock on the door, see if anyone's in there," Holt said.

Holt closed the truck door and went to the truck bed for a moment. When she reappeared, she was carrying a baseball bat.

"You don't knock on the door with a baseball bat," Isabelle said. She called Max and, as requested, the two women were downstairs roughly a minute later. Max was in boxers and a T-shirt, and although Isabelle tried not to notice, Dubs seemed to be wearing nothing but a thong and an extremely threadbare tank top. They were still handcuffed together. If Holt called, in this crew, you came running, regardless of your attire or who you were handcuffed to.

Isabelle couldn't hear what was happening, so she got out of the truck. She wasn't going to be scared and helpless, locked way. Snippets of their conversation drifted over to her. Dubs seemed to be trying to convince Holt not to break one of the Escalade's windows. She didn't understand all of the rapid-fire chatter, but it was possible Dubs wanted to break in herself and take the car out for a joyride.

An agreement was reached, and Holt motioned for Dubs and Max to step back, and they quickly moved away, with Max pulling Dubs slightly behind her. Holt tapped on the driver's side window with the bat head and ducked as low to the ground as she could. Isabelle wasn't a fan of that move, or Holt of feeling like it was necessary.

"No one home, H?" Max asked.

Holt shrugged and knocked harder with the bat. No answer.

Dubs held up her handcuffed hand and Holt unlocked the cuff. Max moved to the windshield and seemed to be comparing something on the car with something in her phone. Isabelle didn't know where she had hidden her phone since she wasn't wearing much. Dubs moved inside the building and returned with a long, thin piece of metal about an inch or less wide.

She moved to the driver side window and looked to Holt. They stepped back and gave Dubs room to work. Holt looked the Escalade over from where she was standing on the passenger's side and sent Max to the front. Holt saw Isabelle out of the truck.

"Hey, babe?" Holt called over. "Does everything look normal to you from where you're standing? Anything look out of place?"

Isabelle looked at the Escalade again. It was parked in such a strange location. Something caught her eye. There was a wire protruding from beneath the left taillight.

"Holt?" Isabelle said.

Holt held up her hand to stop Dubs.

"Yeah," Holt said.

"Can you come look at this? It's probably nothing."

Holt jogged around to Isabelle. She pointed to the wire. She didn't feel like getting actively involved in whatever they were doing. This wasn't the part of working with Holt she enjoyed.

"That's odd," Holt said. She went back to the Escalade and crouched down to examine the wire. She went down to her hip and sprawled out under the car. She was under for fifteen seconds before she shot back out. "Get back! Move!" Max grabbed Dubs and pulled her a good twenty feet from the truck. Holt headed directly for Isabelle. She half carried, half shoved her to the driver's side of the truck, pushed the keys into her hand, and got her inside.

"Drive at least three blocks away from here. Don't stop until you do, understand? When you get at least three blocks away, stop and call nine one one. Tell them the address and say we need the bomb squad."

Isabelle's heart felt like it stopped beating. She felt sweat bead on her forehead. Her mouth was dry.

"I can't. Not without you," Isabelle said. She couldn't leave Holt here.

"You have to. I can't leave. I'm sorry. There are people here that don't know about this. I have to warn them," Holt said. Isabelle saw her work mask drop. Holt was looking at her like she did at home. She was pleading with her.

"I want to beg you to have someone else do it," Isabelle said. "But that wouldn't be who you are. Be careful."

"I will," Holt said. "I'll see you soon."

Isabelle put the truck in reverse and drove quickly away.

Holt felt a measure of relief as soon as Isabelle left the parking lot. There was still a bomb hanging like an ugly metal nutsack from the undercarriage of the Escalade, but at least it wasn't going to blow up and kill Isabelle. Now all she needed to do was make sure it didn't kill anyone at all.

She jogged back to Dubs and Max, who were watching it warily. Max was crouched down, as if keeping an eye on the bomb to make sure it didn't get away. Dubs looked like she wanted to be somewhere else.

"Get inside," Holt said. "Go through this place inch by inch and get everyone out the back door. Max, you clear the second floor. Dubs, you've got a good enough idea of the layout of the first floor. Stand in the middle of the room and yell if you need to. I think Moose or Tuna should be here by now. They can help. Make sure someone goes to the tattoo shop next door. I'm going to hit Jose's shop and the two buildings attached to us. We've got to do this quickly. Isabelle is calling the bomb squad, but I don't know if this is on a timer, or if someone is watching. Who knows. Move it."

Holt watched them scatter. She knew they were scared, but they moved quickly and efficiently, not frantically. She knew Max would keep her cool, but she was happy to see Dubs do the same. It had been a stressful few days, but so far at least, Dubs was handling it. Holt moved through Jose's shop with lightning speed. There weren't many people there that early.

To get to the other buildings, she circled around the back of her office and sprinted along the alley. Their back door was locked. She estimated going back around would take three minutes. She didn't want to wait that long. She picked up a large rock and heaved it through the glass upper half of the door. She tried to be careful letting herself in, but still nicked her underarm on the shattered glass.

Her dramatic entrance caught the attention of the few employees in the first floor office who had arrived early. When she burst through the door, they were already up and headed her way, probably coming to see what the breaking glass was all about.

"I don't have time to explain, but you need to evacuate the building," Holt said. "Please do not go back for personal items, move out into the alley and follow my employees. You need to move far away from the building, as quickly as possible."

"Is this some kind of drill?" one of them asked.

Holt held up her bleeding arm. "No drill. No more questions. Everyone out. Is there anyone that works upstairs?"

She didn't know if it was the blood or her tone, but the crowd got the message. She knew them well enough for a friendly greeting, and she was sure they knew of her, if nothing else. If someone like Holt barged into your office bleeding and said you needed to evacuate, most people took that at face value.

Once she was satisfied they were headed out the door, she continued upstairs. There were three total levels, but no one was in. She was back out of the building in a flash.

As she'd hoped, her crew had taken charge and gotten everyone safely out of harm's way. She ran along the alley toward the large group, and anxious faces and palpable fear greeted her. She debated how much to tell everyone. It seemed unkind to keep the truth from them. She could hear the sirens getting close. Word would spread fast anyway.

"I'm sorry you were rushed out under such terrifying conditions. A car was dropped off in front of my office. Strapped to the undercarriage is what I believe to be an incendiary device. I do not know how much damage it can do, or if it was set to explode at a specific time. I didn't want to take any chances with your safety. The bomb squad is on its way now. I'm sure they can provide more of an update once they know more. I'm going over there now to provide what assistance I can."

Holt sent Isabelle a text, telling her everyone got out okay, and that she was unhurt. She didn't think the flesh wound on her arm was worth reporting.

She got back to the front of her office at the same time the bomb squad arrived. She knew a few of them and shook a few hands. Their leader came over to talk to her.

"What's going on here, Holt?"

"Someone left me a car and I don't like their wrapping paper," Holt said. "There's a wire sticking out of the left taillight. When I took a peek underneath, I thought you guys should probably be the ones doing the inspecting."

"You've got to get better at making friends, Holt."

"I've got plenty of friends. They give me better gifts." She wasn't in a very good mood. This was a little embarrassing, as she preferred to handle her own business. "I cleared the buildings. Everyone's gathered at the gas station a block over."

He gave her a thumbs-up as he walked back over to set up and get to work. They were quick but methodical. This wasn't the kind of work you could rush.

Isabelle texted back to say she was still waiting a few blocks away. Holt called her and told her she should probably go home since this might take a while. Isabelle didn't sound happy, but she agreed and Holt promised to be careful.

Max, Dubs, and Moose joined Holt. "Jose and Lola are keeping everyone entertained back there," Moose said. "What's going on here?"

"They're still working," Holt said. "I can't tell what they're doing, but I'm stressed for them, I can tell you that."

"What do you think would have happened if I'd tried to get that door open?" Dubs asked.

"Best not to think about it," Moose said. "Probably good lughead here didn't go bashing in windows with that damn bat of hers."

"She knocked. Very politely," Max said.

"Why are you bleeding?" Moose asked. "You know how much I hate patching you up. And now there's all this pressure to make it look extra good so Isabelle doesn't worry."

"It's fine, Moose. I'm fine. I just scraped my arm on some glass after I broke the window next door."

Moose rolled his eyes.

The leader of the bomb squad came over and told them to go join the group that had been evacuated. She didn't like being kicked out of the area, but this wasn't really a great time to argue. They were the ones with the expertise and the unexploded bomb. She did what she was told.

When she got back to the large group, who still looked quite nervous, she lasted about fifteen seconds standing around before she got antsy.

"Max, which gang did you say that Escalade belonged to?"

Max told her. "You think they were stupid enough to leave a car with a bomb on your doorstep, H?" Max asked.

Holt shrugged. Probably not, but only one way to find out for sure. She scrolled through the contacts on her phone. She kept a list of all the power players in the gangs, drug trafficking, and other local criminal enterprises in her phone. You never knew when it would come in handy. Like now.

The phone rang a few times before a very sleepy voice answered. He didn't sound happy to be woken up.

"Is this Marcos?" Holt asked.

"Who wants to know?"

"I'll assume that's a yes. This is Holt Lasher. I believe you spoke with two of my colleagues yesterday."

"Bitch, how did you get this number? And why are you calling me so early? We're not friends. This was a dangerous phone call to make. You understand me?"

"You don't want a friend like me," Holt said. She wasn't in the mood to play games. "Do you understand me? This is not a social call. I found your Escalade."

"I told your two yesterday, that got stolen last week. Where did you find it? Are you really calling to tell me you found my car?"

"No. I'm calling to tell you I found your car outside my front door with a bomb strapped to the undercarriage."

There was silence on the other end of the line for a second. Marcos was either trying to figure out a lie, or was shocked into speechlessness.

"Holy fuck, Holt, we had nothing to do with that. I told your people, and I'm telling you, that car was stolen. Why would I pick a fight with you? Like you said, I don't want a friend like you, and I certainly don't want an enemy like you, either."

"See, the problem for you, and for me, is that your car was used in a drive-by shooting, and now this. And you didn't file a police report after it was stolen."

"You really think I would file a police report? That's hilarious. I'm not about to ask for trouble, from the cops or the new cats in town boostin' cars. They wanted my ride, fine, I got a few others. But now, clearly, that's causing me some problems. Look, Holt, I don't want any trouble from you. I'm certainly not stupid enough to try and blow you up. I don't do bombs anyway. That's mob stuff, or terrorists, or some other shit than me."

"Then tell me about the new cats in town, the ones stealing cars, and we'll call it even," Holt said.

"They're real secretive. I don't know much. Just that they work out of the South Side and they're nasty pieces of work. Not for nothing, but I bet those assholes know a thing or two about bombs. But I don't got no names or anything."

"Thanks, Marcos. You've been real helpful. Maybe there's a chance for friendship after all," Holt said. She could hear Marcos sputtering as she hung up the phone.

Holt didn't think he had anything to do with either the shooting or the bomb. She hadn't thought it before talking to him, but she was more certain now. There wasn't really a way to know for sure, but he didn't seem like he was lying. She was pretty good at detecting bullshit, even over the phone, and he didn't have a good reason for attacking her. He was common, petty, small time. Not a bomb-making, drive-by-during-the-day kind of thug.

"I don't think Marcos is our guy," Holt said. "Max, Dubs, think back to your day, retrace your steps, and figure out how someone would have known you were looking for that Escalade. When we're allowed back in the office, I want a list of everyone you came in contact with. Marcos thinks our group is working out of the South Side. I know that doesn't narrow it down, but it's something."

"We were over there looking for the Escalade," Max said. "We've got the list of cars Dubs thinks are their work, and Isabelle is working the financial end. Eventually, we're going to cross-reference enough that we'll get this narrowed down."

"The bomb might tell us something too," Moose said.

"And Shorty's cell phone, right?" Dubs asked, her teeth chattering.

"All of it will help," Holt said. "Are you cold?" Holt asked Dubs.

"Freezing," Dubs said. "But I didn't really have a chance to run back in for clothes. There was a bomb on the doorstep, if you remember. I was only sleeping with underwear on because Max was there. If I'd been alone, I would have evacuated in my birthday suit."

"That would have distracted the bomb squad," Max said. "Might have made our initial evacuation easier though. Just follow the naked woman. She'll lead you to safety."

The bomb squad leader saved Dubs from more embarrassment.

"All clear, Holt. You guys got lucky. That thing could have done some real damage. It was rigged to the driver's side door and ignition. If you had opened the door, or started the engine, the car would have blown. There was plenty of punch under there to take out most of your office too. We'll take it all back with us and have the forensic team do what they do. Maybe we can get some prints or other evidence. We'll be in touch."

Holt shook his hand, unsettled by his news. Dubs had been seconds away from popping the lock and opening the door. Isabelle had been in the parking lot, in harm's way. Whoever dropped off the car seemed to know they would have tried to move it.

"Everyone back to the office," Holt said. She was pissed. On her way back, she called Isabelle to let her know she was fine and the coast was clear. She left the details of how much damage could have been done, and how close a call it really was, a little vague. There were some details she figured Isabelle didn't need to know.

CHAPTER THIRTEEN

Dubs didn't know how Max and the rest of her colleagues worked the way they did. So far, she'd seen a knife fight, been shot at, and almost blown up, and the rest of the time, they'd sat around plotting, or working leads on the computer. She was either bored out of her mind, or running for her life. Max tried to tell her she had just caught them during a bad stretch, at least as far as the life-threatening excitement, but Dubs didn't know whether to believe her.

Then there was Max. Dubs had started flirting with her to pass the time, and to get a rise out of her. But now she was worried about just how much she was enjoying it. One major advantage to all the danger they had been in was that she had gotten to see Max in full superhero mode multiple times. She was insanely sexy. There was no denying that.

Her phone buzzed and she looked at the text. It was Tony. While she had told Max what he had said about the new crew of thieves, she hadn't told her everything he had said to her. He was trying to get her to do a job, a very specific one. So far, she was resisting, although it meant a lot to her, but he was wearing her down. She had taken this opportunity with Holt to find a way to get back on her feet. She didn't know why she was hesitating to take Tony up on his offer. It was precisely the opportunity she had been looking for.

She tossed her phone down with a sigh. Prison had been less complicated.

Max walked in just in time to catch Dubs's sigh. "I told you, things aren't usually so rough around here," she said, misreading Dubs's morose attitude.

"It's not that," Dubs said. "I'm fine. Really."

"Uh huh." Max started rubbing her shoulders. It felt like magic. Max found knots Dubs didn't even know were there.

"Oh my God. Please don't ever stop doing that," Dub said. "How is it you big strong types are so tender?"

Max laughed. "I don't think anyone has ever called me big or strong. I'm pretty sure I've actually been blown over in a gust of wind."

"It's not about what's on the outside, Max." She was close to catatonic she felt so good. Max had amazing hands. "You're big and strong in all the right ways. Your heart, your courage, your kindness. And right now, your massage skills are off the charts."

"Feeling better then?" Max asked. She stopped rubbing Dubs's shoulders.

"Hey, why'd ya stop?"

"Because I'm not sure you were concentrating," Max said, "and I want to make sure you're okay. All of this has been a lot."

"I'm a criminal, remember? I live for danger."

"You're also full of shit," Max said. "But if you don't want to talk about it, that's your business. Who was texting you?"

"Is that an official inquiry, or a personal one?" Dubs asked. She wanted to know if Max was checking up on her for Holt, or if Max was interested in her personally. She hoped Max was being nosy for her own sake, not Holt's.

"Does it matter?"

"It does to me," Dubs said. "I like to feel wanted and valuable to my lady. I don't like to feel owned by my boss. So? Personal or professional?"

"You do realize I'm not your lady, right?" Max said.

"Position's open."

"Two years ago, there were just under twelve hundred motor vehicle thefts in Providence," Max said, apparently ignoring Dubs's offer. "Last year that number was under one thousand. So far this year, we're already over fourteen hundred."

"What's your point, Pretty Girl?" Dubs asked. She liked watching Max work. Her mind worked in a far more detailed and technical way than anyone Dubs had ever met. She was used to people like the rest of Holt's crew, maybe not as impeccably honest and good, but their general type. But she had never met anyone like Max.

"My point is, how do you randomly steal over four hundred cars in less than a year without anyone knowing who you are? Without a security camera picking you up, getting caught by a nosy neighbor, a competitor figuring out what you're up to?"

"You don't," Dubs said. "The kind of theft you're talking about, any theft really, is about opportunity. But a truly random theft is even more driven by serendipity. You stumble on a guy who ran into the gas station, but left his keys in the ignition. Or he left the door open with the spare key conveniently hidden right inside. There aren't four hundred of those just lying around."

"So how do you make your own opportunity?" Max asked. "What or who are we looking for?"

"Someone with access to a lot of cars," Dubs said. "But it's got to be more than that. They had to have access to the right kind of cars, and access for a long time, in a way where they could steal them without anyone noticing, or tracing it back to them. That's not easy to do. These guys are good."

"You kinda sound like you admire them," Max said.

"They tried to torpedo me first, then dropped off a bomb for us today. I'm not a big fan. 'Cause you know who would have been charred like one of those dumb cartoon characters with the slim-jim in her hand? This idiot. I was the one about to open that door and drive the Escalade out of here. Just like they wanted me to. That's a low, dirty, cheap shot."

Dubs had thought she was okay from the events of the day, but perhaps she really wasn't. She hadn't stopped to consider that it would have been her blown to bits. Whoever left the Escalade had to know that. If a stolen car was dropped on the doorstep of another car thief, it was a well known challenge. Maybe it was because she was a threat to them. Or maybe it was because she was selling out and working for the cops. She knew how working for Holt Lasher would go over in their community. Although it wasn't like she had much choice.

But now Shorty was dead, after meeting with her. And Tony was putting even more pressure on her to legitimize herself again quickly in the community's eyes, before it was too late. She sighed, closed her eyes, and tipped her head back. Her hair was down from its ponytail and flowed behind her. It felt good, tugging ever so slightly on her scalp.

She startled when she felt Max's hands on her head, but she didn't open her eyes. She didn't dare move. Whatever Max was up to, she was along for the ride, a willing participant. Max ran her hand through Dubs's hair, stopping when her hand was cupping the back of Dubs's head. Max pulled her forward a few inches and kissed her. Dubs opened her eyes, just long enough to make sure it was real.

Max's lips were soft and full. Dubs tried to deepen the kiss. She reached out to grasp any part of Max she could reach, but Max broke the kiss and pulled away. She gently stroked Dubs's cheek and moved back to the bed, where she had been sitting while they talked.

"What did you do that for, and what the hell did you stop for? I demand you get back over here," Dubs said. That was the best and worst kiss she had ever had.

"You looked like you needed it, I guess," Max said.

"And what if that didn't help?" Dubs asked. "What if I need more of the same treatment? What if I need extended dosing? I think I'm addicted. You wield a powerful weapon and you were not careful with it. Now look what you've done."

"I think you'll survive," Max said.

Dubs could be wrong, but she looked a little flushed too. "If you aren't going to kiss me again," Dubs said, "I'm coming over there to kiss you."

She hopped up and headed for Max. There wasn't anywhere for Max to go in the small room, and Dubs landed in her lap, forcing

Max to either catch her or let her fall on the floor. In the process, Dubs got the upper hand and tipped Max off balance, forcing her on her back on the bed.

Max didn't seem willing to give up easily. She rolled them both over so she was straddling Dubs's waist. She pinned Dubs's hands over her head and leaned over her. Dubs could see the desire in Max's eyes, and Dubs couldn't remember ever being more turned on. Max was sexy, and powerful, but in her own Max kind of way was letting Dubs guide things.

"You got me where we both want me," Dubs said. "You started this, Pretty Girl. You going to finish it?"

Max hesitated. As suddenly as it all began, Max let go of Dubs's wrists and climbed off the bed. "We shouldn't be doing this. I've got work to do downstairs," she said.

"Hey." She sat up and tried to get to Max, who wouldn't even look at her. Dubs wrapped her arms around Max's torso and noticed, yet again, that Max was hiding an impressive amount of muscle on her thin frame. "Don't run out of here. We can pretend none of that just happened if you want, but we still have to get in the same bed tonight, just like every night."

"I'll sleep on the floor," Max said.

"Seriously?" Sometimes women could be idiots.

"It seemed like the right thing to offer," Max said.

"Chivalry isn't dead after all," Dubs said. "Now turn around and talk to me. I'm getting myself in trouble with free access to your stomach."

"I never told you to go exploring," Max said. She turned around and Dubs was happy to see she was smiling.

Dubs kissed her. She didn't prolong it, even though she was tempted.

"What was that for?" Max asked.

"A teaser for when you decide to pick up where you left off," Dubs said.

"You're awfully confident that will happen."

"What can I say? I'm an optimist. Now let's go downstairs and get back to work. I must be an invaluable asset, otherwise people wouldn't be trying so hard to kill me all the time." Dubs wished there were a less true statement, at least the part about people trying to kill her. She didn't know how much of an asset she was. Or wanted to be. Everything was muddled now.

Max took her hand and gave it a squeeze. Dubs intertwined their fingers. Max pulled their two hands to her mouth, and kissed the top of Dubs's hand then let their hands fall free. They headed out the door and back to work.

Chapter Fourteen

Max wanted to get as much space from Dubs as possible. It was difficult to do in the office, however, since she kept having to ask her questions. She was pretty sure Dubs was enjoying the fact that she was avoiding her. She had no idea what had possessed her to kiss her, and her lips still tingled. It was both irritating and exciting.

Lola was the only other person in the office. She was sitting with Dubs, and Max could hear them talking about babies.

"Has she signed all the paperwork?" Dubs asked.

"We met with the lawyer to get that process going," Lola said. "I didn't realize how complicated it is. I thought she just handed over the kid at the hospital and we went from there. Holt is making me do it all the right way. I guess a pregnancy test on your doorstep in the middle of the night and a note saying you don't want the kid isn't binding in court. Who knew?"

"Is the father on board with giving the kid up?" Dubs asked.

"I think he's already signed the papers," Lola said. "Tiffany won't let me meet him though. She said he doesn't want anything to do with the process. It's kinda weird, but whatever he wants, I guess. It's so strange to think this little baby can hear us now, and we're talking about his biological parents not wanting him or her."

"Good thing you do," Dubs said. "Do you know if it's a boy or a girl?"

"No," Lola said. "Tiffany knows. But she said she won't tell me until all the papers are signed and I'm sure this is what I want. She's sort of an ass. Took me a while to see that."

"Cheating on you didn't give it away?" Dubs asked.

"I'm a slow learner," Lola said.

Max couldn't take it anymore. She couldn't avoid Dubs forever, and truth be told, she didn't really want to. On top of that, she wanted to hear more about the baby. Lola was one of her closest friends, and it wasn't fair that Dubs was getting all the juicy bits of news while she was stuck across the room pretending not to be listening. She headed over to the two of them.

"Do you have a crib? Names picked out?" Max asked. "You're going to have a whole office full of really excited, probably overly involved, aunts and uncles. You're prepared for that, right?"

"I don't have anything," Lola said. She looked a little stressed. "I don't know the first thing about kids, actually. I keep looking at these websites online that say I need all this stuff, but the kid is going to weigh less than a watermelon. How much stuff can it really need?"

"Oh, honey," Dubs said. "Didn't we talk about this already? Should I start listing the things you need?"

"Please don't," Lola said.

"Just make sure you have a car seat to get home from the hospital," Dubs said. "A good friend of mine had a baby before I got locked up. He said you can't leave the hospital without one."

"I guess that means I need a car too," Lola said.

"You want me to hook you up?" Dubs said.

"No," Lola and Max said simultaneously, laughing.

"Hey, it was a joke." She looked a little defensive.

"So how do I pick a car seat? Or a crib? Just walk in the store and tell them I need one?" Lola asked.

"Definitely not," Max said. "There are safety standards and stuff with those things, right? I'm pretty sure it's situations like this that the Internet was invented for. Come over here. I'll get you set up."

Holt and Moose walked into the office as Max was reminding Lola of all the intricacies of using a computer. As smart as she was, she didn't really understand technology, which was a constant source of amusement, and frustration, to Max.

Dubs greeted Moose warmly, but only nodded hello to Holt. Max had noticed Dubs had warmed quickly to everyone in the office except Holt. She wasn't unfriendly, or adversarial, toward her, but she seemed to go out of her way to keep her distance. Holt was the closest thing to a prison warden here, so perhaps Dubs resented that. And Holt hadn't exactly rolled out the welcome mat when Dubs arrived.

"Fighting the electronic beast again, Lola?" Moose called across the room.

"Max said it will teach me about car seats," Lola shouted back.

"What is there to learn?" Moose said. "It's a seat. It goes in the car. The kid goes in the seat. Done."

"I hope you never have children," Holt said, putting her arm around Moose's shoulders.

"I'll be a great dad," Moose said. "But apparently someone else will have to do the shopping."

"And we all know who wants that job," Lola said.

Moose blushed a deep crimson. He suddenly had something important to take care of in Holt's office. Their laughter followed him through the door.

"What was that all about?" Dubs asked.

"Jose has had the hots for him since high school," Lola said. "But he's too chicken to do anything about it. So we all tease both of them, mostly Moose, mercilessly. I guess one of them will eventually do something about it."

"Is Moose into Jose?" Dubs asked.

"You know, I have no idea," Lola said. "I don't know what or who Moose is into. He's never shot us down with our teasing, or told Jose to stop. And I've never seen him with a significant other of any kind. I guess I always assumed they would end up together eventually. Maybe Holt knows."

"That reaction seemed to say a lot," Dubs said. "I would blush like that if you teased me about M—"

Max shot Dubs a cease and desist look, and she took the hint.

"I just meant I wouldn't blush like that if I didn't like someone. That's all I was trying to say."

Lola looked at her funny, but let it go.

"Max," Holt said, coming over to join them. "Have you had any luck getting phone numbers off Shorty's cell phone? Do you need help, Lola? You're going to be at that a while if you only use your index finger to type."

"I got this under control, H."

"Of course. That's totally obvious, now that I'm closer," Holt said.

"I do have a list," Max said. "I identified all the numbers except one. That one is a prepaid burner. It was purchased four months ago from the Walmart across town. He got calls once every couple weeks, sometimes less often. He never made outgoing calls. It's consistent with how he described his relationship with the contact he had with the group. He said he thought the person he talked to wasn't close to the main group, but he could have been lying, or not well informed."

"It's worth running down," Holt said. "I want you to stay here and run that number against some of the other leads we've developed. See if it comes up in contact with Marcos, or the Escalade. See what Isabelle has gotten from wading through the financial side of things. That money has to be flowing in and out of somewhere. Start piecing together a larger map of this if you can. I want all the little puzzle pieces on one giant grid. We need to find our first corner and start building from there. Maybe it's Shorty, or maybe this phone number. Hell, maybe it was that Escalade, or that bomb."

"Have you heard anything from the government about the bomb?" Dubs asked.

Max saw Holt's look of confusion.

"Sorry, the police. Have you heard anything from the police about what they found from analyzing the bomb?"

"Nothing yet. And I know what you meant by government. I was trying to figure out what camp you put me in. This has to be hard for you."

"Nobody's killed me yet," Dubs said. "And you can't say they aren't trying."

"I told you before," Holt said, "you're part of my team as long as you're here and playing straight. I protect my own."

"I heard you," Dubs said.

Max knew hearing was different from believing, even after Holt had saved them both from getting shot.

"Go see if Moose is ready to come out of hiding. The two of you should take a trip to Walmart and see if you can find video of someone buying that phone. They probably paid with cash, but you might recognize the buyer. And maybe we'll get phenomenally lucky and they paid with a credit card or had to show their ID for some reason. Stranger things have happened."

"You coming, Pretty Girl?" Dubs asked.

"I've got some chores for Max here," Holt said. "You'll have to do without her for a few hours. Moose is good company. I promise."

"Significantly less hot though," Dubs said.

Max glared at her and Dubs seemed to like it, which annoyed Max even more.

"I'm sure Moose will appreciate your assessment," Holt said.

Dubs went to get Moose and they headed off on their errand. Max watched Dubs's ass all the way out the door, which Dubs turned around and caught her doing. She smiled knowingly as she leaned back in the door to wave good-bye. She was so damned disarming Max didn't even really mind getting caught. She was pretty sure Dubs had been walking slowly and with a little extra sway for her benefit anyway. It would have been rude not to notice.

"Hope you weren't trying not to get caught," Holt said.

"I don't know what you're talking about," Max said, embarrassed Holt had seen her looking at Dubs's ass. She shouldn't be surprised though. Holt noticed everything.

"Uh huh," Holt said. "Let's just hope you're more subtle if you ever do undercover work. Or need to lie convincingly to someone on a job."

"I did just fine undercover as a car thief pretending not to be a car thief. We almost got caught before she could get the car unlocked, but we improvised by pretending to be a horny couple using the parking lot to make out. We were very convincing, I'll have you know," Max said. She didn't think that should really count. Kissing Dubs wasn't that much of a challenge. The hard undercover work Holt was talking about was probably going to be something like pretending to be an important tech power player when she was really just a poor, nerdy kid.

Holt raised her eyebrows but didn't say anything.

"I feel like I handled that okay," Max said. "But overall, how do you know if you're doing a good job in the field?"

"You catch the guy you're chasing, then you did a good job," Holt said.

Max was stunned into silence. She expected some words of wisdom, not that boiled down, plain white rice explanation. "That seems kind of simple, boss," Max said.

"It is," Holt said. "If I had a team I didn't trust, I would give more caveats and explanation. But I trust everyone here to go after the guys we chase the right way. Therefore, if you catch the guy you're chasing, job well done. Simple as that. I'll amend, since you're new to this. Don't cut corners, don't compromise your ethics, watch the backs of the people you work with."

It was amazing that Max used to be terrified of Holt. Sure, she had a temper that made the Incredible Hulk look reasonable and mild mannered, but she was just so...Holt. She was hard not to like.

"How are you doing with watching Dubs? Aside from her backside, that is? You clearly have that well handled."

"It's fine, I guess," Max said. "Hard to keep up with the computer work I'd like to be doing. Seems like there's a lot to do in the world outside this office."

"Now you know why I refuse to give up my time on the streets," Holt said. "I don't want to spend all my time buried under paperwork, although Isabelle would prefer that, I think."

"I don't feel like I'm doing a good job," Max said. She felt relieved saying it out loud. She was worried she was letting Holt down, and now at least she could voice those fears directly to the one person whose approval or disapproval mattered most to her.

"And certainly by the definition you just gave, I'm not. No bad guys yet."

"Yet is the key word there, Max," Holt said. "Why don't you think you're doing a good job?"

"I let Dubs convince me to go to the beach, then she gets far enough away that I can't hear anything she's saying as she chats with an old friend. My first meeting with a potential informant, he's dead. You had to save us, or who knows, I might be dead, or Dubs might. Then a bomb shows up on our doorstep, and I can't help but think that's my fault. I haven't figured out how yet, but I will."

"Do you think Dubs is playing us?" Holt asked.

"I don't know," Max said. Saying it stung, but it was the truth. She really wanted to believe Dubs was one hundred percent on their side and being honest with them, especially her, but she wasn't sure. That fact, maybe more than anything else, is what stopped her from taking things further earlier. "Something's bothering her. I don't know what it is. She's been getting a lot of text messages that agitate her. She says they're from her dad, but I'm not sure I believe her."

"It's good you're aware of that," Holt said. "As far as the conversation with her friend at the beach, I took the cuffs off you two. You can't be by her side at all times. Would it have been ideal to hear what they talked about? Of course. But you have to build trust, which it seems like you're doing. And who knows if he would have talked to her if you were there. I can't imagine we're real popular among her close friends."

That made Max feel marginally better. All of this was so new to her she didn't feel like she had an accurate barometer by which to judge her performance.

"As for the shooting," Holt said. "You did exactly what I would want you to in that situation. You saw something that put you on guard, you got your charges, and you sought shelter. You were heading for the alley, correct?"

Max nodded. She'd registered the Escalade and van approaching, and she just knew they needed to get out of there. She remembered grabbing Dubs and pulling her with her. She was pretty sure she got Shorty too, but she wasn't sure.

"I hope you're never in a situation like that again, but if you are, you'll learn when to keep running, and when to stop and take cover. I simply helped with the take cover aspect."

"I'm not sure Dubs has forgiven you yet for literally covering her with our bodies. She was complaining about being under us for hours. She said you should lay off the gym a few days the next time you're going to land on top of someone on the sidewalk."

"I'll take it under advisement," Holt said, looking amused. "I'm not even going to try and convince you the bomb isn't your fault. Maybe you asked questions and someone got nervous, maybe it had nothing to do with that," Holt said. "It's just a reminder that at times, our job is dangerous. You've got to let that one go."

"I'll do my best," Max said.

"Moving out from behind the computer wasn't ever going to be easy. This is probably the hardest first test case I could have found for you. Give yourself a break. Keep talking to me. You'll make mistakes. We all do. You don't learn from them if you don't talk about them and figure out what went wrong."

Max took a deep breath. "I also kissed her."

"You told me that. Undercover move. I think I've kissed Lola, Moose, Jose, maybe even Tuna, once."

"Nope," Max said. "In my room. No one else around we were trying to fool. She looked a little blue, and I guess I thought it would help."

"So it was a pity kiss? A public service? How many ways are you going to find to kiss this woman that aren't really kisses? I did warn you about just this thing, didn't I?" Holt didn't sound upset, but her tone was serious.

"Yes, you did." Max barely stopped herself from adding "ma'am" at the end.

"Be careful, Max," Holt said. "You said yourself you don't know if you can trust her. For your sake, be careful. She's valuable to what we're doing here, and I'm starting to like her, but all of that will survive without her. I don't want to see you in a situation where you won't."

"I have no idea what I'm doing," Max said, staring at her hands.

Holt smiled knowingly. "Women will do that to ladies like us. I could be wrong, but you seem a lot like me when I was your age. You want to be with someone badly and you'll give your all to the person you're with. That makes you vulnerable, though. Make sure you choose someone who will be good to you. We look tough, but we need care, feeding, and watering to keep us strong and healthy. Trust me, it takes a special kind of woman to put up with someone like me. I suspect you aren't much different, in your own way."

"I'll be careful," Max said. She really appreciated how much Holt looked out for her. She also felt like she wanted to do some kind of spastic happy dance when she thought of Holt seeing herself in Max. Max saw herself as a wafer thin computer nerd, not the female Adonis, superhero clone that was Holt Lasher.

First she had kissed Dubs, and now she was a baby Holt. Sure, each of those brought complications out the wazoo, but right now, life didn't seem like it could get much better.

"Thanks for the chat, H," Max said. "I'm going to get back to work. I want to be able to say I did a good job in my first field assignment."

Holt nodded and headed to her office. "Go get 'em kid. You know where to find me if you need any help."

CHAPTER FIFTEEN

Isabelle poured over the financial data in front of her. She had been sorting through it for weeks, but still couldn't make sense of it, at least not in a way that would blow Holt's case wide open. It was incredibly frustrating. She was used to working on something doggedly, but usually there was an end in sight. Right now, she wasn't even sure what the end looked like. It felt like every time she pulled on one seemingly promising thread, it either tangled another section, or unraveled a week's worth of hard work. Isabelle sighed.

Holt was by her side almost instantly. "What's wrong, sweetheart?"

The loft wasn't that large, but even for Holt, she had moved fast. Isabelle suspected she had been hovering, waiting for an excuse to come over.

"It's problems at work," Isabelle said. "I don't think you'd understand."

"Try me," Holt said, scooping Isabelle up and carrying her to the couch. When she sat down, Isabelle was settled comfortably on her lap. "I can be quite understanding."

"Is that so?" Isabelle asked, playing along. She repositioned so she was straddling Holt's lap. She ran the fingers of both hands through Holt's hair and left her hands framing Holt's face. "Well, I've got a really, really sexy boss, who I've got the hots for. It's very distracting. Makes getting any work done extremely difficult."

"I'm jealous," Holt said. "Anyone I know?"

"Nah." Isabelle moved forward until her lips were only millimeters away from Holts. "Just some lady. But all day long, she struts around in her jeans, and her T-shirts, and her boots. And she's got these tattoos that peek out everywhere. And her muscles? Don't get me started. I know what's under all that clothing, so you can understand how hard it is for me to think about anything but getting it all off."

"I don't strut," Holt said, looking a little offended.

"You walk assertively," Isabelle said. "No complaints here."

Isabelle moved even closer to Holt until she was pressed against her stomach. Holt ran her hands along Isabelle's thighs, let her thumbs linger for a moment where her thighs and torso met, and then moved back and grabbed her ass, pulling her even tighter to her. Isabelle gasped at the quick, pleasurable sensation that shot through her as her center came in full contact with the hard planes and muscled lines of Holt's midsection.

Holt flipped them over so Isabelle was lying on her back on the couch. Holt pulled off first her own shirt, then Isabelle's and then both of their bras. Isabelle shimmied out of her pants and pointed to Holt's, encouraging her to lose hers as well. Once their clothes were off, Holt kissed her way back up Isabelle's body. She never made it as far as Isabelle's lips. She stopped at her breasts, and Isabelle arched up to meet her. Holt teased Isabelle's nipple. She kissed and caressed gently with her tongue, never quite getting close enough to allow Isabelle full ecstasy. It was making her crazy in a wonderful way.

When Holt finally did take Isabelle's nipple in her mouth, it sent a wave of desire rapidly to her clit, the pulsating excitement of it so overwhelming it made her moan and dig her fingers into Holt's hair, encouraging her to continue. She switched to Isabelle's other breast and let her hand wander down Isabelle's stomach until she reached the apex between her thighs. Isabelle wanted to force Holt to move faster, or slow down, or do something other than what she was doing, because she felt as if she was going to explode, but the feeling was so excruciatingly wonderful, she simply experienced it.

Holt ran her fingers gently through Isabelle's wetness, but she didn't seem to be in any hurry to heighten her arousal. She continued to tease her breasts, working back and forth, and then slowly ran her tongue along the underside of one, down her stomach, and along her thigh.

She moved off the edge of the couch and kneeled on the floor. She pulled Isabelle with her, to the edge. She ran both hands along the insides of Isabelle's thighs, her thumbs meeting at Isabelle's clit, once again sending shockwaves through Isabelle's already sensitive system. Holt leaned forward and replaced her thumbs with her tongue.

It took excessive willpower for Isabelle to not come at Holt's first caress. She knotted her fingers in the couch cushions on either side of her and threw her head back, wanting to focus on every exquisite wave of heat Holt was producing throughout her body. She wrapped her legs over Holt's shoulders, and she grabbed her ass and pulled her even closer. That was all it took to send her over the edge.

When Holt moved back up her body to kiss her, Isabelle could see it was going to be a long night. She loved when Holt had that look of need. She kissed her deeply, letting her know they had the rest of the night for each other. Holt half stood from her crouch on the floor, and scooped Isabelle off the couch, never breaking their kiss. Isabelle found it thrilling how physically capable Holt was. She enjoyed the ease with which Holt could carry her to their bedroom if she wished, yet she was still soft and curved in all the right places.

"What are you doing?" Isabelle asked, kissing Holt's neck.

"Now I'm strutting," Holt said.

"Feeling a little proud of yourself?"

"A little," Holt said. "I'm also carrying the most beautiful woman I've ever laid eyes on. I've got a few reasons to strut."

Isabelle kissed Holt as they tumbled onto the bed. Holt landed on her back. Isabelle took a minute, as she always did, to look over every naked inch of her. Holt's tattooed body was a thing to behold, and she marveled every day that it was all hers.

She started at Holt's collarbone and traced her index finger between Holt's breasts, straight down the line of her abs, and finally along the ridge of her hardened clit. Holt shivered under her touch. Isabelle moved further down and entered her. She used her thumb to keep steady pressure on Holt's clit. Holt arched up under her touch and came quickly. When she opened her eyes, Isabelle was taken aback by the hunger in them.

"That was fast, baby," Isabelle said.

"I was a little riled up," Holt said. "It's a good thing we have all night."

Chapter Sixteen

Dubs was invigorated by her investigative success the day before with Moose. She was starting to enjoy the day-to-day work of Holt's crew. She never thought she would say that. When she got out of prison and joined this group, actually catching bad guys wasn't a concern of hers. She had started helping them as a condition of her getting out, but now, it felt different. She wanted to help. She wanted to catch these guys, and she was enjoying the process.

She knew a lot of it had to do with Max. Seeing the way Max went about her work, the dedication she applied to everything she did, was inspiring. If Max weren't so adorably earnest about it all, it would be damned annoying.

Dubs looked around the main office. A few of Holt's crew were working at computer stations. Max was at her desk, typing furiously and staring blankly at her computer screen. She had been running her hands through her hair for the past hour, so now it was sticking almost straight up in all directions. She thought about kissing Max. It had been so unexpected at first she hadn't done anything but react to the pleasurable physical aspect. And it was *quite* pleasurable.

After Max had stopped the kiss from going any further, Dubs had done some thinking. She was glad Max hadn't gotten as carried away as she had. She enjoyed their flirting and definitely the kiss, but she also liked not quite knowing where all of it was leading. She liked Max a lot. If they had slept together, it would have pushed them in a specific direction, probably awkward-friends-with-benefits territory. She didn't want that. In fact, aside from really, really wanting to kiss Max again, she wasn't entirely sure what she wanted. If Max wasn't who she was, and Dubs wasn't Dubs, the answer would be a lot easier. But a car thief and a bad guy catcher didn't really scream happy couple. Opposites might attract, but Dubs thought that combo sounded more like oil and water.

"You done daydreaming?" Moose asked, quite close to Dubs's ear.

"Whoa, giant man. How is it even possible for you to sneak up on people?"

"You were pretty lost in thought," Moose said. "Anything good?"

"Yes," Dubs said, not willing to offer any other details.

"Okay then. Well, I got a call this morning from our favorite security officer at Walmart. He copied the tapes I asked for yesterday. You ready for some exciting feature film viewing with yours truly?"

"Are you going to serve popcorn? Can I be in charge of the remote? Do we get to watch on Max's fancy big screens?"

"Yes, absolutely not, and of course," Moose said. "Curtain goes up in ten. I've seen how much coffee you drink. Make sure you pee first. I'm not going to stop every five minutes so you can evacuate the excess."

Dubs made a face at Moose, who seemed unconcerned. She ignored his advice and instead used her time to visit Max. As she walked the short distance to Max's desk, she pulled her hair out of its ponytail. She got the feeling Max liked her hair better when it was down. For some reason that mattered to her right now. She realized she was slightly nervous, which felt silly, which then made her feel more nervous, because she started to question the original nerves. She thought about aborting, but Max turned around and saw her before she could make a move. Max's smile when she saw her approach was all the confirmation she needed that she made the right move.

"What are you working on over here?"

"Still trying to come up with some kind of matrix that makes sense of all the data points we have for this case. I've got them all entered; now I'm working on a way to cross-reference them to look for patterns or overlap."

"I would think someone was punishing you, except I can tell by the look of exhilaration on your face you actually think this stuff is fun. Seriously, it's close to rapture."

"We all have our things."

"I think it's adorable," Dubs said. She leaned in and quickly kissed Max on the cheek. She wanted to kiss her for real, but she knew Max wouldn't appreciate it in the middle of the office. In fact, she wasn't entirely sure if Max would appreciate it at all.

"If I get stuck at the matinee all day, I'll see you at home later," Dubs said.

Max seemed to try to hide it, but she smiled widely at Dubs's innocent comment, and her face softened at the mention of their current shared dwelling. On the way to the conference room, Dubs felt like she was having an out of body experience. She was insanely happy at Max's reaction to her characterization of Max's apartment as their home, and yet the fact that she was so happy was so unexpected, it was as if she were watching someone else experiencing the moment. It was unnerving.

She glanced back over her shoulder, hoping to be subtle. Max was watching her walk away and caught her eye. So much for subtle. She spun back around quickly, just in time to trip over an office chair. She heard Max chuckle behind her, but she didn't dare turn back again. She let out a huge sigh of relief when she made it safely to the conference room. Moose looked at her sideways, but didn't say anything.

Her cell phone buzzed in her pocket. She pulled it out and read the text message. "Enjoy the matinee." It was from Max.

She wrote back. "Pretty Girl, you're killing me right now."

"I can see you from here. You look very much alive."

"Oh yeah. How's my hair? Do I need to freshen up my lip gloss?"

"Probably, since half of it's still stuck on my cheek."

"Just a little something to remember me by."

"How long are you expecting your surveillance video viewing to last exactly?" Max wrote back.

"How am I supposed to know? I've never done this before. But I do know you're taking me to dinner afterward. I'm already hungry," Dubs replied.

"Deal. Now stop texting me before Moose smashes your phone to bits with his pinky finger," Max wrote.

Dubs looked up for the first time since she sat down. Moose was drumming his fingers on the conference room table, waiting impatiently for her to finish. "Whoops. Just finishing up here. Max had a question."

"Good call, Pretty Girl. See you soon." Dubs put her phone in her pocket.

"Let's get this to-do started," she said. "I feel like we're about to watch something really dirty. Maybe it's the black-and-white, Big Brother feel of it all. Do you feel that way? You probably don't. You do this all the time. It's weird for me though. Clearly, I'm excited. This is going to be fun."

Turns out, it wasn't that much fun at all. It was more like trying to find a specific needle in a stack of needles. They would locate the guy they were looking for on one camera, in one section of the store, but finding him again on another camera, even one that seemed like it was the correct time and store location, wasn't as easy as it should have been. To top it off, the guy they were tracking really liked to shop. He was all over the store.

Dubs wanted to just watch the front entrance video and see when he came in the doors, then go to the parking lot video, but Moose insisted they piece together his time in the store as well. It was possible he bought something before going to get the cell phone. And what if he used a credit card for that purchase? The logic was sound, but the sitting still for hours on end was nearly impossible.

Eventually, they saw their guy making another purchase. However, he used cash for that transaction as well.

"I can see you need a pick-me-up," Moose said. "You watch the front door video. I'm going to get some coffee. Don't wander off, and don't miss him coming in. Think you can handle it?"

"Of course, Big Guy. I got this." Dubs appreciated the confidence Moose was showing in her. Either that or he was getting tired of her constantly shifting positions and twitching legs. Either way, she wouldn't let him down. This part might not be quite as fun as running around town with Max, doing clue gathering and bad guy chasing, but she could see the value.

"When you find him, make note of the time. Then you can switch to the parking lot tapes if I'm not back yet. Start a bit before our guy walks through the front door. And hope he didn't sit in the car on the phone for an hour."

"Hilarious," Dubs said. With the way this guy had wandered around the store, he just might have done that. She hoped not.

Moose headed out, and Dubs settled in with the remote and endless security tapes. A lot of people came through Walmart every few minutes. They all started to look the same after a while. She had only gone back about twenty minutes before she expected to see the man she was looking for walk in, but even in that time, hundreds of people entered the store. By the time the man she was targeting did enter, she almost missed him. He snuck in behind a group of teenagers, almost as if he was hoping to avoid being seen by the cameras.

"Gotcha," Dubs said. She rewound the footage and tried to ascertain which of the two large double doors perpendicular to the even larger set of main doors the man had entered. That would at least give her an idea of which side of the parking lot to search first.

Once she was reasonably sure about where to start her outside search, she made note of the time on the front door tape, and switched to the parking lot footage. There were multiple cameras covering the staggeringly large parking lot. Dubs had to watch each one individually, hoping to catch her man. Although she hoped to get lucky with the first video, she didn't. By the fifth twenty-minute video clip, she hadn't found the phone buyer, but she had discovered a new gold mine for car theft. No one seemed to lock their car doors, and in some cases, even bother to bring their keys with them. And there were so many cars Dubs would have loved to relieve their owners of. It was strange though, watching the videos, seeing the owners leaving their property so vulnerable. She kept thinking of what Max would say if she were to sneak up and drive off with someone else's car. Kissing Max was one thing, but having her pop up as an annoying conscience when she was trying to work when she left here, wasn't going to work.

Dubs was saved more unpleasant daydreaming when she got to the sixth camera footage. In clear view of the camera, her guy pulled in and parked a black Honda Civic. Dubs watched as he carefully locked the door and tucked the keys in his pocket. She paused the video and jogged into the main office space. There wasn't anyone except Max left.

"Pretty Girl, I found him," Dubs said. "Now I need your help."

"Found who?" Max asked.

"The dude who bought the burner phone."

"I thought you found him a long time ago. He paid in cash. What were you guys looking for in there?"

"We were looking for him arriving. To see if we could get his license plate. And now I got it. But I don't know what to do with it," Dubs said. "I figure that's your business."

"Look at you," Max said. "You're all giddy and adorably excited. Are you hearing the siren song of crime fighting?"

"Don't get carried away, Pretty Girl. Not even you have that kind of power over me. Are you going to help me?"

"Of course," Max said. "Bring me the license plate number. Let's see who it belongs to."

Moose returned with coffee just as Max was going to work on her computer. Dubs practically leapt into his arms to get at the latte he had for her. No one else understood when she said coffee helped calm her down, but it did. Right now she was so jazzed up at her discovery she needed the latte even more than she did before.

Dubs caught Moose up on the developments while Max worked.

"Nicely done, Dubs," Moose said. "I thought we were going to be at it all night."

"So little faith in my skill," Dubs said.

"No one has underestimated your healthy self regard," Max said, giving Dubs a wink.

"Just spicing things up around here," Dubs said. "You are all so...I don't even know. Superbly Wonder Bread. You need a criminal around."

"Thank God you showed up then," Moose said.

"I know, right?"

"All right, I got something," Max said. "That Civic is a loaner vehicle for Smith's Auto Shop. The registered owner is the shop owner, but based on the picture, he's not your guy. Even if he hasn't renewed his license in years, his license picture doesn't look like that guy at all."

"Is H still around?" Moose asked.

"Yeah, she's in her office," Max said.

Moose went to fetch her.

"How do you have all this information so quickly? I can barely make my phone work," Dubs said.

Max shrugged. "It's kinda my thing."

"Remind me never to let you near anything of mine with an on/off switch."

"Oh, please," Max said. "I don't need to get near it."

Dubs didn't like the sound of that. She wondered what information Max could access on her, or what information she had already gotten. It would make sense that she did background on her before she came on board, but now it felt overly personal.

"What's up?" Holt asked, following Moose to Max's desk.

"The Wonder Twins here have been hard at work all day and have an update."

"Who the hell are the Wonder Twins?" Dubs asked.

"Weird alien twins with superpowers. One can change into any form of water, and the other can change into animals," Moose said. "They also have a pet space monkey."

"Water? Really?" Max said. "How is that ever useful?"

"What did you two find?" Holt said.

"Oh, right. Well, the guy who bought the burner phone, the one used to contact Shorty, was driving a loaner car from Smith's Auto Shop."

"Is that the shop you and Dubs went to about the Escalade?" Holt asked.

"No, different place," Max said. "And we don't know who the driver is. He's not the registered owner of the car. Maybe an employee?"

"Or he could have had the car as a loaner that day," Holt said.

"Can't we go to Smith's Auto Shop and talk to them? See if anyone recognizes the guy?" Dubs asked.

"Yes," Holt said. "But the last time we poked around, someone left a bomb on our doorstep. I'm inclined to do some less obvious digging for a little while. Print a picture of him and add him to our lookout file. I'll give you a couple more days, Max, to piece this puzzle together."

"I'm on it, H," Max said.

"Let me know when you have something concrete. Dubs, we may need to turn up the pressure again and get you back out on the street. Think about if you feel that would help us, or just complicate an already volatile situation. Now, though, it's late. Go home. I'll see you all tomorrow."

Holt took her own advice and was out the door quickly. Moose followed shortly after.

"The boss lady is a lot faster out the door than she used to be," Max said. "I'm not sure she ever left before Isabelle."

"If I had what they had, I'd be the first one out the door at the end of the day," Dubs said. She didn't know Isabelle well, but she could tell by the way Holt worshipped her that they had something special. She didn't get the sense Holt settled, and Isabelle certainly didn't look like she was willing to just follow along with whatever life put in her path.

"Well, rumor has it you're playing house these days, so you better be getting your butt home soon," Max said.

"Or what?" Dubs said. "Is my ball and chain going to be upset because I don't have dinner on the table? Because I seem to remember demanding that you take me out to dinner tonight."

"Ball and chain? And I was going to take you somewhere nice. Now I'm downgrading to Dunkin' Donuts."

"You might want to rethink that," Dubs said. "I'm not wearing the dress hanging in the closet to Dunkin' Donuts. On the off chance you haven't seen it, take a peek while I shower. I'll leave our dining destination up to you though, totally your choice."

"You're a tease, Dubs. Do you know that?" Max swung their joined hands gently.

Dubs took advantage of Max's overture and took it a step further by perching on her lap. She saw Max look around, but they were alone. "I don't mean to be a tease," Dubs said honestly. "But you make me nervous."

"I make you nervous?" Max said. "How in the world is that possible?"

"Because, for example, right now I want to kiss you, and you also scare me so badly I also want to run out the door and never come back."

"That's not worth it," Max said. "Holt would hunt you down and drag you back to me, never knowing why you ran away. And she'd probably cuff us together all the time again."

"So you're saying kissing you is the safer option?"

"Wow, I backed myself right into that, didn't I?" Max was the one looking nervous now.

Dubs moved closer until her lips were mere millimeters from Max's. They were both breathing more heavily than normal. "All you have to say is no and I'll stop," Dubs said.

Instead, Max closed the distance between them and kissed her. It started tentative, but soon one or the other of them deepened the kiss. Max wrapped her arms around Dubs's waist, letting one hand explore her upper thigh.

Dubs wasn't sure how long their mini make out session lasted. It could have been a second, or an hour. She was completely swept away in the feeling. When they broke the kiss, Max gently put one hand on either side of Dubs's face. "You look beautiful with your hair down. I've been meaning to tell you all day."

"Thank you." Dubs didn't think she'd ever gotten such a genuine compliment.

"Also, you need to shower and do whatever is required for that thing you are calling a dress. I've seen it in the closet and I want to see it on you. No Dunkin' Donuts this evening."

"Excellent," Dubs said. "It fits just like my bikini."

"Lord help me," Max said. "I hope I make it through the evening."

CHAPTER SEVENTEEN

Dubs hadn't been exaggerating when she described the fit of her dress. Max was having a hard time focusing on their conversation. She suspected that was the point of the dress, and also Dubs's intention when she went out of her way to draw attention to its finest features. It was navy blue and formfitting from her hips to her chest. The two straps tied behind Dubs's neck, something she of course had needed Max's help with while getting ready. It was open to the middle of her back, making it impossible for her to wear a bra, a fact not lost on Max.

They hadn't been sitting there for five minutes, hadn't even ordered appetizers, and Max was rapidly cycling through thinking about just how beautiful Dubs looked, how perfect her bare shoulders looked in that dress, the fact that she wasn't wearing a bra, and that she wasn't supposed to be thinking about any of it. She was supposed to be paying attention to what Dubs was saying. She was also uncomfortable in clothes she never wore.

She had panicked after boldly telling Dubs she would take her to one of the nicest restaurants in Providence. She owned exactly one shirt with a collar, and she didn't know if it was appropriate for where they were going. While Dubs was showering, she had snuck down to Lola's apartment and begged for help. Lola had called Jose, who lived nearby, and before she knew what she had done, Jose and Lola had stripped her down to her underwear and were dressing her like a Ken doll.

The end result was a pair of her pants and a dress shirt that belonged to someone Jose knew. He said they'd left it at his house and wouldn't be coming to claim it. No one asked any questions. It fit Max, which was remarkable, since she got teased for being so small. The man who had previously owned the shirt must have been the world's skinniest man. Lola had insisted on a bow tie, which Max resisted at first, but now was really into. They had passed three other people, all under thirty, rocking similar neckwear, so apparently, Lola knew what she was talking about. In reality, it didn't matter what Max was wearing, because everyone was looking at Dubs. Max didn't blame them. She was stunning.

"Did you hear me, Pretty Girl?" Dubs asked.

"I'm sorry. What did you say?"

"Everything okay?" Dubs asked, looking concerned. "That bow tie cutting off circulation to your brain? It's cute as hell, but I don't want you losing brain cells for my pleasure."

"Oh please," Max said with a half grin. "Don't pretend you have no idea why I might be a little distractible this evening."

"Me? I wouldn't know what you're talking about," Dubs said. "I'm just out to dinner with a mighty dapper lady. When you told me where we were going, I had to dress the part."

"Oh, of course," Max said. "Now, what did you ask me?"

Dubs stroked the top of her foot along the back of Max's calf. Oh, those high heels, Max thought. She had forgotten about the heels. *Focus.*

"I asked why you live in Holt's attic," Dubs said.

"Oh." Her body stiffened. She had no trouble focusing now as she thought about the place that felt a million miles away, but was only about fifteen miles away, and a small house about three towns away.

"Hey, wait. No, never mind. I didn't realize that was a bad subject," Dubs said, clearly reading the change in Max's body language. "I want to know all about it. But it doesn't have to be here. I just want to know more about you. How about I start?"

"I'm sorry," Max said. "You just caught me off guard. I don't mind telling you. I want you to know. But it's a rough transition to go from thinking about you in that dress and how good your ass looked when you were walking in here tonight, to the fact that I was homeless for three months last year."

"I didn't mean to cause such a tenebrific atmosphere," Dubs said.

"One more Scrabble word and you shouldn't need dinner," Max said. "That one was quite a mouthful."

"I could totally do better," Dubs said.

"I have no doubts."

"Haven't you worked for Holt for more than a year?" Dubs asked.

"I have," Max said.

Dubs looked angry. "How could she, with all her fake save the world crap, let you live on the streets for three months? That is the worst kind of hypocritical, horrible…How can you work for her?"

Max took Dubs's hand, which was clenched into a fist. "She had no idea. No one on the crew did. She still wouldn't have any idea probably, except Isabelle found out. Although I think Moose was starting to figure it out, too. As soon as I told her, she practically marched me upstairs and moved me into my place. I've been there ever since. I barely pay rent. There are people you can get mad at in this story, but Holt isn't one of them. Okay?"

"Fine," Dubs said. She unclenched her fist and instead wound her fingers through Max's.

Max considered removing her hand from Dubs's. Holt had just warned her, for the second time, about getting involved with Dubs, and they were in a very public place. But this felt so good. Perhaps she would get burned, but she would worry about that later. Besides, making out in the office was probably much riskier than this. If Holt were able to look at it objectively, her falling in love with Isabelle while someone was trying to kill both of them probably wasn't the smartest move, but that had worked out all right. Max wasn't equating the two, but for the moment, she was going with what felt right.

"So how did you end up running my mean streets?"

"I'm tougher than I look, if that's what you're wondering," Max said. She didn't exactly like reliving those days, but she had survived them fairly well.

"You look plenty tough," Dubs said. "You're like a little Holt clone. Except you're sexier, and you have more heart. Or at least, that's how I see it. But the 'don't mess with me' vibe, the ass-kicking stance, the powerful way you walk into a room, total alpha butch. Be still my heart. And I've seen you fight, so I know you're tough. I was just wondering what would have precipitated your arrival on the street."

Max was rather shocked by Dubs's assessment of her. It wasn't that long ago that she felt like she cowered in Holt's presence. Now Dubs thought she was as powerful as Holt. Surely that was Dubs flirting, but it still felt nice to hear.

"Not even you with your rose-colored glasses can think I come close to Holt and those muscles," Max said, flexing her right bicep for effect.

"You've got everything I'm looking for," Dubs said.

Max had to give her credit, Dubs was nothing if not direct. Max just wasn't sure how much of it was real and how much of it was outrageous flirting. She felt like she was starting to develop real feelings for her, but she was scared to allow herself to until she could understand exactly what Dubs was feeling, and what side she was working for. She didn't even know how to go about doing that.

"Uh huh," Max said.

"I'm serious, Pretty Girl. No games. Now tell me how you ended up on the street. I want to know."

Max sighed. "From as long as I can remember, it was just me and my mom. She's…old school, I guess you could call it. She still has one of those big butt TVs. You wouldn't be impressed with her car. We've never really gotten along. I've never been everything she was looking for in a daughter, and it got worse as I got older. When I got into computers, I at least had an escape, but that seemed to make her hate me. It was like I was some kind of freak or something. She said I was a criminal and a hacker."

"That's just mean," Dubs said. "How could your own mother say such horrible things?"

"Well, some of it was true," Max said. "When I was thirteen, I didn't cover my tracks well enough when I was practicing some hacking jobs, so I sort of got caught. The police showed up to question me. I had covered up just enough they couldn't prove anything, but my mom was pissed. I've never been caught since, though. That was a good lesson."

"Wait, you? A criminal?" Dubs looked beside herself. "I want to rip that bow tie and shirt off of you right now and whisper unimaginable things in your ear until you have no choice but to clear off this table and make me yours."

Max thought that all sounded amazing, except for the public performance aspect. "I only use my powers for good, never evil," she said.

"For the record, we're not staying through dessert," Dubs said.

"Oh really?" Max said. "I'm telling you my sob story and all you can think about is getting me home?"

"I'm twenty-two. I'm out to dinner with a criminally good-looking woman, who I find out is just like me and actually can sometimes be a criminal, but for the good guys. You're like my wet dream. What do you expect from me?"

"Do you want to hear the rest of my story?"

"Yes, of course," Dubs said. "I want to know all of your hurts and triumphs."

Max didn't know what to say to that. It was such a sweet sentiment.

"Well, anyway, things got rougher and rougher with my mom. We were barely speaking through my senior year in high school. When I graduated, I went directly to Holt and asked for a job. I think that was the scariest thing I've ever done. You've seen the mellowed out Holt, but she was a different beast before Isabelle. She was the same person, just more intense. Version 2.0 is the improved model. At first, my mom was thrilled I had a job and was gainfully employed. She didn't ask anything about it. I think she assumed I would be a good for nothing loser and she'd be supporting me the rest of her life. A few months after I started working for Holt, a detective came by the house looking for me. He was just following up on a case. I think I had forgotten to sign some paperwork or something like that. Maybe he was looking for Moose or Lola, who knows. Anyway, my mom freaked out. All of a sudden she wanted to know who, what, and where I was working."

"And let me guess, Holt Lasher didn't pass inspection? Or working for a bounty hunter?"

"No, definitely not. Either one. She didn't want me working for that lesbo. So I told her I, too, was one of those lesbos. I've never seen anything quite like what happened next. My mother looks nothing like me, and isn't in the best shape, but she sprinted around the house like an Olympic-caliber athlete and collected every item that belonged to me, or may have been mine, and dumped them all out the nearest window. She just started throwing things out every window in the house. My favorite cereal went flying out the kitchen window, my shampoo and towels out the bathroom window. All my clothes out my bedroom window. She tried to fit the mattress out the window, but it didn't fit, so she winged it down the stairs and out the front door. Desk chair, out the window. Literally anything that didn't belong to her was flung out the nearest window. It was insane. I was able to grab my computer before she tossed that, luckily. It took her less than an hour to purge me from the house. I was able to get my stash of cash and a few other things from my room while she was ripping through the bathroom. I sorted through what I wanted from the yard, and I haven't been back since. I left most of my clothes with a friend for a while, but I couldn't stay with her for more than a few days."

"Holy shit, Pretty Girl," Dubs said. "That's so horrible. Have you talked to your mom since then?"

Max shook her head. "Not a word. She knows how to find me. She's clearly not interested. Her last words weren't all that kind. I don't think she wants to have a daughter anymore."

"I'm so sorry." Dubs seemed at a loss for words, a rare occurrence.

"Thanks," Max said. "I bounced around for a while, then just started camping out on the street when it was warm enough. I stayed at the office overnight when I felt like I could get away with it. I was trying to save up enough to put down money for an apartment, but then Isabelle discovered my secret. And now I've got a beautiful little shoe box in, as you call it, Holt's attic."

They sat in comfortable silence for a while, only interrupted by the waiter taking their order.

"What do you want to do after this case is over?" Max asked.

Dubs looked startled. "What do you mean?"

"I mean, what do you want to do with your time? Will you go back to stealing cars? Will you get a desk job? Will you become an astronaut?" The answer was important to Max. She couldn't imagine having to one day chase down Dubs and toss her in jail. She also couldn't imagine a future for them if Dubs was planning on resuming a life quite so far outside the law.

"I honestly have no idea," Dubs said. "When I first got out, I figured working for you all would be a good way to get started back up again. Remake my name. But now…" She trailed off.

"But now?" Max wasn't going to let her get away with that answer.

"Now I don't know. I don't think I get to keep seeing you like this if I'm stealing cars for a living. And I've grown to like what we're doing. It feels good waking up in the morning. Not just because you're usually sprawled all over me. What's up with that, by the way?"

Max shrugged. "I'm a snuggler. And I'm asleep. I can't be held responsible for my actions."

"No complaints," Dubs said. "None at all."

"I feel like there's a 'but' to this fairy tale and unicorns."

"There's some business from my past that won't quite leave me be," Dubs said. She looked phenomenally sad. "It has to do with Levi."

"Will you tell me about Levi?" Max asked. She had shared a great bit of herself with Dubs, and she wanted to know more about her too.

Dubs pulled back from the table a few inches and ran her hand through her hair. Max loved the way it flowed through her fingers and cascaded back over her neck and shoulders.

"I knew you would ask me about him eventually."

"You don't have to tell me," Max said, although she really did want to know.

"It's not that," Dubs said, her eyes soft. She took Max's hand again. "It just still hurts, badly. Levi was like my kid brother, and I should have been the one driving the car the day he died, not him. Maybe no one needed to die that day."

"I remember seeing the news story," Max said, which was partially true. She did see the news story once she Googled it after meeting Mrs. Otis. "It said he died in a high-speed chase with police."

"That's the story of his death," Dubs said. "But it tells nothing of his life. And if he hadn't been defending my name, he would have just pulled over and taken his jail time or, since he was a first-timer, probably just probation. But that day, he couldn't get caught, or at least he didn't think so."

"I don't understand," Max said.

"My mother died when I was three," Dubs said. "I don't remember her. The two people who raised me were my father and Mrs. Otis. They're both world-class car thieves. I learned everything from them."

"Mrs. Otis? Really? Who knew." Max was surprised, although she shouldn't have been. She had learned not to be surprised by anything.

"You should have seen her in her heyday. My God, she was amazing. Anyway, she was mostly retired by the time Levi was old enough to learn anything, so he learned from me. He's four years younger than I am. He was."

"Somehow we really let dinner take a morose turn," Max said. "Sorry about that."

Dubs laughed. "It is a little weird to be in this restaurant, with you in that bow tie, and us talking about Levi dying. But I do want you to know."

"And I want to hear."

"Okay, but after dinner, no more talking about bad things," Dubs said. "Only happy talk."

"Like how hot you look in that dress?" Max asked.

"That totally works. But I have to finish my story first. Before our dinner arrives. Levi and I were just starting to really make a name for ourselves before I got arrested. It was different than it is now. There were only a few organized groups working sections of the city, stealing cars and chopping them up and selling the parts. We were the best of the bunch. We were making a lot of money. Some of the older fellas didn't like that. A challenge was laid down. We had to earn our place in town. It's been that way for years. My dad had warned me the challenge was coming. We were getting too good."

"What was the challenge?" Max asked.

"They're always impossible tasks. Or nearly impossible. Technically difficult and exceptionally risky. Most of the old guard probably couldn't pull it off these days, but the younger ones have to earn their way in. That's what we had to do."

"What happens if you fail?" Max asked.

"You can't work in the city. But if you succeed, you get to carve out a little game for yourself. That wasn't enough for me. I wanted to rule. I mouthed off. I talked about how easy their stupid challenge was going to be. Usually the rules for completion are malleable, since the task is so hard, but since I was an idiot, it was full completion, or failure. There was no wiggle room. My counter offer was, when we succeeded, we not only got to keep our territory, we ruled the city."

"I think I can see where this is going," Max said. Her heart ached for all the pain Dubs must feel for the loss of her friend and the part she played in it.

"Yeah," Dubs said, sounding sad and resigned. "I still believe I could have pulled off what they were asking. But Levi wasn't ready. I think even he knew that. But I got arrested a month before the challenge was supposed to take place. I wasn't even doing a job. I just saw a stupid car I thought was too beautiful to pass up. And it was beautiful, and the acceleration…Well, that's what got me in trouble. I got careless. And booked. I know Levi held them off as long as he could. My father and Mrs. Otis tried to help too. But once the challenge has been thrown down, you can't get out of it. We said we were a package deal. I had made that clear. At the time I thought I was helping him, because I wanted him to be protected, part of my crew, associated with me. Turns out that got him killed."

"You couldn't have known that," Max said. She wanted to pull Dubs to her and hold her, to make the sadness go away. She knew there wasn't anything she could do, but it sucked being so unable to help.

"He tried on his own. From what I've heard, he made it through the first half, but the police found him eventually. He couldn't give up though, because of what I did, because I mouthed off. If I had kept my mouth shut, getting as far as he did probably would have been fine. But he had to make it through to the end. He had to lose the cops. So he ran. And the rest you saw on the news."

"I know it might not mean anything, but you know it's not your fault, right?"

"Oh, beautiful Max. That little, wonderful, gorgeous boy is dead because of me. It might not technically be my fault, but my hubris put him in the ground. Somehow his mother forgives me, a fact I will be forever grateful for. She texted me the other day and told me to never stop being a cocky little bitch. I told her my friend, the woman she met, tells me I'm overconfident all the time."

"I do no such thing," Max said in protest.

"They're still after me," Dubs said. "The challenge is still out there. Only this time, it's not just for my territory. Since I saw my friend on the beach, they've been in contact. They say Levi died a failure. The only way to clear his name of that shame is to prove I wasn't full of shit. They're trying to use his death against me."

"Is that normal?" Max asked. "Does one member have to step in and win back the honor of a fallen colleague?"

"I don't know," Dubs said. "This is kind of uncharted territory. And like I said, things have changed now. I don't know what to believe. But there's a lot of pressure. Daily. Hourly, sometimes."

"Are those all the text messages you keep saying are from your dad?"

"Some of them are," Dubs said. "He's getting it from them, too."

"You're not going to do it though, right?" Max said. "We're working on something bigger now." Max didn't like the idea for multiple reasons. She was sure Holt would veto it for one, and it sounded dangerous. She didn't like the idea of Dubs in that much danger, at all.

"I don't know," Dubs said. "What would you do if someone was smearing the good name of Holt, or Moose, or Lola? What if something had happened to them and you were the only one who could set the record straight? You'd do anything in your power to do that, right?"

"Yeah, I guess I would. But this feels like manipulation, not honor. We should talk to Holt, see if she can figure out what's going on. She knows a lot of people in a lot of places all over the city."

"No," Dubs said. "No one else hears about this. Just you and me. I trusted you with this information. Please don't break that trust. I'll figure out what to do. Maybe that will mean going to Holt, but not yet. If I do end up doing it though, it might help us. It could draw more attention to me, make the new guys think I'm getting back in business. Put more pressure on. That would be a good thing, right?"

"Yes," Max said. "But only if it's done in a controlled manner. We apply pressure carefully, otherwise it can blow up in your face. Please don't do anything stupid, Dubs."

"I'll try," Dubs said.

Max wasn't entirely convinced, but their dinners arrived before she could get more of a promise from her. As agreed, they moved the conversation to less loaded topics.

As Dubs had suggested, they didn't stay for dessert, however neither of them were quite as frisky as they had been to start the evening. When they got back to Max's apartment, they held hands as they walked up the stairs. Max unlocked the door and led them inside.

"Will you help me out of my dress?" Dubs asked. "Then will you just hold me tonight?"

"Of course," Max said.

Dubs moved to Max's dresser and pulled out a T-shirt and a pair of boxer shorts. She turned around in front of Max expectantly. Max gently moved her hair away from the knot holding the halter top in place and untied the dress. She moved lower, her fingers skimming along Dubs's bare back, and unzipped the lower half. Dubs half turned around. "Thank you."

She wriggled out of her dress, her back still to Max, and slipped into the T-shirt and boxers. Max had to sit down. She had tried not to stare, but the apartment wasn't that large. She might have survived the bare back and no bra, but Dubs's thong had just about killed her.

Dubs grabbed a hair tie from the dresser and turned around, pulling her hair back loosely for bed. "Pretty Girl, are you planning on sleeping in the bow tie?"

"Um, no," Max said. She wasn't sure she trusted her legs just yet.

"Here, let me help," Dubs said. She moved between Max's legs and untied her tie. Then she pulled Max's shirt from her pants and began to unbutton it. Max was frozen in place. Her hands were firmly planted on either side of her on the bed, and it was taking all of her willpower not to reach out and pull Dubs down onto the bed.

Dubs had cleared the buttons over Max's chest and was working on the ones over her stomach. Max couldn't take it. She scrambled away. "I'll take it from here," she said. "Why don't you get in bed? I'll be right there." She had no idea that having Dubs unbuttoning her dress shirt would be such a turn-on. It made her feel sexy and powerful. Not the things she was supposed to be feeling when Dubs had asked her to simply hold her.

"You okay?" Dubs asked. She looked amused.

"Fine, thank you," Max said.

"I still think you're the hottest woman I've ever laid eyes on," Dubs said. "And I really wish you'd let me finish getting that shirt off you. I was enjoying myself. I'm just feeling a little sad after I told you about Levi. Tonight, I wanted to feel your strength wrapped all around me. You always end up wrapped all over me anyway, I thought you might not mind starting out that way. Is that okay?"

Max felt a little like an ass. All she could think about was sex, while Dubs was grieving for her friend. "Of course that's okay. Anything you need," she said. "Let me get some different clothes on. I'll be right there, big strong arms at the ready."

It probably should have felt stranger for Dubs to want her to hold her, but they had been sharing a bed since the second night they knew each other. They already had an intimacy most people didn't. Plus, there was whatever was growing between them. Max changed quickly and climbed into bed next to Dubs.

"Come here," she said, opening her arms. Dubs slipped into Max's embrace. "I'm all yours."

CHAPTER EIGHTEEN

Isabelle didn't quite register why she was awake at first. She knew her usually soft, snuggly pillow was now squirming away from her. She tried to pull Holt back, but it was no use. When she did open her eyes, "work Holt" was wide-awake, standing next to the bed. That was enough to chase the remaining remnants of sleep from Isabelle's consciousness as well. That's when she heard the knocking.

"Who's there?" she asked, as if Holt could see through walls.

"I don't know," Holt said. "Stay here."

Isabelle didn't know why Holt always insisted on issuing that command. She never followed her instruction, and she didn't think Holt expected or wanted her to. Well, maybe she *wanted* her to, but she certainly knew Isabelle better than that. They were a team, which meant more often than not, Isabelle was by Holt's side, especially when it involved their home. Big scary work things? Those were all Holt's.

Isabelle's heart was racing as they moved into the living room. She always felt safe with Holt, but someone had tried to blow up her office recently. And kill her. Those things made a girl jumpy.

As they got closer to the door, they could hear a voice on the other side. It was Lola. Holt yanked the door open and dragged her inside.

"What the hell are you doing at my door at two in the morning?" Holt said.

Isabelle knew Holt had every reason to be upset. She also knew Holt's anger was coming mostly from fear, but Lola was in tears. Now probably wasn't the time to rip into her.

"Sweetie, why don't you get Lola something to drink? And put some pants on."

"I'm really sorry to barge in here so late," Lola said. "I didn't really even know what time it was."

"You're always welcome here, Lola," Isabelle said. "Maybe next time you could call first, though. Then you won't get the dragon all grumpy, thinking someone's breaking into her castle."

"I can hear you, you know," Holt said from behind the room divider that separated their bedroom from the rest of the loft.

"I'm well aware," Isabelle said. "I can also hear you. What are you doing in there? Are you going to have any clothes left? It sounds like you're ripping them apart."

"Lola, I swear to you. Don't pull this crap again, no matter how upset you are. Not after Decker."

"Oh come on, H. I knew you didn't have any guns in the house. The worst you could have done was rip the front door off its hinges and land on me. I've seen worse than a pipsqueak like you surfing a door. Hell, I got shot in the head recently. I'm still here."

"Shot in the head? Don't be so dramatic. That bullet barely nicked you."

Holt had reemerged from the bedroom. She looked considerably less angry and Lola was no longer crying. Isabelle didn't understand either of them.

"Seriously, though, you scared Isabelle," Holt said.

"Oh no, leave me out of this," Isabelle said. "If you're having emotions you need to talk about, don't use me as your fall guy."

"Fine, you scared me. And Isabelle."

Isabelle kicked Holt in the seat of the pants, making her smile.

"I'm sorry, H. But I need to talk to someone and you're the one I trust the most for this sort of thing."

"Well, next time text or something," Holt said.

Holt and Lola hugged each other. It was an awkward, yet deep, hug. The kind of hug you see between two people who rarely have physical contact with each other, but mean the world to one another. Isabelle thought it was one of the cutest things she had ever seen.

"What's going on?" Isabelle asked. This didn't seem like it was going to be a quick conversation, so she started a pot of coffee and some water for tea.

"This didn't just happen today. I don't want you to think that," Lola said. "Everyone's been asking me all about the baby. Dubs and Max were asking me whether I had all the stuff I needed for the kid. I didn't even think about that. Then I was looking online at what you need. It's a lot of stuff. I've been moving furniture around in my apartment all night. I think if I get a twin bed and maybe one of those folding dining room tables, I could fit all the kid's stuff in there too."

"Lola, if space is the issue, we can make that work," Holt said.

"I mean, that's part of it," Lola said. "Or it started there. But I don't know the first thing about kids. I mean, nothing. I've never even held a baby. Well, Superman I guess, but he's not a baby."

"And I would like to point out, he loves you," Holt said.

Isabelle's heart was aching for Lola. She was so clearly confused and hurting. Isabelle had no idea how to help, and Holt didn't look like she did either.

"The more I started reading, the less confident I started feeling. I don't think I can take this baby. I mean, I work insane hours, in an occasionally dangerous job. I know it was just a nick, but I did have a bullet make contact with my head fairly recently. I thought I wanted this, you know, because I've always wanted kids and I really did love Tiffany, but now I don't know."

"What do you need from me?" Holt asked. "Do you need me to help you work through your decision? Do you need me to convince you that you'll be a good parent? Or have you made up your mind and you need me to help you plan your next steps?"

"I don't know," Lola said.

Isabelle wasn't sure she believed her. It seemed liked Lola wanted to say something, but wasn't quite ready to.

"Anyone want a cup of coffee?" Isabelle asked.

"It's three a.m.," Lola said.

"I don't think we're in danger of going back to sleep anytime soon," Isabelle said. "This is more important."

"Sure," Lola said. "Coffee would be great."

Holt got up to help Isabelle. When Isabelle looked back at Lola sitting on the couch, she had her head in her hands. "Baby, there's something she's not telling us."

"I know," Holt said. "She'll get around to it. Lola always does. Give her time."

When they got back to the couch, Lola wanted to talk about Dubs and the case. Lola, it seemed, was a Dubs fan, at least on an interpersonal level. She also noted Max seemed to be a very big Dubs fan. Isabelle hadn't noticed that, but now she would pay more attention.

"Well, I shouldn't keep you up any longer," Lola said when she finished her coffee. "I'm really sorry to barge in like that."

Isabelle was stunned. Lola hadn't said anything significant, not even a hint as to why she was really here.

"Sit your butt down," Holt said, not getting up or moving at all. "You're not leaving until you've had breakfast with us, and you've gotten whatever it is you came here to say off your chest. Your choice which comes first."

"You make me insane, H," Lola said.

"I know it," Holt said. "You've been saying that since we were kids."

Lola still didn't say anything for a long time. Isabelle considered trying to prompt her, but she didn't know what to say, or what Lola needed. Holt had known her much longer, and Holt was waiting her out. Isabelle followed her lead.

"I guess I really came here hoping for two things," Lola said. "Right off the bat, you should know, neither one is really fair of me to ask. But I still have to. Maybe it's the only thing I'll do as this little unborn baby's mother. But if I do, and you agree, then it's the greatest gift I could give this little one."

"Good Lord, Lola, spit it out," Holt said.

Isabelle loved Holt more than anything in the world, but she didn't have an over-abundance of patience for this kind of thing.

That said, Isabelle was a little on edge herself. Lola was being cagey, and it sounded like she had some strange ideas about just who should end up with Tiffany's baby.

"First, I would like you to tell me you don't think I'm a bad person for not being able to take the baby," Lola said. She looked near tears again. "I've always looked up to you, H. If you say I'm good, then I know I am. I feel like after George died, you're the only family I've got, and this feels like a family moment to me. That's really why I came here tonight."

Holt took Lola's hand. "You know you're family to me too," she said. "And I think not taking a child when you can't take care of him or her is a courageous decision. You were pressured into this by someone who was supposed to love you, but you had no agency. You didn't make this baby, or even get a say in whether or not it was created. I'll make sure you're able to find the best possible home for the little one if that's what you want. There are a lot of good adoption agencies out there, and a lot of families who really want children."

"So," Lola said. "You're right in that I didn't have a say in whether this child was mine, or whether it was created in the first place, but I've gotten kind of attached to the idea of it, you know? I don't just want a good family. I want the best. It's not any of my business, but I happened to overhear you and Isabelle talking about maybe wanting kids one day at work a couple of weeks ago. I was hoping maybe one day could be in about two months."

"Wait, what?" Holt looked stunned. "You want us to adopt Tiffany's kid?"

"I said I wanted the best for the little critter," Lola said.

Isabelle felt completely blank. She had no emotional or physical reaction at all. It was as if Lola's suggestion had stunned her very cells into inaction. Sure, she and Holt had mentioned children, but in a vague, preliminary kind of way. Holt looked like she was experiencing the same level of shock.

"What makes you think I'm in any way qualified to be a parent?" Holt asked. Unlike Isabelle, Holt still seemed able to speak.

"Everything, I guess," Lola said.

"Well, that narrows it down," Holt said.

"Look how great you are with Superman."

"I get to send him home at the end of the day," Holt said, sounding a little panicky.

"You're wonderful with him, sweetie," Isabelle said.

"And can you think of anyone in the world more qualified to raise a kind, courageous, intelligent human being than Isabelle?" Lola asked.

"Nope," Holt said. "You've really thought this out, haven't you?"

"Why do you think it took me until the middle of the night to get over here?"

"What would Tiffany think of a change in adopter?" Isabelle asked. She still didn't know how she felt about it, but it was worth finding out if it was even possible.

"She's fine with it. She's willing to sign the papers for you, me, whoever. The father already signed away his parental rights. I'm going to go home now, but will you at least think about it? There's a little time to decide. I'm sorry to just spring it on you. I just…I really want this baby as part of my life. But I'm not the one to raise it. This way, it stays with me, in my family." She shrugged and looked at them both searchingly, and the silence hung thick in the air.

Holt walked Lola to the door. Isabelle heard Holt tell her that if they did decide to adopt the baby, she was buying them the car seat, and maybe the crib. Lola seemed willing to take that deal because they shook hands before Lola departed.

"Holy fuck," Holt said, sitting as close to Isabelle as she could without actually sitting on her lap. She kissed her cheek.

"Couldn't have said it better myself," Isabelle said. She still was having trouble feeling anything. It was all so overwhelming. "What do we do, baby?"

"I have no idea," Holt said with a smile. "The thought of a kid, that I'm responsible for, scares the hell out of me. But then I picture you holding our child, and hear that little kid calling you 'Mom,' and I think a little piece of my heart blows up. Don't get me wrong, I'm under no illusion that it will be all sunshine and roses. But some of it would be, and Lola's right, you would be the best person on this entire planet to raise an outstanding child."

"I do want kids," Isabelle said. "But two months from now? How long ago was I telling you that we can't have a kid in this loft? And you were worried about your job."

"Houses can be found. They only take money and time," Holt said. "And I was worried about my job for a change, but you weren't."

"It sounds like you want to do this." Isabelle smiled. It was so cute to see Holt's face lighting up at the prospect of motherhood.

"I don't know what I want," Holt said. "I just don't think we should let the obvious, and easy, reasons not to do it prevent us from even considering it."

"If there's no easy answer to this question," Isabelle said, "and we can't take the easy way out, how do we decide?"

"I have no idea," Holt said. They both laughed. "Flip a coin?"

"Fantastic," Isabelle said. "If we pick correctly we could name the kid Tails Rochat-Lasher."

"There's a name," Holt said. "I can't even get started on this decision without breakfast. I'm making us eggs."

"There's bacon in the fridge too," Isabelle said. "I'll put on more coffee. You should call the office. I don't think either one of us is going to be in this morning."

CHAPTER NINETEEN

Dubs carefully reapplied her makeup as she sat on the park bench, studying her reflection in the small mirror in her makeup kit. She always dressed up for a job, something which Levi and some of the other guys she was friends with used to tease her about, but it was her profession, and she wanted to look professional. Now, truth be told, she was doing it at least fifty percent for Max. She liked the way she felt when she caught Max watching her, or the appreciative look Max had when she first saw her in the morning. Max always had that look, makeup or no, but Dubs felt best with it on.

They had been sitting on this park bench, watching the world, and quite a few very nice cars, go by for over an hour. Max was getting antsy, but Dubs was quite content. When she was working, her usual restlessness melted away.

"How many cars do you need to browse before you find the perfect one?" Max asked.

"Picking a car is like dating," Dubs said. "You don't settle for the first pretty thing that drives by. I want to make sure she's my type, that she's into me, and in the case of the car, that she's not going to start screaming with one of those alarms I can't turn off in five seconds or less."

"There are so many jokes to be made with what you just said," Max said. "But I'm going to just let it be."

"What fun is that?" Dubs asked.

"Uh huh," Max said. "I'm trying to focus on work over here. You're the one with the least compliant makeup on the market. And did you just happen to forget to put your hair up this evening? For the first time on a job since we've been working together? You wouldn't be trying to distract me, would you?"

"If I were, how would I hypothetically be doing?"

"It's been a long hour," Max said. "Hypothetically, of course."

Dubs was putting on a bit of a show. She loved the way Max made her feel sexy, and worthwhile, and like the most important person in Max's orbit.

"I'm so sorry to hear that," Dubs said.

"You are not," Max said. "Look at you. You're enjoying torturing me. Every minute of it. You're a cruel woman, Dubs."

"I'm no such thing, Pretty Girl," Dubs said. "I'm very, very nice." Dubs kissed Max, first on the check, then on her neck.

Max sat perfectly still, her back ramrod straight, her hands clenching the bench seat tightly.

"I'm not just a tease, you know," Dubs said. "You're more beautiful to me than any car I've ever seen. I know that sounds dumb, but until you, there was nothing more beautiful to me in the world."

"You're really sweet, Dubs. Now, why don't you take a look at the second most beautiful thing to you, because I think our ride just pulled in."

Dubs looked up. Max was right. Holt had sent them back out to steal another car and see what they could shake up. They hadn't heard anything or had any new leads on the theft ring since they got the license plate number from the security tape. Hopefully, this would help.

Max scooted closer to Dubs and ran the back of one hand along Dubs's cheek, and the other on her thigh.

"What are you doing?" Dubs asked. Her blood pressure was suddenly through the roof. If this was what Max had been dealing with for the past hour, she felt terrible for what she had done to her.

"The car owners are looking over here. I'm just giving them a reason to not be concerned with our presence," Max said.

"I'm pretty sure you're giving them a reason to stare," Dubs said. "And if you keep it up, you're going to have to call an ambulance for me."

Max kissed her. It didn't last nearly long enough for Dubs's liking. When Max broke their kiss, she patted Dubs lightly on the cheek. "I think you'll survive."

"You're killing me," Dubs said. "But you're saved because it's time to move."

Max hopped up and took Dubs by the hand. They strolled hand in hand toward the car Dubs had identified as their target. The car was parked in such a way that the driver's side door was shielded enough from the street that Dubs could slide a slim-jim in the window and get the door open. She was anticipating an alarm and was ready to cut the wires under the dashboard to control the squawking, but when she opened the door, there was no alarm. Either the car didn't have one, or the owners never bothered to set it. She got in the driver's side door, unlocked the door for Max, quickly hotwired the ignition, and they were off.

This was Dubs's favorite part of the get, when she first pulled away in whatever car she was taking. The rush was greater than almost anything else she had ever felt. There was the adrenaline of having pulled off the theft, and also the anxiety of whether she was truly going to get away. The combination was intoxicating. She looked over at Max. She could tell by the look on her face that she felt it as well.

"It's an amazing feeling, isn't it?"

"I'm not saying I'm changing careers, but it is a rush," Max said. "I didn't believe you when you told me it would be."

Dubs put her hand on Max's knee as she drove. "This might be my dream scenario right here," Dubs said. "Maybe we should just keep driving forever. If we head west we could go for a long time."

"Hell no," Max said. "That little dress of yours and that eye-patch bikini are still at home. If we go west where they have killer beaches and amazing weather all year round, we're taking those with us. Or at least, that would be my must pack list if I were given control of that sort of thing."

"Is that right?" Dubs said. "Well, in that case, that red pair of skinny jeans you have, and the Batman T-shirt that somehow lost its sleeves? Both coming with us. Also, your black boots. And that damn bow tie. You might just get to wear that every day."

"With the Batman shirt and the jeans and boots?"

"Nope, just the bow tie."

"Oh, I see. We should probably find a private place then," Max said. Her cheeks were a little red. She stiffened. "Dubs, there's a cop."

"Don't worry, Pretty Girl," Dubs said. The car shouldn't have been reported stolen yet, but even if it had, she was confident she could lose one police officer. "Put your sun visor down and slide the cover off the vanity mirror," Dubs said. "Keep an eye on the gov behind us. Don't turn around or check the side mirror."

Max did as she was told and Dubs kept an eye on the rearview mirror. She drove the speed limit and followed all traffic rules. This was the time when amateurs could blow it. They would start running, or do something stupid like start driving erratically. There was no reason to start acting wild until absolutely necessary. So far, she had no reason to do anything but drive to the drop site.

Dubs could tell Max had her adrenaline pumping. Part of the deal when they left the office this evening was not to get caught. Holt had made that clear.

"It's going to be fine, Max," Dubs said. "I got you."

"I know." Max looked her straight in the eye, and Dubs knew she meant it. "I trust you."

Dubs's heart melted a little bit. She couldn't remember anyone ever putting so much faith in her. Not even Levi. He trusted her with his life, but they depended on each other in a very different way.

The cop followed them for about five blocks before turning off to continue whatever it was he was up to for the evening. Dubs suspected both she and Max let out a small sigh of relief.

They pulled into the same downtown location they left the previous car they'd stolen and parked. They wiped down the car for prints and locked the doors on their way out. They took off at a good clip away from the car. Max texted Holt that they were safely away. Holt would probably call it in and give the cops a heads up where to find the car. She would say it was a tip she got when she picked someone up, but whether they believed her or not was another story.

"I always feel like I could fly after I pull off a job," Dubs said. "That rush is what I always imagined crack is like."

"I was just starting to come down," Max said, "and then that cop started following us. That just shot the adrenaline back through the roof. You're a bad influence on me."

"I hope you don't mean that."

"Only in the best kind of way."

"How are we getting home?" Dubs asked.

"In a hurry?" Max looked amused.

"I've got my normal post job buzz, I've got you walking next to me, flirting away, and the whole time I was working, I had you sitting over there in the passenger seat, looking so good I considered pulling over and letting you drive, just so I could stare at you. So yeah, I'm a little eager to get home."

"I like that you're the one in charge when we're working like this," Max said. "It's hot as hell."

"Tell me more about that."

"Probably can't really do that," Max said. "It's kind of hard to explain."

"That's too bad," Dubs said. "I was really looking forward to hearing about it."

"Hmm," Max said. "I wonder if there's something else I could do."

"You're brilliant, Pretty Girl. I'm sure you'll think of something." She was enjoying this back-and-forth so much she barely registered that they weren't moving anymore. Max had pulled them to the side. They were stopped against the brick façade of one of the old mill buildings that littered the city.

"Why are we stopped?" Dubs asked.

"Well, we're waiting for our ride," Max said. "And I also figured out how I can explain just how damned hot it is to see you hot-wiring a car and driving like a boss."

"I can't wait to hear it," Dubs said. It felt like her whole body was pins and needles with anticipation.

"Only way to do it is to show you," Max said quietly. She leaned against the wall and pulled Dubs to her. She put one of her boot soles up, flat against the wall and wrapped her arms around Dubs's waist.

Dubs didn't wait for Max to kiss her. As soon as Max pulled her close, she wrapped her arms around Max's neck and initiated an aggressive, greedy kiss. She didn't feel like she could get enough. Apparently, Max felt the same way, as she deepened the kiss and pulled Dubs even closer, cupping her ass tightly and holding her close.

As their tongues danced together, their lips meeting and parting again, Dubs let her hands wander, first over Max's short-cropped hair, then over her thin, strong shoulders. Max had her hands all over Dubs's back and ass.

When they took a second to catch their breath, Dubs nuzzled into Max's neck. She felt the excitement of kissing Max throughout her body, but the sensation in her stomach wasn't arousal; it was an emotion-driven feeling she had only ever felt one time before. It reaffirmed what she suspected. Max meant a lot to her. Maybe too much.

Max trailed a line of kisses from Dubs's earlobe down the side of her neck. It was all Dubs could do not to take this further. She almost didn't care they were in public.

"You ladies need a ride home? Or should I circle the block? I can see it wasn't a hardship that I got stuck in a little traffic," Lola said from behind them.

Dubs tried to pull away quickly, not wanting Max to be uncomfortable in front of Lola, but Max didn't let her go right away.

"It's okay," Max whispered. "Lola won't say anything." Max kissed her lightly, and this time the kiss felt filled with affection.

Dubs let her hand slide off Max's shoulder and down her chest before she turned toward Lola and the truck.

Dubs climbed in, taking the middle seat on the bench. Max followed.

"So," Lola said. "How was the job? Anything exciting happen?"

"Easy as pie," Dubs said. "Car's at the drop spot, so our line's in the water. Hopefully, we get a few bites."

"Well, you two…Oh, never mind, that's just too easy," Lola said. "Were you practicing your undercover work?"

"Clearly," Dubs said. "How'd it look? Convincing?"

"Very good," Lola said. "I think half the block will need a cold shower this evening. For real, though, I'm not telling Holt anything other than the official report. You know that, right, kids?"

"Thanks, Lola," Max said.

"That's not going to stop me from giving you my advice," Lola said. "Which is, be kind to one another." They were already back at the office. "And for this evening, remember that the walls in this place are thin, and I'm only one apartment away. I don't own earplugs."

"Screw you," Max said with a laugh as she got out of the truck. Dubs followed.

"I didn't know I was invited," Lola said.

"You're not," Dubs said, winking at Lola and slamming the truck door. She and Max walked hand in hand as fast as they could to Max's apartment.

CHAPTER TWENTY

Max had barely closed the door to her apartment before she felt Dubs's hands wrap around her waist from behind and spread across her stomach. She braced her hands on the back of the door and let Dubs explore.

First, Dubs moved over her stomach, then over her sides. When Dubs pressed her palms flat over Max's chest, she turned around and took Dubs in her arms.

"You're not stopping this again, are you?" Dubs asked.

"Only if you want me to," Max said.

Dubs kissed her, and Max took that as her answer.

"You've been staring at my chest all night," Dubs said. "You finally going to do something about it?"

Max spun her around so Dubs was against the door.

"Not my fault," Max said, kissing a line down Dubs's neck. "You wore that tank top to drive me insane."

"You're still all talk, Pretty Girl," Dubs said, although she sounded far more out of breath than she had before.

Max bit down gently on the exposed skin just above the line of Dubs's low-cut tank top, then pulled the tiny tank top over Dubs's head and tossed it across the room. Before Max could focus any attention on Dubs's bare chest, Dubs kissed her, hard and started moving them toward the bed. Max pulled Dubs close and enjoyed every naked inch of her back and lower torso that she could get her hands on.

When Max's calves made contact with the edge of the bed, Dubs pushed her back, forcing her to sit, and then straddled her lap. Dubs was taller than Max by just enough to provide Max access to her breasts. Max ran her tongue around them, without touching a nipple until it was hard and Dubs was begging her for more. She finally gave in and took the nipple in her mouth, teasing Dubs's other breast with her hand. Dubs held on to Max's shoulders and rocked her hips against Max's stomach.

Max held Dubs's ass tightly, encouraging her. She switched back and forth between Dubs's breasts until it became clear Dubs couldn't take it anymore. She tried to push Max back onto the bed, but Max flipped Dubs onto her back instead.

"You've got too many clothes on, Pretty Girl," Dubs said. She pulled Max's T-shirt over her head and off, taking her sports bra with it.

"So do you," Max said. She helped Dubs wriggle out of her jeans. As soon as they were off, Max worked hers off as well.

Max took a moment to admire how truly beautiful Dubs was. She knew if she didn't say it right now, she might not find the courage, so she blurted it out. "You're incredibly beautiful. Maybe the most beautiful woman I've ever seen."

"And you, Max, are more than I know what to do with."

Max saw real, true, vulnerable emotion for a moment in Dubs's eyes. That alone was overwhelming. The fact that it was replaced by a hunger so strong it hit her like a wave pulse practically made her brain short-circuit.

"Can you see how bad I want you?" Dubs asked.

"Show me."

Dubs kissed her again, so intensely the kiss in and of itself felt like enough to send Max soaring. It was certainly enough to make her feel a frenzy unlike anything she had felt before. She had to make Dubs feel pleasure right now, in all ways she could think of. She reached between their bodies and dipped her hand into Dubs's wetness.

She rolled them both over so Dubs was now on top and slid her hand farther down. Dubs straddled her stomach, and Max slipped two fingers inside. She matched the rhythm of Max's hand with her hips. She threw back her head and looked to the ceiling in pleasure as Max moved her thumb along her clit in motion with their movement. With her other hand, she worked from one of Dubs's breasts to the other, making circles around first one nipple then the other.

Dubs came hard, collapsing onto Max's chest. She slowly withdrew her fingers, but kept a steady rhythm on Dubs's clit, eliciting another orgasm.

Dubs grinned at Max and moved down her body, kissing her as she went. Max bunched her hands in the sheets. She could barely stand what Dubs was doing, and she was only trailing kisses down non-sensitive areas.

When Dubs reached the apex of Max's thighs, she spread Max's legs slightly and ran her tongue along the length of Max's clit. Max thought she was going to come off the bed with pleasure. And when she did it again, Max twisted her upper body sideways.

"Pretty Girl, you're wound so tight," Dubs said. "I bet I can help."

Max couldn't even respond. She was helpless under Dubs's touch.

Dubs took Max's clit in her mouth, sucking it in. Max was wound so tight she came almost instantly. Dubs continued to run her tongue along Max's clit until she came twice more, until she was begging her to stop.

"I've wanted to have sex with you since I first laid eyes on you," Dubs said, nuzzled in Max's arms. "It's better now though, now that I know you, and care about you."

"I like you too," Max said. "And this."

"Maybe after the case is over, I could stick around and we could still sleep in the same bed, and sometimes it could even be naked," Dubs said.

Max thought she sounded shy, which was very unlike Dubs, and was also completely adorable. "I would like that very much."

"Good," Dubs said.

They fell asleep in one another's arms.

CHAPTER TWENTY-ONE

Dubs heard her phone text alert, forcing her from sexy dreams into the unpleasant world outside Max's apartment. Dubs checked the text, although she knew what it was going to say. It was the same as the last six or seven she had received from various acquaintances from her past. The pressure to take up their challenge was getting more and more difficult to resist.

This text was different. It didn't give her the same options and reasons for why she should take the challenge and clear Levi's name. This one simply said, "Last chance. It's on in an hour. State House. Move your ass."

She considered waking Max up and talking to her about the text, but she knew what she would say. This wasn't a problem for Holt. What could she do? This was her problem to solve. Her past to put to rest. She checked to make sure Max was still asleep and slipped out of bed.

She dressed quickly, for the first time forgoing her makeup as she got ready to work. She was about to walk out the door when she paused. She felt guilty for thinking of handcuffing Max to the bed, but she also didn't want Holt to think Max had let her go freely. She wondered if Max would forgive her for slipping out, or if she was fracturing the bond they had spent the last weeks building.

She grabbed the handcuffs that usually tied the two of them together in the evenings and carefully slipped one end around Max's wrist. She attached the other side to one of the rails on Max's headboard. She stopped to blow Max a kiss before she snuck out the door, and tried to ignore the way her heart felt as though it were fractured glass.

Once she was in the hallway, she moved as fast as she could out of the building. The last thing she needed was Lola spotting her and keeping her from getting to the State House. She texted one of her past contacts and asked for a ride. She wasn't about to steal one of Holt's cars. She wasn't going to cross that line.

Tony, the man who had found her at the beach what seemed like ages ago, picked her up. "Took you long enough, Dubs," he said.

"What's it to you?" Dubs said. "You never cared about my reputation. Levi's either. You didn't even like the guy."

"Things change, Dubs," Tony said. "And they're saying nasty stuff about you. Besides, I want to see if you can do what they're asking. They say you're a pussy now. You're working for the government and you've lost your balls."

"I don't even know where to start with that," Dubs said. "What do they want me to do?"

"The governor is arriving in about thirty minutes in a caravan. You have to steal the lead car and deliver it to a group waiting for you down by the docks. The trick is not having a soul on your ass when you get there."

Dubs didn't think much of the challenge. It wasn't a challenge for a car thief. It was a challenge for a stunt driver. This felt off, but she didn't say anything to Tony. The lead car in the governor's caravan was likely to be a state police SUV, and stealing it was probably as hard as sitting in the driver's seat and pushing the gas pedal. In her experience, the cruisers were usually either still running, or at the very least still had the keys in the ignition. This was nothing like what Levi had to do.

When they got near the State House, Tony dropped Dubs off, wished her luck, and sped off. She saw a familiar face, Rich waiting for her on the corner.

"Did Tony tell you what you have to do?" Rich asked.

"Sure," Dubs said. "What the fuck for, though?"

"Because that's what the challenge is," Rich said. "You stepping up or not? You going to go down in flames like your boy Levi?"

"Fuck you," Dubs said. "You want me to prove to you I can put a car in drive and not hit anything on the way out of a driveway, fine. You want me to be able to keep a fucking car on the road, hey, I can do that too. Maybe tomorrow I can use a knife and a fork and fully masticate my food."

"What?"

"Never mind, you dumb fuck." She was thinking about Max, wondering if she had woken up yet and realized she was gone. Her heart ached when she thought about seeing her again, especially when she considered that Max might not want anything to do with her anymore. This hardly seemed worth it, but it was what they wanted from her. It was the code of the street.

"You're up," Rich said.

Dubs moved closer to the State House. She leaned on the marble railing surrounding the courtyard in front of the main entrance. She could see the caravan making its way up the street toward her. She waited until they pulled into the courtyard before she moved closer.

As she suspected, the first car was indeed a state police SUV. The governor of Rhode Island was protected by the state police, so most of the vehicles in his caravan were marked or unmarked state police cars.

The governor and his handlers, escorts, protection, and other staffers got out of vehicles and made their way inside. A few officers stood near the back of the line of cars, but for the most part, the caravan was unattended. Dubs found that strange, but she proceeded with her task at hand.

She moved swiftly but stealthily to the first SUV and opened the door quietly. As she suspected might be the case, the keys were in the ignition and the engine was running. Once she was in the driver's seat, she wasted no time getting out of the courtyard and onto the roadway. She glanced in the rearview and saw the officers who had remained with the other caravan vehicles running to cars, flipping on lights and sirens, and coming after her. As a general rule, after stealing a car she drove slowly and calmly to avoid detection. Now she had the pedal to the floor.

She flew along the surface streets around the State House, weaving in and out of what little traffic was on the road at this hour. She ran four red lights before she had gone a mile. She made three quick turns and circled back the way she came, effectively losing her police pursuit for the time being.

She pulled into an alley for a moment and backed in as far as she could. The alley had outlets on both ends and an escape midway in, so she felt relatively safe taking a moment to plot her fastest, most effective route to the docks. She didn't want to get into a high-speed chase with the police through downtown Providence if she could avoid it.

Before she had time to fully consider her options two large, black SUVs pulled into the alley, one in front and one behind her. They were moving fast. Dubs's heart rate jumped a few beats per minute. She knew aggressive, unfriendly driving when she saw it. She slammed the SUV in gear and headed for the mid alley escape route. She always left herself multiple outlets, but she was especially glad for it now.

She hit the tee outlet hard, clipping the back bumper of the SUV as she made the tight turn. The two pursuing cars had to slam on their brakes and come to a full stop, as neither had yielded to the other, before they could follow. It bought her valuable breathing room and she didn't waste it. She shot out of the alley, nearly hitting another car, and sped off down the side street.

The gas pedal was almost to the floor, even on the surface streets, as she tried to get away from whoever was behind her in those SUVs. She didn't think they were police. That meant her problems were compounded now. She considered the possibility she had been set up and thought about the bomb-laden SUV at Holt's place. Her stomach turned.

As she took a corner on two wheels, the tires squealing in protest, one of the black SUVs shot out from a perpendicular side street and slammed full speed into the passenger side door. Dubs slammed against her seat belt. Her adrenaline was pumping so wildly she didn't know if she was hurt. She also didn't wait around to find out what her new friends wanted with her. She threw the SUV in reverse, disentangled the vehicles, and jammed her foot down on the gas pedal again. A highway entrance ramp was just ahead. She took it, heading south, toward the water. She didn't think anything good was waiting for her there, but for now she didn't know where else to go.

Once she was on the highway, there was significantly more traffic. Unfortunately, there were also two more unfriendly vehicles that seemed intent on running her off the road. She was amazed at the lack of police pursuit. She was in a stolen police cruiser, and the state police didn't seem all that concerned. As soon as she thought it, she saw flashing lights and heard sirens behind her. *Great. More fun.* She knew the police were less willing to take risks with the public safety than the other guys after her. At least she knew what she was up against. Good guys and bad guys. She had no idea which one she was anymore.

She checked her rearview and saw the third SUV, the one that had smashed into her a few moments before, join the chase. She watched the three of them set up behind her.

The first SUV moved next to her, on the passenger side. They were flying along between eighty and ninety miles an hour, weaving in and out of traffic. Fear made Dubs's hands slick on the wheel, and sweat dripped down her neck. She wondered if this was what Levi felt before he died. Then she thought of Max. She wanted to talk to her and tell her how she felt. But this wasn't the time to get distracted by mushy, squishy feelings. If she survived this, she'd damn well tell her how she felt. If.

The second SUV moved up to her left. She glanced over and saw the driver. It was Mr. Malevolent from the auto shop she had visited with Max. "What are you doing, trying to kill me?" Dubs said out loud. She pushed the SUV to its maximum and shot ahead of her two escorts. She pulled the wheel hard to the right, cutting off one side of the box. When she was past the enemy on the right and driving on the shoulder, she slammed both feet on the brake, skidding and sliding her way to a stop. She shifted quickly into reverse and hit the gas as hard as she could. *Thank God for standard issue police acceleration.*

She kept an eye on the SUVs pursuing her. It took them a few minutes to come to a stop, but they didn't bother reversing down the highway. All three had turned and were driving along the shoulder the wrong way, straight at her. She didn't see the police lights at all anymore. *What the fuck? What's that about?* Dubs looked behind her. The exit she was aiming for was less than one hundred yards. It was going to be close, but she thought she would make it.

She floored it in reverse. When she was close enough, she hit the brakes hard again, shifting gears, and slammed down on the gas once again. The SUV barreled off the exit into oncoming traffic. Dubs hopped lanes, barely avoiding the honking cars. She didn't know how long she would be able to keep her pursuers from winning this battle. She was going to have to ditch the car or make a phone call. Neither option was all that appealing. She checked her mirror and saw the three SUVs, lined up one after the other, gaining on her. She picked up her phone.

CHAPTER TWENTY-TWO

Max knocked on Holt's door. It was the last place she wanted to be. She was filled with sadness, hurt, and mostly embarrassment. She had no idea how she could have been so stupid on so many levels. And now she had to face Holt and tell her how badly she had screwed up.

Holt finally answered the door, looking wide-awake, alert, and ready to tear Max's head off if she needed to. The fact that she was in a T-shirt and boxer shorts was the only sign that she had probably been asleep. It was four in the morning, after all.

"It's Max, baby. No need for alarm," Holt said over her shoulder.

"Invite her in," Max heard Isabelle say. "And put on some pants. We should move your dresser to the front entry since you seem to be getting so many late night visitors. I'll make some coffee."

"Come on in, Max," Holt said. "What's wrong?"

Max didn't even get all the way in the door before she blurted out what she came to say. "She's gone, Holt. I screwed up, and now she's gone."

"Who's gone?" Holt asked.

"Dubs. She handcuffed me to the damned bed and snuck out. I failed you."

Holt didn't look happy, but she didn't freak out, which Max thought was a marginally good sign. "Do you have any idea where she might be? Or why she left?"

"I might, actually," Max said. "She's been talking about a challenge laid down by some other people in the car thief community. Something about avenging her friend Levi and clearing his good name. She said they've been putting a lot of pressure on her to accept their challenge. I told her to talk to you, but she said no. My guess is she finally caved."

"Do you know what this challenge entails?" Holt asked.

"Will she be okay on her own?" Isabelle asked.

"I don't know," Max said. Much to her horror, she felt herself getting emotional. She was pissed as hell at Dubs, and she also knew the last time someone took one of these challenges, they ended up dead.

"I put a tracer on her cell phone, but I've only been using it to see who was calling her. I haven't been tracking her text messages since she's pretty open about who's texting. Or at least, I thought she was. I brought my laptop. We can pull up the messages themselves now. Maybe it will help."

"Do it," Holt said.

Max felt so stupid for trusting Dubs, and for getting so wrapped up in her desire for her that she had let this happen. *Stupid. So stupid. I'm an idiot. And if something happens to her...*

"I'm sorry I let you down, H," Max said.

"Max," Holt said. "We don't know enough about Dubs's motivations to understand why she did what she did, but it's highly unlikely you could have prevented her from walking out your door tonight. Maybe she let us both down, or maybe she has reasons that make no sense to us, but are pure to her. It's too early to pass judgment. We work the case like always. What can you tell me about those texts?"

If Max hadn't loved Holt before that moment, she loved her more than ever in that instant. She had expected Holt to yell or berate her, but what she said made sense. Max knew Dubs's motivation, but not enough to explain to Holt. They needed to find her.

"I don't know where she is now," Max said. "But two hours ago she was headed for the State House."

Holt's cell phone rang. "I wonder why the head of the state police is calling me so early," Holt said, pinching the bridge of her nose.

Max's heart sank and she felt tears welling. Isabelle must have seen her distress.

"She means a lot to you, doesn't she?" Isabelle asked.

"No, she's a total asshole," Max said. "She deserves anything she gets for acting like a fool. If a tear happened to slip out of my eyes right now, it's just a sign of how incredibly angry I am at her for handcuffing me to the bed and causing so much hassle."

"Well, obviously," Isabelle said. "I remember shedding a few 'go to hell' tears over Holt too."

"Why does everyone assume I'm all emotionally wrapped up in this?" Max asked. Isabelle's understanding and kindness wasn't helping her pull herself together.

"Oh, sweetie, it's written all over your face. I won't tell anyone, though, if you don't want anyone to know. And you can feel free to be as mad at Dubs as you like when she gets back. But from the sound of Holt's conversation, Dubs might be in trouble, and she might need a hero to come rescue her, if you're into that sort of thing."

Max hadn't been listening to Holt's end of the conversation at all. She was too far into her own head. She tuned in.

"No, sir," Holt said. "I understand how dangerous that is for the general public, but I assure you, she's highly skilled. Those three SUVs aren't part of my crew. I take no responsibility for their actions." Holt listened for a moment, her expression stormy. "Sir, excuse me for a moment, but don't you think if we were trying to draw out the group of thieves you were interested in us finding, that perhaps that's exactly what happened?"

Max could hear the man on the other end talking loudly. Holt even held the phone away from her ear for a time.

"Well, I'm sorry that things got a little messy. I'm guessing that's why you passed the job off to us. If you wanted it, and it was going to stay clean, you probably would have had your guys do it. Sir, I'm going to have to put you on hold. I'm getting another call."

Holt held the phone away from her ear and switched lines. Max had thought she was bluffing with the angry state police captain, but she was wrong.

"Dubs, where the fuck are you?"

Max didn't know if she was relieved to not have gotten Dubs's phone call, or incredibly hurt that Dubs had reached out to Holt instead. Mostly, she was happy Dubs was safe, or at least safe enough to be making a phone call.

Holt listened intently. She moved to the kitchen island and grabbed a piece of paper and a pen. She jotted down a few details and motioned Max over. Max looked at the note.

Dubs. Stolen state police SUV, damaged. Pursued by 3 black SUVs, no plates. Intent to kill. Mr. Malevolent driving. Needs escape.

Max felt a little woozy. She had a moment picturing Dubs inside the state police SUV, airbags deployed, her body smashed, and mangled, and lifeless. She couldn't let that happen. She needed to focus.

"Where is she?" Max asked. She pulled out her phone and pulled up an app she had created for Holt's crew. It sent an emergency text to anyone who was working at that moment. She typed in the message "response needed for protection of crewmember driving state police SUV. Pursued by 3 black SUVs. Protect by all means necessary. Location to follow."

Holt relayed Dubs's current position and Max pulled up a map on her phone. She looked for a location that would make an ambush easiest. "Got it," she said, mostly to herself. She relayed the address and cross street to Holt to pass along to Dubs, while she sent a second emergency alert text to the team.

Max moved back to her laptop and pulled up the GPS locators on the crew-issued cell phones. Seven signals were converging on the location she had sent. If Dubs could make it there in one piece, she would have plenty of backup.

"Let's go," Holt said. "We've got to meet her there. My police friend is itching to throw her back in prison."

"Isn't he still on hold?" Isabelle asked.

"Must have lost signal," Holt said with a wink.

"You two go," Isabelle said. "Do whatever it is you do. I'll be fine here. I'll have some coffee, read the paper. You know, normal person things on a Saturday morning."

"I love you," Holt said. "I'll be back in a few. We've got some things to talk about."

"Shoo," Isabelle said.

Max was intrigued, but she knew better than to ask. Instead, she sprinted after Holt, who was jogging to her truck. Luckily, the location Max had chosen was only a few blocks from Holt's loft.

When they arrived, it was clear they were late to the party. Max's stomach dropped, and she thought she might be sick. The stolen police SUV was upside down in the middle of the intersection.

Holt's crew had positioned their vehicles around the overturned SUV and were standing defensively in a large perimeter. No one, not even the angry looking state police officers, were allowed inside. Max couldn't see Dubs anywhere.

"Did any of those idiots check to make sure Dubs is okay?"

"Go check on her," Holt said. "I'll talk to our trooper friends. If she needs rescue, you come directly to me, no middle men delivering a message, okay?"

Max nodded and shot out of the truck as soon as it had slowed enough. She ran full speed for the overturned SUV, past the line of her co-workers, who parted to let her through. In truth, she might be smaller than any of them, but she didn't think there was one of them there this morning that could have stopped her. She had made the decision back in Holt's loft to see this through completely, to make sure Dubs was safe, and if she needed it, cared for. She would be pissed, hurt, and betrayed, later.

She dropped to her knees when she got to the driver's side window. She peered inside. Empty. There was blood on the steering wheel.

"Dubs?" Max called out.

"Pretty Girl," Dubs said from nearby. She sounded tired and pained. "I'm over here."

Max moved to the front of the SUV. Dubs was sitting on the pavement, her legs stretched in front of her, leaning against the passenger side headlight. Max knelt beside her and looked her over. Her hand was bleeding, and she had a cut on her forehead, but there weren't any other obvious signs of injury. That didn't mean there weren't any.

"Are you hurt?"

"Remarkably, no," Dubs said. "I do know I never want to be in a car when it gets rammed like we're playing bumper cars, though."

"I'm glad you're okay," Max said. "You should probably get checked out."

Dubs looked so sad it was making it hard for Max to keep her professional resolve to work the case and keep emotions aside. She wanted to be angry, if she was going to feel anything, but right now she wanted to pull Dubs into her arms, hold her, and tell her everything was going to be okay.

"I thought I was going to die out here," Dubs said. "And all I could think about was you. I thought how mad you probably were at the way I left and that just ate at me. I started out flirting with you because I knew I could get a rise out of you. But that's not what it's been for a while now. That's not what it was last night. I know I'm going back to prison, and you won't want anything to do with me, but I wanted you to know. You know, in case it means anything."

Dubs sounded desperate and defeated. Max didn't know what to do. She had spent so long believing Dubs was just messing with her, and here she was telling her that was true. Now it was hard to know whether this was more of the game. It didn't feel like it, though. Last night, and the weeks prior, sure hadn't felt like a game. She was saved from having to answer by Holt.

"Max, you find her?"

"Over here, Holt. She says she's okay," Max said.

Holt squatted in front of Dubs. "You okay? You look a little worse for wear."

"I'll survive. I'm sorry about this. Thank you for what you did. I owe you," Dubs said.

"What you owe me, and Max, is an explanation. But that will have to wait. You need to come with me. We're going to talk to some very angry police officers. You're going to stand next to me and you aren't going to say a word. Do you understand? Not a single word. I know that's not in your nature, but it's important. Not a word."

"I'll do my best," Dubs said.

"No," Holt said. "You'll do better than that. You'll do what is expected of you as a member of this team. You'll do what I just asked you to do. You'll keep your mouth shut. Understood?"

Dubs looked surprised. Max wondered what part of Holt's statement caused the look. Personally, she was surprised by Holt's characterization of Dubs as a member of the team.

"Yes, ma'am," Dubs said.

"Oh no," Holt said. "That's my mother. You call me Holt, H, hey you, or whatever else you like. Not ma'am. Ask Max how well I enjoy that endearment."

Max shook her head when Dubs glanced her way.

As they got up to leave, Max fell in to join them. Holt held up her hand to stop her. "You stay here, Max. Get the crew back to their posts. When that's done, head back to the office and get to work. Figure out who the hell was in those SUVs. I'll bring Dubs by in a bit. She's going to need a shower and a nap before she gets back to work. You'll need to keep an eye on her. I haven't decided if the cuffs go back on full-time."

"H, with all due respect, it might be better if someone else took over that job for a while." Max couldn't imagine having to be handcuffed to Dubs twenty-four seven again. She couldn't even imagine having to live with Dubs after last night and the events of this morning.

"Are you ill?" Holt asked.

"No."

"Injured? Planning an unscheduled vacation? Unfit for duty?"

"No. It's just that—"

"Whatever it is, Max, work it out. We'll be back soon."

"Yes, boss," Max said.

She hadn't had the urge to salute in months. She did now. She watched them walk off and couldn't help but feel the familiar sense of attraction when she looked at Dubs. She sighed.

"Rough day," Lola said.

"The worst," Max said. "You've had recent trouble with women. How did you handle it?"

"You get Dubs pregnant last night?" Lola said with a knowing smile.

"Really? That's the kind of help you're going to offer?"

Lola laughed. "I can't help you, kid. You've got to work it out between the two of you. Besides, I've got horrible taste in women, and from what I can tell, you've got pretty good taste. So what kind of advice could I offer anyway? You'll figure it out."

"Well, at least wait around and give me a ride," Max said.

"Sure thing. I'll just be here, by the busted ass police car. Take your time."

Max stomped off, wondering what in the hell she had gotten herself into.

CHAPTER TWENTY-THREE

Dubs stood in Holt's office completely silent. She hadn't said a word since Holt told her not to speak by the wrecked SUV. She'd been following Holt around, but the past hour had been so surreal, she didn't have anything to say anyway.

"Sit down, Dubs." Holt offered her a chair. "We need to talk. I need to understand what happened this morning. Why did you take off?"

"Can I ask you a question first?" Dubs had about a hundred questions.

"I promise I'll answer any questions you have, but it might be best if we start from the beginning. It might help our relationship continue to develop if we have all the background context."

"Okay. You're the boss. Did Max tell you about Levi?"

Holt nodded.

"Of course she did. Did she also tell you about the challenge that was presented to, first him, then me?"

"She told me you were getting pressure from some old acquaintances. She thought it had to do with Levi and maybe avenging his death or clearing his name. She wasn't sure of the specifics."

Dubs thought it was interesting that Max had shielded her personal failings from Holt. She appreciated it greatly, but it surprised her. She didn't think Max would keep anything from Holt. She hoped it was a sign of how much Max cared about her. Maybe enough to work past this betrayal. She had seen the hurt in Max's eyes. That was going to be hard to overcome.

"That's more or less it. Levi died attempting the challenge on my behalf, because I was in prison. Since he failed, it was the same as if I had failed too. It was also as if his good name was ruined by that failure. It might not make any sense, but it was the code of the street at the time. Things seemed to have changed since I've been gone."

"And since you've been out, there has been pressure to take up the challenge he died trying to complete?"

"That's what I thought," Dubs said. "It would have cleared his name, and mine. But today when I got there, that wasn't a challenge. It was a suicide mission. And that's before those other dudes showed up."

"Too bad they didn't stick around once our people showed up for the party," Holt said. "Guess they prefer three to one odds."

"I don't think we'd be here talking if everyone hadn't shown up when they did," Dubs said. "They rolled me and were lining up for the kill shot when the cavalry arrived."

"Max has always had good timing," Holt said.

"Max sent all those guys?"

"She was worried about you. She mobilized every crew member working and sent them to your location."

"I'll be damned," Dubs said.

"Why did you wait to call me until after you were in trouble?" Holt asked.

"This doesn't have anything to do with the case."

"That doesn't answer my question."

"Max asked me the other day what I planned on doing when this case is over. I couldn't answer her," Dubs said. "When I got out of prison it was with the goal of either helping you bring down this new crew so that I could reestablish myself, or if you couldn't bring them down, at least I could get back in the game, get my name back out there, and set up my contacts again. But now, I don't know. Things are different. I'm different. I don't know what I'll do. I guess I thought I needed to handle that on my own, see if I still could.

Maybe I hoped the world I remembered was still the one I was walking out into."

"That's the problem, Dubs. You're thinking like an individual. You're part of a team here. You're part of my team. A valuable, and until this morning, a trusted one. If you were worried about what you were going to do after, you should have come to talk to me. You should still come talk to me. There are more options than your old life, going back to prison, or wandering the streets with nothing to do."

"I think I completely blew it for the opportunity I really want," Dubs said. It wasn't until the words came out of her mouth that she realized it was true.

"Which is?"

"I guess it doesn't matter now," Dubs said. "But I really like the work I've been doing with you and everyone who works for you. I couldn't have imagined that when I stepped out of the prison yard. That's for sure."

"Dubs," Holt said. "Your ability to work for me is not hindered by the stunt you pulled this morning. Well, at least not for the reason you think. Everyone came to your rescue today because Max asked them to. They trusted her and they knew a team member was in trouble. That's important. We lean on each other, depend on each other, trust each other. That's the thing you don't get yet. I understand why you did what you did for your friend. I told you I lost a friend. If someone was sullying his reputation, I would do anything to defend it."

"Can I ask you something?" Dubs asked.

"Sure," Holt said.

"Why did you tell the state police my jaunt this morning was part of our investigation? You could have sent me back to prison."

"I've told you this a number of times. I take care of my own. You are one of my own. You screwed up. That's not enough for me to abandon you. Did you listen to anything I just said? You're not an island anymore."

"I didn't think you liked me much."

"I wasn't sure if I could trust you," Holt said. "That's not the same thing. That's why I made sure Max was close by. From the look of things, that kind of backfired on me."

"It backfired on me. That's for sure," Dubs said. "She's just like you. Strong, capable, principled, team player. I don't know if she's as willing to forgive and forget though."

"I'm not forgetting, Dubs. All I said was I understand your reasoning. As for Max, if I'm reading the looks you two were giving each other correctly, she's not thinking with the same rational detachment I am. That's a pain in the ass for me, but it's something else entirely for you."

"Think you could help me out? Max would listen to you if you said I didn't mean to completely betray her trust," Dubs said. She didn't get her hopes up, but it would go a long way if Holt could help her out. She wanted to make things right with Max.

"Oh no," Holt said. "You two paddled yourselves out into the middle of a fast moving stream and then took a machine gun to the bottom of your row boat. I'm not getting involved."

"Yeah, okay."

"Look," Holt said. "I'm the last one to talk about not falling in love with someone you're working with intimately on a case, but be careful. Especially with Max. If you're just fucking around because you're bored."

"Holt—" Dubs couldn't believe Holt would think that after how much she had been floundering around since Holt had come to her rescue this morning.

"Hey," Holt said. "I am in no way saying that's what's happening. I can tell you're hurting here, but Max is too, so be careful. That's all I'm saying. I don't want either of you to get hurt."

"I'm not sure I have to worry about that anymore," Dubs said.

"Jesus," Holt said. "I do not want to be doing this. Listen. If Max is anything like me, and if she feels about you like you seem to feel about her, then she'll come around. She was scared. You were in danger, and there wasn't anything she could do. And you shut her out of something really important. And you handcuffed her to the bed. Not cool."

"Well—" Dubs said.

"Stop right there," Holt said.

Dubs smiled, but didn't dare actually laugh, smirk, or giggle.

"Now, do you have any other outstanding challenges I need to know about?"

"Nothing at all. My life moving forward is conflict free. Assuming we figure out who tried to kill me tonight, obviously."

"No arm wrestling contests? Poker tournaments? Pissing contests you're forgetting about?"

Dubs shook her head. Even if someone came forward and called her every nasty name she could think of, told her she was fat, and ugly, and her dress was hideous, she wasn't going to engage. At least not for a week or two.

"And the concept of teamwork is something you'll let sink in?" Holt asked.

"It's a steep learning curve," Dubs said. "But I'm highly motivated. I like you all. You're a good group. For a bunch of government agents."

"Government agents?" Holt asked, looking incredulous. "Get out of here, Dubs. Are you in any danger of scampering again?"

"No," Dubs said seriously. "I'm not going anywhere. I'll swear on anything you like."

"Your word is fine with me."

"Then you have it."

Holt nodded and Dubs left her office. She saw Max across the room and her stomach knotted up. There was no use putting off the inevitable. She headed for her.

"Hi," Dubs said as she came alongside Max's desk.

"Hello," Max said. The reception wasn't a warm one. "You going back to prison?"

"Remarkably, no."

"That's good," Max said. She still hadn't looked up, but she did at least sound a bit relieved that Dubs wasn't getting locked up again. "Is Holt insisting we be cuffed together again?"

"She didn't say anything about it," Dubs said. "She made me give her my word I wasn't going anywhere. I'm not. I promise you that."

"Well, you know, I would have assumed that last night too," Max said. "And that didn't do me a lot of good. So I don't care what Holt thinks. The cuffs go back on." Max grabbed the handcuffs, which Dubs hadn't noticed next to her computer, and fastened them around first Dubs's wrist, then her own. "My one job is to keep you with me and out of trouble. Since I failed so completely at that this morning, we're back to this."

"You didn't fail." Dubs felt like a little part of her was dying. "I let you down."

"Yes," Max said. She still hadn't looked at Dubs, not in the eye. "But I thought I could trust you, and I was wrong, so I failed."

Dubs sat in the chair next to Max and leaned in close to her, trying to force eye contact. "Look, can we talk about this?" Dubs asked. She knew she sounded like she was begging.

Max finally looked her in the eye. Her eyes were pain filled and watery. "We can talk about the case," she said. "You told Holt you saw one of the men from the auto shop we visited driving one of the three SUVs that were trying to run you off the road. Is that right?"

"Max," Dubs tried again. "Please, I'm sorry. What can I do to get you to talk to me?"

"You can tell me about Mr. Malevolent," Max said.

Dubs sat back in her chair with a sad sigh. Her arm jerked as the handcuffs came taut. Max shot her a look as her hand was pulled off the keyboard. This was a far cry from the awesome evening they had enjoyed last night.

"Yes, the really grumpy guy we saw skulking at the auto shop, shooting venomous looks our way, was one of the drivers," Dubs said.

"That's weird," Max said. "Why would he be part of the challenge, and then try to kill you?"

She wasn't sure, but it sounded like "kill you" caught in Max's throat. Dubs was grasping for any sign that Max wasn't completely emotionally detaching. That was one she was going to hold on to.

"I think the challenge was a setup," Dubs said. "I think the point was the 'kill me,' or at least get me out of the picture. I don't really know why. Threat, message, warning, who knows? I don't think I'm such a menace to them that they needed to specifically take me out. They were determined. I'll give them that."

"Was it the same challenge Levi did?" Max asked.

"No. It wasn't even a challenge, really. I think the point was to get me in an easily identified car and force me to drive. The SUV had the keys in the ignition and was running. It wasn't even a challenge."

"Do you think it's possible the people we're looking for were the ones you played bumper cars with?"

"Seems the most likely idea. I think I'm generally a pretty likable person. Not too many people hate me enough to hold a grudge long enough to wait for me to get out of prison and set all that up."

"That does make me feel better, seeing as I'm handcuffed to you currently," Max said.

"Your choice, Pretty Girl."

"Don't call me that," Max said.

"You can't ask me to stop," Dubs said. "You're beautiful, and it just comes out. Please don't say there's no chance to go back to what we had. To what we were starting to create. I really care about you, and I feel like my heart is breaking."

"Why didn't you think of that when you snuck out on me this morning?" Max asked. "Do you know how horrible I felt when I woke up and you were gone? You think your heart is breaking now? I had to deal with the fact that you had walked out, and I had to go and tell Holt that you were gone and I had no idea where you were. My one job was to know where you were, all the time. And I had no idea. We work as a team around here. You went lone wolf on me. I don't know how to trust that. And after—" She looked away, swallowing hard.

"I just got this chat from Holt," Dubs said. "I'm not used to working as part of a team. It never occurred to me that you, or she, or anyone else here, could help me, or would even want to. Well, I knew you wanted to, but I thought you would get in trouble with Holt. I'm willing to learn. For you, I think I'm willing to do just about anything."

"And what happens the next time something comes up that needs your attention?" Max asked. "I can't take that chance. I was stupid to get swept up in you the first time around. It's a wonderful place, but it's not reality."

"Wait a minute." Dubs felt cold panic sweep up her spine. "It totally can be reality. I take a couple steps your way, and you take a step my way, and then we're right there together. And we're already handcuffed together, so we have to meet in the middle or our arms are going to start hurting. We're practically destined to meet in the middle. It's fate. We were meant to be."

Max tried to hide it, but Dubs saw the smile hinting at the corners of her mouth. Dubs shook her handcuffed wrist, rattling the cuffs all the way to Max's wrist. "Just one little step my way?" Dubs asked, sliding her foot toward Max's foot. When their feet made contact, Max pushed back against Dubs's foot.

"Too many steps, Dubs. You're incorrigible."

"And now you're using Scrabble words too, Pretty Girl."

"Let's solve this case," Max said. "There's plenty of time for talking after."

Hope replaced panic, at least for the moment. Max was engaging with her again, bantering back and forth, and she hadn't repeated her request that she not call her Pretty Girl. Maybe they could work this out after all. She leaned forward in her chair and thought about the SUV driver.

"Auto shops," she said.

"Huh?" Max asked.

"You asked me a while ago what a car thief would need to steal so many cars in such a short time. I said easy access to a lot of cars. The two guys we are reasonably sure are connected to this theft ring work at auto shops. Easy, unimpeded access. They could make a copy of the key, disable the alarm, install an alarm kill or remove a GPS tracker, and the owner wouldn't even know. Plus, they have home addresses for all their clients."

"But these two guys don't work at the same shop."

"No, they would need more than one. Probably three or four," Dubs said. "You would need a high volume of cars so you could pick the ones you want to target. Plus, you have to make sure not every car that comes through the shop gets stolen. Otherwise it's easy to trace back."

"If your theory is correct, we can call all the owners of the stolen cars you think were hit by the ring we're tracking and find out where they took their cars for service, and when their last repair was."

"Exactly," Dubs said. "How are we going to call all those people?"

"Teamwork, remember?" Max said. She leaned back in her chair and called over to Moose. "Moose, I need whoever's free to make some phone calls. Dubs and I may be on to something."

Holt overheard and came over with Moose. "The Wonder Twins are hard at work, H. We should keep them in bracelets all the time. It seems to activate their powers," Moose said.

"You're just hilarious," Max said. "You got time to bust my ass, or do you want to hear what we found?"

"Spit it out," Holt said.

Max looked so excited. Dubs thought she was adorable.

"We know where our bad guys are getting their cars," Max said. "We also know where at least two of the group members work."

"And?" Moose said.

"This is like pulling teeth," Holt said. "You're quite proud of yourselves."

"Max worked really hard figuring this out," Dubs said.

"Auto shops," Max said. "They're scouting the cars at auto shops and stealing them later. We know at least two that are being used. It seems like the two guys we've tracked down probably work at these shops."

"And you want people to make phone calls to all the stolen cars we have on our list?" Moose said.

"Exactly," Max said. "See if they were serviced recently, and if so, where."

"It's worth a try," Holt said. "It makes sense they would be using a place like auto shops for access. Make sense to you, Dubs?"

"Perfect sense." She appreciated Holt allowing her to be part of this conversation. She wanted to learn the flow of working as part of the team. "I was telling Max, when a car was in the shop for service, a key could be made, an alarm system disabled, or a kill switch installed. If there was a GPS tracker on board, that could be removed. It's the perfect time to be all over a car without raising suspicion. Also, what better way to know exactly what you're getting when you go back for the car later? I mean, they could already have buyers for all the parts and accessories prior to stealing and chopping the car. It's brilliant, really."

"Get anyone who's not working a priority case," Holt said. "Let's call everyone on that list. Max, you and Dubs put together the phone numbers and car makes and models. You two will be in charge of a master list of what our callers find out. Report back to me as soon as you have something worth talking about. But, Wonder Twins, if it's after seven, call Moose. I'm busy this evening."

"We're on it, boss," Dubs said.

Dubs saw Max give her a funny look. She couldn't tell if it was amusement, annoyance, or amazement. Perhaps it was a combination of all three.

"What was that look for?" she asked when Moose and Holt walked away.

"That's the first time I've heard you call Holt 'boss.' It caught me off guard. That's all," Max said.

"She's winning me over," Dubs said. "Should we get to work?"

"Let's dive in," Max said. "We've got a long night ahead of us."

CHAPTER TWENTY-FOUR

Isabelle always looked forward to date night with Holt, but tonight carried more weight than usual. They hadn't had a chance to really talk about Lola's proposal that they adopt Tiffany's baby, so tonight would be their first chance. Holt had even volunteered to let Isabelle be in charge of the Batphone, Isabelle's name for Holt's work cell phone, which effectively meant a work free evening.

When Holt emerged from the bedroom portion of the loft, she took Isabelle's breath away, as she always did when Isabelle hadn't seen her for more than a few minutes. She had traded in her white T-shirt for a white button-down shirt, untucked over her jeans, and black boots. Isabelle was happy she had chosen to wear a skirt and sleeveless top or she wouldn't have stood a chance next to Holt.

She got up and rolled up each cuff of Holt's shirt. "You're going to be too hot, baby," she said. "But don't you dare change."

"Sweetheart," Holt said. "I could parade down Main Street naked and if you were walking next to me, not a soul would notice. You look amazingly beautiful. I wonder every day when you're at work showing everyone that you're the smartest woman in the room, or winning over a crowd at the coffee shop, or right now when you're so stunningly beautiful that my heart actually hurts, how I got so damned lucky."

"You're so rock hard on the outside, with your muscles, and tattoos, and toughness, but you have the squishiest insides I've ever come across," Isabelle said. She kissed Holt quickly. "I love you. Now let's get going before we miss the lighting."

"Yes, ma'am," Holt said.

They headed downtown to WaterFire, a hugely popular and uniquely Providence outdoor community event. On Saturday evenings throughout the summer and fall, cauldrons suspended in the three rivers running through downtown were lit on fire. Music was piped in along the route, and vendors lined the streets, dance floors were erected, and local restaurants moved their bars outdoors for the evening. Thousands of people, sometimes tens of thousands on the really popular lightings, walked the route, lost in the magic of the flames and mystery of the water and fire.

Isabelle loved WaterFire. She loved the smell of the wood fires and the peaceful feeling of the crowds as they strolled along the rivers. Since she had started coming with Holt, WaterFire had taken on an almost magical feeling. She felt like she was in Venice, or some unnamed, uncharted romantic location where she could happily reside forever.

The largest collection of cauldrons resided in a basin surrounded by amphitheater-type seating and restaurants. Those cauldrons were lit by silent black boats manned by volunteers who constantly floated along the river, stoking the fires.

They found seats and settled before the first cauldron was lit. Isabelle sat in front of Holt, between her legs, and leaned back in her arms. Holt held her tightly.

"Have you told anyone about the baby?" Holt asked.

"I almost told my sister," Isabelle said. "But you know how well she keeps a secret. My mother would know, probably before I got off the phone with Ellen. She would be beside herself. She'd probably call your mother. It was overwhelming to think about."

Holt was laughing and Isabelle knew Holt liked her family a lot. Her sister was an amazing person, and she and Holt got along really well, and she really was terrible with secrets.

"I probably would have told Amy, if it had come up," Holt said. "But it didn't."

"You expected Amy to ask you if anyone had offered you a baby to adopt? Really? That was never going to come up in any reasonable conversation," Isabelle said. "Did you chicken out?"

"Me?" Holt asked. "No way. It's just she would have had a lot of questions I couldn't answer. So it was better to wait for her to ask me about it."

"Which you knew she was never going to do. What kinds of questions were you worried about answering?"

"Just little stuff really," Holt said. "You know, are you going to do it? That kind of thing."

"Oh, right, the little stuff," Isabelle said. She felt butterflies in her stomach. "I suppose we do need to talk about that."

"Of course," Holt said. "Kind of mind blowing. I can't stop thinking about it, actually."

"Me either," Isabelle said. "What do you think, you know, when you're thinking about it?"

"Well, I have a lot of concerns," Holt said, looking serious. "But I think about when you asked me a while ago if I wanted kids. I wasn't sure at that time, but now I am. I do want kids. And I want to raise them with you. So the question becomes, I guess, is now the right time, and is that the right child for us?"

"I want to do it," Isabelle said, blurting out feelings she wasn't even one hundred percent sure were hers until they were leaving her mouth. Once they were out, she was sure though, very sure. She hoped Holt felt the same way.

Holt smiled widely. "Are you sure?"

"Yes," Isabelle said. "Very sure."

"I was hoping you would feel that way." She reached into her pocket and produced a small square jewelry box. "I brought this along because I thought we might be having a baby."

Isabelle's hands were shaking as she opened the box. Inside was a necklace made of two overlapping hearts. Three small diamonds were nestled in the metal where they met at the top. Held gently inside the hearts were two beautiful stones. Isabelle recognized her birthstone, but she didn't know the other.

"What is this one?" she asked.

"That's the baby's birthstone," Holt said. "I asked Lola the due date. It's smack in the middle of the month, so early or late, I figured I had a good chance at getting it right. If I'm a month off though, I'll change it. The hearts are you and me. The three diamonds are for our new family."

"This is the most amazing gift," Isabelle said. She felt tears forming and slipping down her cheeks. "I can't believe we're going to do this. I know we talked about it a few times in passing, when we could catch a minute, but I thought this would take so much longer to decide."

"I think it's something we both really want," Holt said. "But now I owe you a new house. I'll move anywhere you want. If you're willing to find a realtor, I'll look at every house in the state until we find the perfect one."

"Deal," Isabelle hadn't known happiness like this existed.

"I have one last present, if you can just let me see my phone for a second," Holt said. "I promise no work."

Isabelle handed over Holt's phone. She was perplexed when Holt sent a text message, but she trusted Holt's motives. A short time later Holt got a text reply.

Holt tapped the screen a few times and then held up a picture for Isabelle to see.

"Lola was going to see Tiffany today, and she told her she was talking to us about adoption and we were interested. Tiffany was in a sharing mood, apparently," Holt said.

Isabelle looked at the screen. She gasped out loud. On Holt's phone was an ultrasound picture, clear as day. The baby was in profile and sucking its thumb. "Holt…"

"Isabelle, I'd like to formally introduce you to our son."

CHAPTER TWENTY-FIVE

I don't know why you needed to sacrifice my car to this cause," Amy said. It had been two weeks since Max and Dubs had figured out the link to the auto shops. Their phone call blitz had revealed two other shops involved. As chance would have it, Holt's best friend, Amy, got her car serviced at one of the places on their list. Somehow, Max didn't know how, and clearly Amy was having second thoughts as well, Holt had talked her into using her car as bait.

"You take your car there already," Max said. "If one of us showed up, it would be really suspicious. Even Isabelle would probably raise alarms."

"But I've been taking my car there for years. Wouldn't they have already stolen it if they wanted it so badly?" Amy asked. "And couldn't I have taken the car seat out? Superman finally decided he liked this car seat."

"I'm sorry," Max said. "It's for the greater good?" She knew that sounded lame. She also knew Amy had been friends with Holt long enough to understand what she did and why Holt was asking.

"This is a new crew that just started working recently," Dubs said. "They didn't have their structure in place the last time you took your car in. And if you took your car seat out, that would look really sketchy. We're hoping they don't know you're friends with Holt."

Max didn't add that they were also hoping the thieves couldn't see through the artificial engine trouble Jose created, and that they didn't find the GPS tracker Holt hid on the engine block. There were a lot of "ifs" before they even got to the part where they had to actually steal the car for their plan to work. If it did work, it would be beautiful. They could just follow Amy's car right to the bad guys.

"It might not be any of my business," Amy said. "But why are you two handcuffed together? Is Holt hazing you or something?"

Despite the time since Dubs's elopement, Max hadn't budged on keeping her close. She sometimes wondered if she was doing it out of a sense of duty, or because it was an excuse to keep her close, without admitting to anyone, herself included, that she was, once again, struggling to keep her distance. This way she didn't have to try.

"It's a long story," Dubs said. "Good thing we like each other, right?"

There was so much less spark in Dubs's eyes these days. Max missed the Dubs that was constantly flirting with her, wearing clothes she knew would make her crazy, or talking nonstop. The new Dubs wasn't a flight risk; she was a diligent worker, and seemingly learning to integrate herself into the team, but she had lost some of the spark Max found so alluring.

"You good here, Amy?" Max asked.

"Oh sure," Amy said. "I'm going to watch your computer screen and see if my dot moves. Holt better be back by day care let out time. I'm currently car- and car seat-less. She's got the only spare."

"Where are Holt and Isabelle today?" Dubs asked.

"Looking at houses," Max said. "I think I overheard Holt say they're looking at ten this morning. I don't know how you can even keep them straight after a while."

"She remembers everything," Amy said. "And she's spent so much time in every baby store in the state trying to pick out the safest and best of everything, she probably has a spreadsheet of the exact dimensions she needs. I'm sure she's already made Isabelle insane. The nesting instinct has hit her hard."

"They're going to be such good parents," Max said.

"Isabelle's going to be amazing," Amy said. "Holt's gotta take it down a beat or two, or she's going to exhaust herself before the kid's even here. I guess she only knows one speed though."

"I think Isabelle will balance her," Dubs said. "They seem good together."

"None better," Amy said.

"Come walk with me," Max said to Dubs, tugging lightly on their joined wrists.

"I go where you go," Dubs said.

They headed out of the offices and down the street. It was a beautiful day. Max knew the handcuffs made them stand out, but she didn't care. She was miserable, and had been since things got weird between the two of them.

"I miss you, Dubs."

"How is that possible?" Dubs asked. "I am eighteen inches from your side every waking minute."

"No, I miss the cocky, sexy, motor-mouth, constantly flirting, Dubs. The one who wore that killer dress just because you knew it would make me wild for you. I miss the one who talked my ear off, and was so outrageously full of herself because she had every reason to be. Your hair has been up and you haven't worn makeup since the accident. You don't have to wear clothes, makeup, or your hair down, for me, obviously. But you seemed to take enormous pleasure in all of it. Mostly, I miss your enthusiasm."

There was a small city park near the office, and Dubs pulled them over to a nearby bench. When they sat down and Max looked at her, she was shocked to see tears streaming down Dubs's face. She reached up and, using both hands, wiped them gently away.

"I'm sorry," Max said. "I didn't mean to make you cry. On top of it all, that was the last thing I wanted to do."

"It's not your fault," Dubs said. "I've spent the past few weeks doing a lot of thinking. The conclusion I've come to is that I'm unequivocally, completely, certainly, totally, fully in love with you. It sort of snuck up on me, somewhere between trying to make you a little crazy, and our amazing night together. But the me you say you miss so much is the one you don't trust anymore. And now I'm handcuffed next to you every waking minute, and my chest hurts all day from things not being how they were."

"Oh, God, Dubs," Max said. She pulled Dubs to her, holding her tightly. She felt like an ass. She knew she had a right to be angry with the way Dubs had snuck out, but she had also been far too dismissive of how Dubs was feeling, which was wildly unfair. "I'm sorry I've been so cruel. I have missed you. I care about you deeply. I was embarrassed, and hurt, and angry, when you went off on your own, but I'm sorry for making you feel badly now."

"I didn't think about how it would make you look in front of Holt," Dubs said. "I didn't stop to consider that part. I knew you'd be pissed I didn't let you help me, but I didn't want anything to happen to you."

"You know," Max said. "All us tough guys around here are going to get a reputation if our ladies keep being the ones rescuing us, keeping us from danger, and generally doing the macho stuff we like to think only we're capable of doing."

"You know that's bullshit, right?" Dub asked, smiling up at Max from her position nuzzled against Max's neck.

"Shh," Max said. "My ego might not be able to hear that kind of thing."

"So now what?" Dubs asked. "For the record, I'm completely satisfied staying right here until I starve to death."

"I don't want to lose you over this." Max didn't realize how true that was until she considered the chance it could happen. "But I guess we have some rebuilding to do. Maybe we can rewind a little and go from there? Do you want to go out tonight?"

"Depends," Dubs said, looking at Max, sparkle firmly back in her eye. "Will you wear the bow tie?"

"Yes," Max said. "But do you have something a little less 'thirty-five on a scale of one to ten' you can wear? I know it's not your style, but take pity on me."

"A fifteen is my final offer," Dubs said.

"Who am I to complain?" She leaned down and kissed Dubs gently. She felt it throughout her entire body. She deepened the kiss momentarily and then broke it. They were taking things slow, after all. Her body wasn't having any of the same qualms about returning to the feelings she had been building for Dubs. She hadn't told Dubs the whole truth when she said she cared about her deeply. She knew she was falling in love with her. She also knew it wouldn't take much to tip her over the edge. Right now though, she was hanging on to that edge for dear life. She didn't want to go over until she was sure Dubs wasn't going to disappear on her again. It felt real, but it had before too. Falling in love with someone only looking out for themselves would lead to heartbreak. And she didn't know if Dubs was returning to her criminal life. There was still so much up in the air.

As if reading her mind, Dubs said, "Whatever happens between us, I'm done with the life I had. I don't know what I'll do instead, but it will be on this side of the law. I like what I've become now. It's because of you, and Holt, and Lola, and the rest of the group. I just wanted you to know."

Max kissed the top of Dubs's head. "You'll be a very good non-criminal. Whatever you decide to do."

"It'll take some practice."

Both Max's and Dubs's cell phones buzzed. The texts were from Holt. Amy's car was done at the shop. Lola was taking Amy to pick it up. Now the real fun began. They had to wait and hope someone came and stole it. From the spreadsheet Max and Dubs had put together, the cars were usually stolen two to ten days after work was done. Max was surprised no one had put this together sooner, but all of the auto shops had good reputations. In fact, one of them had a contract with the Providence Police Department and serviced all of the police cruisers. The irony of that was astounding.

"We should head back, I guess," Dubs said.

"We do need to pick where we're going tonight," Max said.

"I was thinking more along the lines of we should finish our work day," Dubs said, looking amused.

"Oh, that too, of course. How will your dad and Mrs. Otis feel about you giving up stealing cars? It was their life's work, right?"

"They already know," Dubs said. "They're really supportive. They were both so pissed at me when I ended up in prison. And they don't like how much things have changed now. There's so much money, and drugs, and other influences on the streets now. It's dangerous. Look at what's happened since I've been out. I've been shot at, flipped, and had a bomb dropped off for Holt. I need a nice, safe job, like a desperate housewife."

"Somehow I can't see that one working for you."

"I have no idea how to cook," Dubs said. "So you would be the desperate one."

They started their stroll back to the office. Along the way, their cuffed hands joined and they finished the walk hand in hand. Max felt more settled than she had in the past two weeks. She also felt lighter and significantly happier.

When they got back, no one was at any of the desks in the main office space. Holt's door was closed. Max checked the GPS tracker on Amy's car and saw it heading back toward her house. She texted Isabelle, asking if she had changed her mind about Max "borrowing" some IRS employee tax information from the auto shops of interest. Isabelle said no, not yet. There wasn't much left for her to do. It was still early, but they headed upstairs to get ready to go out. Max uncuffed them while they got dressed. "I don't think we need those tonight. No one should be trying to run away," Max said.

She turned around just in time to see what Dubs was wearing for the evening. One look at her and there was little doubt she would be anywhere but by her side all night. If this was Dubs's idea of toning it down and giving her a break, Max thought she needed to work on her definitions.

"I thought you were going to take it easy on me tonight," Max said, her voice squeaky.

"What?" Dubs said. "This is easy. You've seen my other dresses. I have another one, but I don't think you'd like it."

"I'm sure I'd love it," Max said. "But we'll go with the safer one."

"Put your tie on and let's go," Dubs said. Max didn't think she looked at all sorry that Max was suffering.

Max was getting used to fancy meals with a beautiful woman on her arm. She felt herself puff out her chest a little when she walked in with Dubs holding her hand. More than one patron looked their way and took a look at Dubs.

"What was it like in prison?" Max asked once they were seated. "I can't imagine what you put up with in there."

"It wasn't so bad," Dubs said. "Not having any freedom sucked. But it was dorm style sleeping, not individual cells, and the other women were nice enough. The jumpsuits were comfortable. They didn't do much for you looks-wise, but they were good to lounge around in."

"I don't know that they have fashion high on the priority list," Max said, teasing.

"I didn't have anyone to impress either. Although they have all kinds of people to talk to you all the time. There are researchers coming in all the time, and AA volunteers for those that need it, doctors, social workers, nuns. I liked to flirt with the researchers. They were usually so young, and I was bored."

Max fought off a wave of jealousy. She didn't like the thought of Dubs flirting the way she flirted with her, with anyone else. "How did they handle a full dose of you?"

"I was like a job competency screening," Dubs said. "Some got flustered and couldn't even finish whatever they were doing with me. Others were annoyed with me, and the really good ones didn't even miss a beat. One woman was really amused by me, but never stopped asking her questions. I couldn't even get an eyebrow raise."

"That must have been crushing for your very healthy ego," Max said.

"It was," Dubs said. "I knew you'd understand. The worst part of prison was always having to watch your back. Most of the women were fine, and most of the officers were cool, but some of them were nasty business. All the women were grouped together, from pot dealers to murderers, so there was quite a range of personalities."

"It's no wonder you were so independent when you started working with us," Max said. "I would be too, after something like that."

"I've got you to impress now," Dubs said. "I'm cleaning up my act."

"I'm not the one you have to impress at work. Holt is," Max said. "But outside that arena, I have to say you clean up well." She gave Dubs an exaggerated look up and down.

"Pig," Dubs said with a huge smile on her face.

"Don't think I'm only interested in your hot little body," Max said. "You're also probably the smartest woman I've ever met."

"Max," Dubs said, her cheeks pinking, "I already told you I'm in love with you. You don't have to prove that you're practically perfect."

"I'm so far from perfect," Max said. "But I wanted you to know that I think you're pretty amazing. And sexy."

"I do have a real question. It's important."

"I can't wait to hear it," Max said.

"Just how slow are we going? Because I'm flashing back to taking your tie off and unbuttoning your shirt, and it's got to be one of the hottest things I've ever done."

"We didn't even have sex that night," Max said.

"Something to look forward to," Dubs said.

"Focus on the task at hand," Max said, pointing her fork at Dubs's entrée.

"I think I am," Dubs said.

"Well, I'm not really in the mood for dessert tonight. I'm not promising anything, but my back is getting a little sore from sleeping on the floor."

"I give excellent massages," Dubs said. "But you can't have a shirt on for that. I'll have to take it all off. I promise it will be worth it."

"I'm sure it will." Max hoped she was doing the right thing.

"Look," Dubs said. "I don't want you to sleep with me just 'cause it's fun. I mean, I want it to be fun, but I'm not into sex just for sex. If that's all it is for you, tell me. I know we talk all the time about the physical side of stuff, but I'm the only one who talks about love."

Max cringed slightly. She didn't want Dubs to think she was only attracted to her physically. That felt horrible. The emotional connection she felt for her was so deep and so strong, it scared her, especially since she still didn't fully trust it, or Dubs. The past couple of weeks had helped that a lot, but she was still a little wary.

"Dubs," Max said. "I hope you know me better than that. What I feel for you sometimes scares me so much I don't want to let myself feel it. I've never only viewed what we had or have as purely physical. If I haven't made that clear to you, I'm sorry."

Dubs took Max's hand. "Pretty Girl, you can feel those things. I'm not going to hurt you."

Max wanted to believe her, but she wasn't sure how.

CHAPTER TWENTY-SIX

Holt walked through the colonial just behind Isabelle. She took in as many details as she could, but was finding it hard to not get carried away picturing raising her family here. This was the second time they had seen the house. They both loved it. Their realtor was pointing out things that needed fixing, and highpoints of the property, but she was picturing small feet running along the gorgeous hardwoods, and making breakfast for Isabelle and their son on a lazy Sunday morning in the large airy kitchen. She knew she was breaking every rule in the home buying-manual, but she didn't care. Isabelle and the realtor were the level-headed ones.

"Holt, babe, did you hear me?" Isabelle asked.

"Yes, of course."

"Really?" Isabelle said. "You have experience reroofing a house and installing a new boiler?"

"Oh," Holt said, totally busted. "My mind might have wandered."

"I guess so. But the kitchen is beautiful."

"How do you always know what I'm thinking?" Holt asked.

"For someone who has the rock hard abs you do, you think with your stomach an awful lot of the time." Isabelle let her hand drift across Holt's abdomen.

"I work out a lot," Holt said a little defensively.

"I don't want to pressure you," the realtor said, "but the market on the East Side is very hot, and this house is in superb condition.

I know there are at least two offers already. If you're interested, we should probably jump in now."

Holt looked at Isabelle. She knew she loved the house and the neighborhood. It wasn't the industrial, slightly more worn around the edges neighborhood they lived in now. This one had trees every couple hundred feet on the edge of the sidewalks, plenty of young families, farmer's markets, and local small businesses within easy walking distance. On top of that, there were two playgrounds Holt could think of that were quite close. It would be a huge change for her, but was much more similar to the neighborhood Isabelle had lived in prior to meeting Holt, minus the swimming pool.

"I love it," Isabelle said. "What do you think?"

"I love it too," Holt said. She did love the house, and she could see them being quite happy there, but more than anything, she loved the way Isabelle's eyes lit up every time they walked in the door, or entered a new room. She wouldn't have said yes to a house she hated just based on that, but it was enough to sell her on this house. "What's it going to take for us to get it?" she asked the realtor.

"Well, the asking price is competitive," she said. "I wouldn't be surprised if the other two offers are at asking, or even a few thousand above."

"Fine," Holt said. "Our offer is thirty thousand above asking and we'll pay cash."

Isabelle laughed out loud at the look on the realtor's face. Holt saw very few advantages to coming from a wealthy family, but this was certainly one of them.

"Will that get it done?" Holt asked. "If not, raise it. And see what you can do about the closing date. We'd like to be in as soon as possible."

"Don't mind her," Isabelle said. "She's used to getting her way."

"With that much money above asking, and a cash offer," the realtor said, "you will probably get whatever you want. If you want to walk up to the coffee shop, I'll write up the offer sheet and send it over. We might be back here this afternoon."

Holt's cell phone rang. "Holt," she said. It was Max on the other end. She listened to Max's excited update. "Send someone to get me." She gave Max her location. "I'll call my friend at the state police and give him a heads up. You gather the troops. We're going in big."

Holt made the second phone call, which didn't last long. Isabelle didn't look too pleased when she got off the phone. "Amy's car just got stolen," Holt said by way of explanation.

"I'm so sorry," the realtor said.

"Believe it or not," Isabelle said, "that's actually good news."

The poor realtor looked confused, but didn't ask more questions.

"Can I sign some paperwork now?" Holt asked. "I'm going to have to leave a bit earlier than anticipated."

"Sure." The realtor pulled out an offer sheet and had Holt sign it blank. Isabelle would make sure it was for the amount they talked about.

Isabelle walked Holt outside. "I know you'll be careful and not take any unnecessary chances," she said, "but I didn't like the sound of 'going in big.'"

"We've got to catch these guys," Holt said. "They've come after Dubs three times now, and they're getting more aggressive and reckless each time. They haven't stopped stealing cars, and it's probably tied up with all kinds of other nasty stuff. You know I'm always careful. My top priority every day when I leave for work is coming back to you at the end of the day. Goal one-A is getting the rest of my team home safely too."

"Don't you want to break your rule and take a machine gun or something this time? Maybe a tank?" Isabelle asked.

"You know my rules," Holt said. "Besides, I don't have a tank, and even if I did, I don't know how to drive one."

"I'm sure Dubs would be happy to steal you one if you asked," Isabelle said. "And Jose can drive anything. He'd love to show off his tank driving skills for Moose."

"We'll be careful," Holt said. "I love you."

"I love you too. You better call me after you're done and tell me you're in one piece. We've got a baby on the way, and I love you too much to lose you over some stupid stolen cars."

"God, I don't think I will ever get tired of hearing you say that," Holt said.

"Which part?" Isabelle asked.

"All of it." Holt pulled Isabelle to her and kissed her, pouring everything she was feeling, which was quite varied and deep, into their kiss. Isabelle clung to her, digging her fingers into the T-Shirt on Holt's back. When Moose pulled to the curb, he had to roll down the window and call her name before Holt finally let Isabelle go. "I'll call you soon. Go get us a house. I can't wait to hear about your victory on that battle. Go as high as you need."

"Be careful. I love you," Isabelle said.

"I love you too."

Holt climbed into the passenger seat and Moose pulled away from the curb. "Everything set?" Holt asked.

"Yep. We're ready to move out. How are the Staties taking being second fiddle?"

"They're fine," Holt said. "They're still pissed about Dubs's wild adventures through town, so I think they'd be fine if we get there and there's nobody home. I don't blame them. If one of their guys did something like that to us, I'd hold a grudge too."

"Guess we better hope the Wonder Twins actually found something then," Moose said.

When they got to the office, most of Holt's crew was huddled around Max's computer. Dubs was sitting on Max's lap. Holt chose to ignore that. After all, there was a lack of seating with all the people around. The crowd parted to let Holt and Moose through.

"Update," Holt said when she got behind Max's chair. Dubs flew off Max's lap and stood next to her. Holt tried not to laugh at the look of mild horror on Dubs's face.

"Amy's car pulled out of her driveway at seven thirty this morning," Max said. "I couldn't get a hold of her to confirm it wasn't her driving until eight forty-five because apparently, she and Superman had walked somewhere to get breakfast and then went to the playground and her phone was on vibrate. She was a little surprised when her car wasn't in the driveway when she returned.

The GPS tracker is working perfectly. The car moved across town and has been in an abandoned old mill building on the Pawtucket line."

"Why do all the bad guys in this state choose old mill buildings?" Holt asked.

"There are a lot of them," Moose said. "It's a good spot for a creepy lair."

"How easy is the approach? Can we do it without being seen?"

"They must be bringing the cars in here," Dubs said, pointing to the blueprints Max had on her computer monitor. "That was the route Amy's car took, and it's the only one that makes sense. That means they're probably chopping them in this location, or prepping them for resale."

"So unless we come in through the building, or are sneaky as fuck, they're probably going to know we're there pretty quickly," Holt said.

"Too much open space," Moose said. "But we can do sneaky as fuck."

"I've never seen you sneak anywhere," Lola said. "Sheer size alone means you're not sneaky."

"I could try it out," Moose said.

"Look," Holt said. "We're going to have plenty of police backup. We'll get as close as we can. We need to catch them in the act, confirm they're running a chop shop, or doing bad things to good cars, and then we can all move in. The police can do the arresting, get their photo op for the media, and we can all go home, happy and safe. No heroes today, okay? I want everyone in one piece. Watch each other's backs. Protect each other. No unnecessary risks. Everyone understand?"

The entire crew mumbled their understanding.

"Gear up," Holt said. "We move in ten."

Max got up with the rest of the crew to get ready to move out. Holt stopped her. "Max, I know you've been working this case hard from the beginning. I put more on you than was probably fair. I want you to know, you did a great job."

"But, H, we don't know if we've caught the bad guys," Max said. "You can't judge my performance yet."

"Yes, I can," Holt said. She was proud of what Max had done. She'd grown by leaps and bounds on this case. She'd made mistakes, like they all had on their first case in the field, but she had come through at the most important time. Holt had learned a lot about Max, and she liked everything she saw.

"Thanks, H. But if it's all the same to you, I'd like to reserve judgment until we get these bastards."

"Suit yourself," Holt said. "Let's go get 'em."

CHAPTER TWENTY-SEVEN

Dubs couldn't remember ever having an adrenaline rush quite like this. The moment Holt said "gear up," her heart rate shot up and she had been riding the high ever since. She felt like she was in a superhero action movie. She didn't believe this stuff actually happened in real life. What were they going to do when they got there? She didn't have a gun. Neither did Holt or Max. She didn't know about anyone else, but it seemed unlikely that they were going to be going in guns blazing.

She didn't have long to wait. Nothing was far away from anything else in Rhode Island. They parked a few blocks away from the building they were targeting. The state police were there too, in unmarked cars. Dubs knew some of them were SWAT. She had grown up being forced to learn to recognize police officers in crowds. Her father made her practice at the mall, movie theaters, restaurants, anywhere there were crowds of people.

"You two are with me," Holt said to Max and Dubs. "We're moving ahead together and scouting. We'll radio back what we see."

Dubs could tell Moose and Lola weren't happy with that plan. They didn't seem to want to let Holt go off on her own, particularly with novices. She admired their loyalty to their friend. It was the kind of dedication to each other that she had been observing over and over since she had joined this team. She and Levi had that kind of bond, but outside of that, there was no one she felt connected to, and she and Levi had been practically family. But now, she was a part of this crew, and integrated into its inner workings. She understood, or at least thought she was starting to understand, what it meant to feel like she belonged to something important and meaningful. She liked the feeling, and she liked watching how each crewmember cared for each other and was completely dedicated to Holt.

They made their way to the mill building, first along the sidewalk, then picked their way through an alley, then crawled carefully across an overgrown field, and Dubs was glad Max hadn't insisted on the handcuffs today.

She tried to follow Holt and Max's lead and stay low to the ground and behind as many natural obstacles as possible, but this was a skill set that didn't come naturally to her. Luckily, there were plenty of natural barriers, and when they reached a decent observation point, it seemed as though they had made it without notice.

Holt peered around the wooden pallets they were hiding behind and spent a few minutes observing. When she ducked back to them, she looked triumphant. "Well, Amy's not going to be happy," she said in a whisper. "Her car is being hacked up completely. There are six other cars there right now. Must have been a busy morning. Dubs, will you take a careful peek and see if there's anything that stands out to you? Don't get spotted."

Dubs knelt carefully and used the same peephole Holt had used. She was astounded at what she saw. The amount of equipment and the sophistication of the operation was staggering. There were at least twenty guys working on the six cars, rapidly breaking them down into parts. Dubs had helped chop cars before, but this was unlike anything she had seen before. She felt like she was watching it happen in fast-forward. She was about to duck back when Mr. Malevolent came into view. He had a handgun stuffed into the waistband of his pants. He seemed to be barking orders and surveying the jobs.

She sat back down. "Our old friend Mr. Malevolent is here," she said. "I think he's the big boss. Or in charge of this portion of the operation, anyway. He's armed."

"I think we've seen all we need to see," Holt said. "Time to call in the cleanup crew."

The three of them sat back against the pallets and waited for their backup. Holt checked the chop shop behind them occasionally to make sure no one was coming their way to take a leak or check the perimeter. It was incredibly hard for Dubs to sit still while she waited. She noticed Max wasn't having the easiest time either. Holt looked annoyed with both of them.

After what felt like an hour and a half, but was probably only fifteen minutes, Dubs sensed movement all around them. Heavily armed state police moved into position. Just after they were past their location, one of the officers identified themselves to the men at the chop shop and indicated they were under arrest.

Max, Dubs, and Holt watched from behind the pallets. Most of the men dropped their tools and put their hands up. Dubs thought it seemed a little too easy. She noticed Mr. Malevolent wasn't complying. He had taken cover behind one of the cars and had pulled the gun out of his waistband and was holding it in his right hand. It seemed to be keeping the police officers from moving further forward, although he was careful not to point it at them. He seemed to know that would be a death sentence.

Dubs jumped out of her skin when Moose asked how it was going from right behind them. When she looked more closely, Holt's crew was interspersed with the state police officers fanning out covering the area. Moose must have come to check on Holt.

"I'm worried about the leader," Holt said. "I don't like his body language. And he's armed."

"I agree," Moose said. "He's got that look."

No sooner had Moose said that, then Mr. Malevolent started shouting. "Get out here, bitch. Come see what you've done. I know it was you. Get out here now. Now!"

A woman cautiously, and clearly with great trepidation, emerged from the building. She was very pregnant.

"No, no, no, no," Holt said.

"Who is that?" Dubs said. Holt was white and Dubs couldn't think of anything that would scare Holt, which made it terrifying.

"That's Tiffany," Max said, looking scared herself. "Lola's ex. She's pregnant with Holt's kid."

"Holy shit." Now she understood why everyone's tension had just shot up.

"You led them here didn't you?" Mr. Malevolent screamed, his voice angry and full of hate. "I knew you didn't need so many meetings with that stupid bitch you used to sleep with. You betrayed me."

He walked to her, still protected behind the car, and struck her across the face. Moose had to hold Holt by both shoulders to keep her from running to Tiffany. The officer in charge of the police contingent shouted for him to stop and put his hands up. They moved closer.

Mr. Malevolent faced the officers and the field where they were crouched behind the pallet. "Where are you, cowards? Dubs, I know you're there. And you, Holt Lasher. Face me. Face me now!"

Dubs wanted to stand up and show herself, but Holt held her back, even though she looked like she was fighting every instinct she had. "Wait," she said. "Let the troopers handle this right now. He doesn't actually know we're here."

He pointed the gun at Tiffany's head. "Show yourself, or I kill her."

The police officers stopped, waiting for a signal from someone.

"We've got to step out," Holt said.

"What's to stop him from shooting you on sight?" Moose asked.

"Nothing," Holt said. "But if we stay here, he's going to get more hyped up. I'm worried he's going to do something bad. I can't watch that happen. Dubs, you don't have to pop up with me. But if you do, stay behind me when we move forward. Always stay behind me. I'll provide cover. You understand?"

"Who's covering you?" Dubs asked. She didn't like the idea of either one of them standing up.

"Stay behind me," Holt said. "Got it?"

Dubs nodded. Holt stood. Dubs popped up right behind her. Holt was so much taller than she was, she could barely see what was going on in front of them.

"You wanted to talk to me," Holt said. "You've got me. What's on your mind?"

"I knew it was you," Mr. Malevolent said. "Call off your attack dogs. I don't like guns pointed at me."

"And yet you've got one pointed at me," Holt said, stepping forward.

"That's because I can't trust you," he said. "Or her." He turned the gun back to Tiffany. "Tell me how you led them here. Tell me how she betrayed me." He turned the gun back to Holt. Dubs watched under Holt's upraised arms, showing she wasn't armed.

"Let Tiffany go. She had nothing to do with your current situation. Believe it or not, we figured it out all on our own."

"I don't believe you. I signed the adoption papers on the first day that stupid lawyer came by. Why did she need to meet with Lola so many times? And that lawyer? She was spying on me and feeding your puppy information."

"If he's the father, H, you better hope nurture is way stronger than nature," Dubs murmured.

"Shut up, Dubs," Holt said under her breath. She sounded like she was holding back laughter.

Dubs stepped to the side just enough so she could see better. Not being able to see was more nerve-racking than potentially catching a bullet. She didn't like the idea of Holt being her personal bulletproof vest, either.

Mr. Malevolent turned the gun back to Tiffany. "Tell them how you spied. Tell them. You betrayed me. You don't deserve to carry my baby." He was ramping up the anger again. His face was red and he was waving the gun erratically.

"Holt," Dubs said.

"I know."

"Hey," Holt said. "She's innocent. If you want to be mad at someone, point that at me. Take out your anger on me." Holt sounded desperate.

Dubs watched him scream at Tiffany. She had seen this kind of single-minded focus before. She didn't think he could hear anything but his own heart beat and deluded sense of justice. She moved out from behind Holt, closer to Tiffany. She had only been in one other situation where someone was held at gunpoint in her presence. It had been terrifying, but she hadn't felt in danger, because she knew she would never get involved. She wasn't scared now.

She didn't know how she knew he was about to fire, but she did. She also didn't know where the overwhelming urge to protect a woman she'd never met, and a baby that hadn't yet been born, came from, but in that moment, it was the only thing she was on this earth to do. As soon as she knew he was readying to shoot, she sprinted for Tiffany. She had heroic plans of grabbing her and pulling both of them to safety, but instead ended up in a leaping, flailing body shield in front of her.

Her heart was beating so fast and hard she didn't even hear the gunshot. She wondered how that was possible. The searing pain in her abdomen, on the left side, about even with her belly button, took her breath away. When she hit the ground she wasn't sure if she would ever be able to breathe again. She looked toward Mr. Malevolent, just in time to see Holt fly over the car he was hiding behind, seemingly unconcerned that the gun was now pointed directly at her, and slam him to the ground.

Dubs put her hand down on her stomach where it burned so badly. It was wet. She pulled her hand back and saw it was covered in blood. How pretty, she thought.

Tiffany was by her head, lying on the ground, moaning quietly. Dubs tried to pull herself to her. She started out okay, making it about a third of the way before her progress stopped. She didn't know why.

"Dubs, stop. Baby, please, stop."

Dubs looked up. Max was holding her. "I'm trying to get to Tiffany," Dubs said. "Can you help me?"

"You've already done enough," Max said. "She's fine. She's going to be just fine. Someone else is helping her." Max was crying. Dubs didn't like that.

"Why are you crying?"

Max was kneeling next to Dubs, her hands pushing down on the painful part of Dubs's stomach. Dubs really wished she wouldn't do that. It hurt.

"We need rescue," Max shouted.

Dubs tried to sit up.

"Don't do that," Max said. "You're going to make it worse."

"But you're crying," Dubs said. "You held me when I was crying. It made me feel better. Let me hold you."

"You just scared me is all," Max said. "You just did something heroic, and selfless, got yourself shot, and I wasn't sure I was going to have the chance to tell you I love you."

"I would have gotten shot a long time ago if I knew you were going to tell me that afterward," Dubs said.

"Don't ever do it again," Max said. She gently stroked Dubs's cheek and she leaned into the touch. It felt nice. She wished Max would come up by her head and hold her more tightly. Her stomach hurt so bad. The light was taking on a funny tinge, too, and she didn't like it. "I'm sorry," Max said. "I've got to use both hands for pressure."

"I'll do that," Holt said, appearing next to Max. "She looks like she needs a pillow."

"Thank you," Dubs said. "Did you read my mind or did I say that out loud?"

"Thank you," Holt said. "You saved Tiffany's life, and the baby's."

"I kind of like being part of the Avengers," Dubs said. "All for one, and one for all."

"That's the Three Musketeers," Max said.

"Whatever. I just got shot. Give me a break." Her stomach was hurting badly, but Max cradled her head and stroked her forehead. That helped. Plus, she could look up and see Max's face. But she was tired. She really just wanted to close her eyes, more than anything.

"Did you really mean what you said?" Dubs asked. "It's not just because you were scared because I got shot?"

"You mean am I sure I'm in love with you? Yes, absolutely. Never more sure about anything. And now I've got Holt as my witness. You know I'd never lie in front of her, not even to make you feel better."

"Next time wear a bulletproof something when getting shot," Holt said. "You heal up faster, while still getting at least some sympathy."

"No," Max said. "No more getting shot, for either of you, or me, or anyone else."

"So many rules," Dubs said. "Is Isabelle going to be mad at me?"

"Oh, so pissed," Holt said. "And really mad at me. I'm supposed to keep you safe."

"I kinda took off on you there."

"You do have a habit of doing that," Holt said.

"I'm working on it."

"Your ride's here," Max said.

"You're coming with me, right?" Dubs asked. She didn't want to go to the hospital alone. She wanted Max there with her.

"I'll be by your side as long as you'll let me," Max said.

"That's going to be a very long time," Dubs said.

As they loaded her onto the stretcher and into the ambulance, Max didn't let go of her hand. The paramedic made Max let go for a moment while he hooked up an IV and got her strapped in. Dubs panicked. She tried to sit up again and flailed around looking for Max. She calmed when she felt Max's hand wrapped tightly around hers.

"Don't worry, sweetheart. I'm not going anywhere."

CHAPTER TWENTY-EIGHT

Isabelle couldn't believe the turn the day had taken. She started off with only a second showing on a promising house on her to-do list. Since then, she and Holt had made an offer on the house, Holt had found the bad guys she'd been chasing for months, Dubs had gotten shot protecting Tiffany and the baby. In all the stress the baby's heart rate had gone through the roof, and Tiffany was induced, and now, Isabelle had just gotten off the phone with their realtor. Their offer on the house had been accepted. She could remember a time when her life could have been described as boring. With the exception of people getting shot entirely too often, she wouldn't trade her new life with Holt for anything in the world.

She was in the lobby of Women and Infants Hospital awaiting word on the birth of their baby. Dubs had been taken to the trauma center of Rhode Island Hospital, which was a separate hospital, but connected to this one by a walkway a few floors up. Holt had been bouncing back and forth checking on Dubs, and especially Max, since Dubs had needed surgery to repair some internal damage. Luckily, she was going to be fine. From the sound of it, Holt's entire crew was up keeping Max company.

"Are you Isabelle Rochat?" a hospital employee asked.

"Yes," Isabelle said, her anxiety spiking. What if something was wrong?

"Tiffany wanted me to get you. The baby is still stressed and has now flipped into a breach position. They're going to do a C-section.

She thought you, or your partner, might want to be in the room when the baby is born."

"Yes. Of course, yes. Can we both be there?"

"I'm sorry, no. Only one of you. But since it's an adoption, after the baby gets checked, we can bring you and the baby out to one of the labor and delivery rooms if there's one available and you can have some time as a family while they're finishing the surgery."

"I'll get Holt and we'll be right up," Isabelle said. She couldn't believe she was about to become a mother.

"You have about ten minutes. They're prepping everything now."

Isabelle called Holt. "It's happening now. They're doing a C-section. One of us can be in the room," Isabelle said. "The other one has to be outside, but then we can all be together right after."

Holt said she was already on her way back. She wasn't kidding. She was in the lobby in less than two minutes. Her smile looked permanent.

"This is the greatest thing," Holt said. "I can't wait to meet him. You should be in the room with him when he's born. I want him to see your face first. If I were a baby, I would want to see someone as beautiful as you as my first introduction to this world."

"You are so sweet," Isabelle said. "But he would do quite well being introduced to someone as amazing as you right away."

"I'll be right outside the door to meet him," Holt said. "You should be there. Let's get up there. I don't want to miss anything."

They went up to the labor and delivery floor. Isabelle changed into scrubs and was ushered into the operating room. She took a seat by Tiffany's head. She had never met her, but despite that, Tiffany looked happy to see her.

"I'm glad they're getting him out, so you can meet him," Tiffany said. "Holt and that other woman saved my life."

"Okay," one of the doctors said. "We're just bringing him out now."

"They'll take him for a quick exam," a nurse explained, "and then they'll bring him over to you."

Isabelle nodded. She felt anxious, and excited, and completely overwhelmed. She wished Holt were here for this moment.

Before she knew it, she heard the sound of a tiny baby cry. It was the most beautiful noise she had ever heard. Shortly after the baby was born, a nurse delivered the swaddled baby boy to Isabelle. She took him in her arms and stared down at him in awe. He was so beautiful. He was crying and scrunching up his tiny face, and she would do anything to make him happy.

"Would you like to see him?" Isabelle asked Tiffany.

"Can I talk to him for a minute?"

"Of course." Isabelle held him up close to Tiffany's face. She wanted to get him out to meet Holt, but she felt like this was the least she could do.

"Baby boy," Tiffany said. "I'm not giving you up because I don't love you. But I know you can have a better life with these women. I know them. They're good people. They're going to give you the world, and keep you safe, and teach you to be a good man. I couldn't do that. Be good, little boy."

Isabelle had tears in her eyes. She moved her son closer to Tiffany so she could kiss him on the forehead.

"We're going to have to move you and the baby out now while we finish the surgery," the nurse said.

"Raise him well," Tiffany said. "Thank you for taking him."

"Thank you for him," Isabelle said. "We'll love him dearly."

She held him tightly as she was led out of the operating room. Holt was right outside the door as she promised. She still had the same smile on her face. It got bigger when she saw Isabelle and the baby.

"Look at how beautiful he is," Isabelle said.

"Look at how beautiful you are holding our son," Holt said. "Look at my family. Can I hold him?"

"Yes, of course, yes." Isabelle handed him to Holt. A nurse ushered them down the hall to a labor and delivery room. She said they would have plenty of time there to bond as a family and feed the baby for the first time. As they settled in, the nurse reminded them that skin to skin contact was the best thing for their baby.

Isabelle sat in the large recliner in the room. Holt leaned on the bed with the baby.

"You should do the skin to skin," Holt said.

Isabelle removed her shirt and bra and Holt unswaddled him and handed him to Isabelle.

"I am fully aware that when we get home we'll probably feel we've lost our minds," Holt said. "But right now, I feel like my life is about as perfect as it can get."

"I love you so much," Isabelle said.

"You are talking to me, right?" Holt said. "I feel like I need to check now."

"Yes, you brute. Although I love him too. More than I thought would ever be possible."

"Me too," Holt said.

"Is Dubs out of surgery?" Isabelle asked.

"Oh. Yes. I was coming back to tell you that," Holt said. "She's all settled in her room. I think my whole crew is jammed in her room. Max has probably moved in by now. I tried to warn Max away from Dubs, but I'm glad they ignored me. They're so happy together. I thought Max was going to lose it when Dubs got shot."

"Can you blame her?" Isabelle asked. "I'm not pleased with any of you for that, but I'm too happy to scold. Do you think they'll let us go for a walk with this little guy? It seems like there's a party going on across the way that we should join. And Dubs should get to meet him. She did save his life."

"I'll check with the nurses," Holt said. She left the room for a moment. Isabelle gazed at the tiny creature now sleeping on her chest.

Holt returned with a bottle and a smile. "Got some traveling snacks and I secured a ride," Holt said. "Even better, the nurses said we can be discharged anytime as long as we're fine with a nurse coming to the loft to visit a couple of times over the next week. He is in perfect health even if things got a little dicey right before he was born. I guess it was lucky the bad guys waited to steal Amy's car so close to his due date. Oh, and security has to check that I installed the car seat correctly on our way out the door and remove his baby lojack."

Isabelle offered their son the bottle, which he greedily took. Since his stomach was about the size of a marble, he filled up quickly. She burped him and they were ready to move out.

"What do you think of these wheels?" Holt asked.

There was a pram on wheels waiting for them just outside the door. Isabelle laid the little boy inside and Holt wheeled it down the hall, grinning from ear to ear the entire time.

"We're not supposed to stay very long," Holt said. "The nurses weren't thrilled with the idea since there are a lot of germs in a hospital. I told them we'd be quick and this little dude wouldn't touch anything."

Holt knocked on the door to Dubs's room. Tuna was closest. "Hey, Holt and Isabelle and the new prince are here!"

"Wait, seriously, they brought him?" someone said from deeper inside the room.

"He's here?" Isabelle heard Max say. "Bring him in."

"Clear a path," Holt said.

As they walked in, many hands patted Isabelle on the back or rubbed her shoulder. She felt more and more comfortable in this group the longer she spent with them. They had started to feel like family. She knew why Holt was so attached to them.

When they got to Dubs's bedside, Holt rolled the pram right next to her head. Max was sitting on the opposite side of the bed, looking like she was carefully avoiding jostling Dubs, but wanting to be as close to her as possible.

"What do you think, Dubs?" Holt asked. "Was he worth it? This is the little guy you saved."

"He's beautiful," Dubs said. She still looked a little woozy from the surgery. "What's his name?"

Isabelle smiled. "I'm glad you're all here to meet our son," she said. "Please welcome George Rochat-Lasher."

"Prince George," Lola said. "It's perfect."

"So are you on full-time mom duty now, H?"

"Don't be ridiculous," Holt said. "I'm still the boss around here. Nothing's changing."

"That's not true at all," Moose said. "That guy is now the boss around here."

Isabelle joined in the laughter. George started to cry. She scooped him up and snuggled him. He settled and she marveled that she could calm him like that. She knew it wouldn't last, or at least wouldn't always be that easy, but it was still miraculous.

"So what are we going to do with ourselves while you're playing mom?"

"We've still got cases," Holt said. "And quit trying to put me out to pasture."

"Seriously though, boss, anything big coming up?"

"Well, we've got a newbie to break in," Holt said.

Isabelle didn't know who Holt was talking about. She followed everyone else's glance. They were all looking at Dubs.

"Me?" Dubs asked. "You want me to join this team?"

"If you're interested," Holt said. "We'd be lucky to have you."

There were a chorus of "amens" and "welcome aboard" from around the room. Dubs might have still been groggy, but she was clearly happy. Isabelle thought it was sweet how excited Dubs was, and Max was obviously thrilled as well.

"So that will take about a minute and a half," Moose said. "We'll all babysit fifteen minutes a day. That will keep us busy, fifteen minutes a day. You're going to have to think of something to fill up our time, H."

"Why the sudden interest in your timekeeping?" Holt asked, sounding exasperated.

"Well, you've got this cute kid, you're buying a house. We don't want you to misplace the Batphone and forget about us."

"Oh, please," Holt said. "You know the Batphone never stays silent for long."

About the Author

Jesse Thoma is a project manager in a clinical research lab and spends a good amount of time in methadone clinics and prisons collecting data and talking to people.

Jesse grew up in Northern California but headed east for college. She never looked back, although her baseball allegiance is still loyally with the San Francisco Giants. She has lived in New England for over a decade and has finally learned to leave extra time in the morning to scrape snow off the car. Jesse is blissfully married and is happiest when she is out for a walk with her family and their dog, pretending she still has the soccer skills she had as an eighteen-year-old, eating anything her wife bakes, or sitting at the computer to write a few lines.

Books Available from Bold Strokes Books

Pedal to the Metal by Jesse J. Thoma. When unreformed thief Dubs Williams is released from prison to help Max Winters bust a car theft ring, Max learns that to catch a thief, get in bed with one. (978-1-62639-239-7)

Dragon Horse War by D. Jackson Leigh. A priestess of peace and a fiery warrior must defeat a vicious uprising that entwines their destinies and ultimately their hearts. (978-1-62639-240-3)

For the Love of Cake by Erin Dutton. When everything is on the line, and one taste can break a heart, will pastry chefs Maya and Shannon take a chance on reality? (978-1-62639-241-0)

Betting on Love by Alyssa Linn Palmer. A quiet country-girl-at-heart and a live-life-to-the-fullest biker take a risk at offering each other their hearts. (978-1-62639-242-7)

The Deadening by Yvonne Heidt. The lines between good and evil, right and wrong, have always been blurry for Shade. When Raven's actions force her to choose, which side will she come out on? (978-1-62639-243-4)

Ordinary Mayhem by Victoria A. Brownworth. Faye Blakemore has been taking photographs since she was ten, but those same photographs threaten to destroy everything she knows and everything she loves. (978-1-62639-315-8)

One Last Thing by Kim Baldwin & Xenia Alexiou. Blood is thicker than pride. The final book in the Elite Operative Series brings together foes, family, and friends to start a new order. (978-1-62639-230-4)

Songs Unfinished by Holly Stratimore. Two aspiring rock stars learn that falling in love while pursuing their dreams can be harmonious—if they can only keep their pasts from throwing them out of tune. (978-1-62639-231-1)

Beyond the Ridge by L.T. Marie. Will a contractor and a horse rancher overcome their family differences and find common ground to build a life together? (978-1-62639-232-8)

Swordfish by Andrea Bramhall. Four women battle the demons from their pasts. Will they learn to let go, or will happiness be forever beyond their grasp? (978-1-62639-233-5)

The Fiend Queen by Barbara Ann Wright. Princess Katya and her consort Starbride must turn evil against evil in order to banish Fiendish power from their kingdom, and only love will pull them back from the brink. (978-1-62639-234-2)

Up the Ante by PJ Trebelhorn. When Jordan Stryker and Ashley Noble meet again fifteen years after a short-lived affair, are either of them prepared to gamble on a chance at love? (978-1-62639-237-3)

Speakeasy by MJ Williamz. When mob leader Helen Byrne sets her sights on the girlfriend of Al Capone's right-hand man, passion and tempers flare on the streets of Chicago. (978-1-62639-238-0)

Venus in Love by Tina Michele. Morgan Blake can't afford any distractions and Ainsley Dencourt can't afford to lose control—but the beauty of life and art usually lies in the unpredictable strokes of the artist's brush. (978-1-62639-220-5)

Rules of Revenge by AJ Quinn. When a lethal operative on a collision course with her past agrees to help a CIA analyst on a critical assignment, the encounter proves explosive in ways neither woman anticipated. (978-1-62639-221-2)

The Romance Vote by Ali Vali. Chili Alexander is a sought-after campaign consultant who isn't prepared when her boss's daughter,

Samantha Pellegrin, comes to work at the firm and shakes up Chili's life from the first day. (978-1-62639-222-9)

Advance: Exodus Book One by Gun Brooke. Admiral Dael Caydoc's mission to find a new homeworld for the Oconodian people is hazardous, but working with the infuriating Commander Aniwyn "Spinner" Seclan endangers her heart and soul. (978-1-62639-224-3)

UnCatholic Conduct by Stevie Mikayne. Jil Kidd goes undercover to investigate fraud at St. Marguerite's Catholic School, but life gets complicated when her student is killed—and she begins to fall for her prime target. (978-1-62639-304-2)

Season's Meetings by Amy Dunne. Catherine Birch reluctantly ventures on the festive road trip from hell with beautiful stranger Holly Daniels only to discover the road to true love has its own obstacles to maneuver. (978-1-62639-227-4)

Myth and Magic: Queer Fairy Tales edited by Radclyffe and Stacia Seaman. Myth, magic, and monsters—the stuff of childhood dreams (or nightmares) and adult fantasies. (978-1-62639-225-0)

Nine Nights on the Windy Tree by Martha Miller. Recovering drug addict, Bertha Brannon, is an attorney who is trying to stay clean when a murder sends her back to the bad end of town. (978-1-62639-179-6)

Driving Lessons by Annameekee Hesik. Dive into Abbey Brooks's sophomore year as she attempts to figure out the amazing, but sometimes complicated, life of a you-know-who girl at Gila High School. (978-1-62639-228-1)

Asher's Shot by Elizabeth Wheeler. Asher Price's candid photographs capture the truth, but when his success requires exposing an enemy, Asher discovers his only shot at happiness involves revealing secrets of his own. (978-1-62639-229-8)

Courtship by Carsen Taite. Love and justice—a lethal mix or a perfect match? (978-1-62639-210-6)

Against Doctor's Orders by Radclyffe. Corporate financier Presley Worth wants to shut down Argyle Community Hospital, but Dr. Harper Rivers will fight her every step of the way, if she can also fight their growing attraction. (978-1-62639-211-3)

A Spark of Heavenly Fire by Kathleen Knowles. Kerry and Beth are building their life together, but unexpected circumstances could destroy their happiness. (978-1-62639-212-0)

Never Too Late by Julie Blair. When Dr. Jamie Hammond is forced to hire a new office manager, she's shocked to come face to face with Carla Grant and memories from her past. (978-1-62639-213-7)

Widow by Martha Miller. Judge Bertha Brannon must solve the murder of her lover, a policewoman she thought she'd grow old with. As more bodies pile up, the murderer starts coming for her. (978-1-62639-214-4)

Twisted Echoes by Sheri Lewis Wohl. What's a woman to do when she realizes the voices in her head are real? (978-1-62639-215-1)

Criminal Gold by Ann Aptaker. Through a dangerous night in New York in 1949, Cantor Gold, dapper dyke-about-town, smuggler of fine art, is forced by a crime lord to be his instrument of vengeance. (978-1-62639-216-8)

The Melody of Light by M.L. Rice. After surviving abuse and loss, will Riley Gordon be able to navigate her first year of college and accept true love and family? (978-1-62639-219-9)

Because of You by Julie Cannon. What would you do for the woman you were forced to leave behind? (978-1-62639-199-4)

The Job by Jove Belle. Sera always dreamed that she would one day reunite with Tor. She just didn't think it would involve terrorists, firearms, and hostages. (978-1-62639-200-7)

Making Time by C.J. Harte. Two women going in different directions meet after fifteen years and struggle to reconnect in spite of the past that separated them. (978-1-62639-201-4)

Once The Clouds Have Gone by KE Payne. Overwhelmed by the dark clouds of her past, Tag Grainger is lost until the intriguing and spirited Freddie Metcalfe unexpectedly forces her to reevaluate her life. (978-1-62639-202-1)

The Acquittal by Anne Laughlin. Chicago private investigator Josie Harper searches for the real killer of a woman whose lover has been acquitted of the crime. (978-1-62639-203-8)

An American Queer: The Amazon Trail by Lee Lynch. Lee Lynch's heartening and heart-rending history of gay life from the turbulence of the late 1900s to the triumphs of the early 2000s are recorded in this selection of her columns. (978-1-62639-204-5)

Stick McLaughlin: The Prohibition Years by CF Frizzell. Corruption in 1918 cost Stick her lover, her freedom, and her identity, but a very special flapper and the family bond of her own gang could help win them back—even if it means outwitting the Boston Mob. (978-1-62639-205-2)

Edge of Awareness by C.A. Popovich. When Maria, a woman in the middle of her third divorce, meets Dana, an out lesbian, awareness of her feelings brings up reservations about the teachings of her church. (978-1-62639-188-8)

Taken by Storm by Kim Baldwin. Lives depend on two women when a train derails high in the remote Alps, but an unforgiving mountain, avalanches, crevasses, and other perils stand between them and safety. (978-1-62639-189-5)

The Common Thread by Jaime Maddox. Dr. Nicole Coussart's life is falling apart, but fortunately, DEA Attorney Rae Rhodes is there to pick up the pieces and help Nic put them back together. (978-1-62639-190-1)

Jolt by Kris Bryant. Mystery writer Bethany Lange wasn't prepared for the twisting emotions that left her breathless the moment she laid eyes on folk singer sensation Ali Hart. (978-1-62639-191-8)

Searching For Forever by Emily Smith. Dr. Natalie Jenner's life has always been about saving others, until young paramedic Charlie Thompson comes along and shows her maybe she's the one who needs saving. (978-1-62639-186-4)

A Queer Sort of Justice: Prison Tales Across Time by Rebecca S. Buck. When liberty is only a memory, and all seems lost, what freedoms and hopes can be found within us? (978-1-62639-195-6E)

Blue Water Dreams by Dena Hankins. Lania Marchiol keeps her wary sailor's gaze trained on the horizon until Oly Rassmussen, a wickedly handsome trans man, sends her trusty compass spinning off course. (978-1-62639-192-5)

Rest Home Runaways by Clifford Henderson. Baby boomer Morgan Ronzio's troubled marriage is the least of her worries when she gets the call that her addled, eighty-six-year-old, half-blind dad has escaped the rest home. (978-1-62639-169-7)

Charm City by Mason Dixon. Raq Overstreet's loyalty to her drug kingpin boss is put to the test when she begins to fall for Bathsheba Morris, the undercover cop assigned to bring him down. (978-1-62639-198-7)